AND OTHER TOXIC STORIES

HAZMAT
& Other Toxic Stories

by

Lawrence Watt-Evans

Misenchanted Press

HAZMAT & Other Toxic Stories

Published by Misenchanted Press

Cover design by Lawrence Watt-Evans

CONTENTS

~~~~~~

Introduction

I grew up reading science fiction, fantasy, and mystery. My father loved science fiction, and enjoyed mysteries and good fantasy, so our house was full of the stuff.

Not horror, though. Dad didn't like horror. Some of it crept in anyway, one way or another – often because it was written by an author (Ray Bradbury, for example) who my parents considered a science fiction writer – but that only amounted to perhaps a dozen or so of our thousands of books.

I realized as a kid, though, that *I* liked horror, even if Dad didn't. And later on I realized that my *mother* loved horror, but hadn't been buying it because she didn't want to annoy my father and we had plenty of other stuff to read.

So I checked horror stories out of the library, and bought horror comics (such as they were in the Comics Code Approved 1960s), and watched horror movies on TV when I could. Once I was old enough to drive I even saw a few of those movies in the theater.

And once I was an established writer, I began thinking about writing horror...

Well, actually, I had been thinking about it for a long time. I wrote my first horror story for a class assignment in fifth grade, lifting much of my plot from the Vincent Price movie "The House on Haunted Hill." But I only started thinking about writing horror *professionally* in the late 1980s, when I had already published a good bit of fantasy and science fiction.

At the time horror was booming, particularly the subgenre known as "splatterpunk," so it seemed like a good idea to get in on it, and I tried, but alas, I was behind the curve. By the time

1

my first horror novel, *The Nightmare People*, saw print, the boom had gone bust.

But I had tasted blood, and all through the 1990s I wrote short horror stories for various markets.

Around the turn of the century, though, I ran out of steam. My mood changed, and horror was less appealing. There weren't as many markets anymore, and due to health problems I wasn't writing much short fiction of any kind, so I pretty much stopped. I had unfinished stories lying around, and a complete but unsold story or two, but I had lost interest. They stayed unfinished and unsold.

At that point I had been thinking for years that I should put together a collection of my short horror stories. I wanted to call it *Toxic Stories*. Then I started writing "Hazmat," and decided it should be *Hazmat & Other Toxic Stories*.

But I needed to finish "Hazmat" first, obviously, and... well, I'd stopped writing horror. So for the next fifteen or sixteen years, I never got around to finishing it.

But finally, in March 2016, I did. Which meant I could assemble that collection.

And here it is.

This is not all my short horror. I haven't included any stories that are in any of my other collections. That means no vampire stories, because I collected all those in *In the Blood* back in 2011. It means a few others, such as "Real Time," aren't here, since I'd included them elsewhere – they fit neatly into other genres, in addition to horror.

And there were a couple of stories that I decided just didn't deserve to be here, for one reason or another.

But this is most of it. Nineteen older stories are reprinted in this collection, and two new ones, "Hazmat" and "Slash," are published here for the first time. (I never tried selling those two anywhere else; it just wasn't worth the trouble. If a market had come looking for them... but none did.)

These stories were not all written as straight-up horror; a few were even intended as humor. Still, they are among my most disturbing creations. They all have a definite dark side, even the funny ones.

I hope you'll enjoy them.

– Lawrence Watt-Evans
Takoma Park, 2016

HAZMAT

~~~~~

Hazmat

Jennie didn't hear the crash or the sirens, but when she got off the late bus at the corner she could see the flashing lights in the distance, blue and red and yellow, on the highway behind her house. If the sun had been shining she probably would never have seen them, but the rain had only just stopped and the skies were still dark and threatening, so that the lights were plainly visible.

She knew her mother was expecting her inside, and she didn't want her to worry, but she wanted to see what was happening, and it would only take a few minutes, so she dropped her school-bag on the porch and ran on around to the back yard.

Her parents hated the highway; they complained about it all the time, and Jennie always said she didn't like it either, but the truth was that she found it fascinating. At night she would watch the cars from her bedroom window, the lines of red and white lights flowing by in either direction, the white turning red as they passed. During the daytime, when she played out back, she would sometimes stop just to listen to the steady rumble of traffic, the trucks and cars streaming by endlessly.

Where did they all come from, where did they all go, what were all those people who drove them like? Did they have families, and children, and homes?

She ran down the slope, and hopped from tussock to stone to cross the ditch; she could hear voices on the embankment ahead, and the colored lights were much brighter now. A raindrop splashed in the puddle beside her; apparently the storm was not over at all, but had merely paused.

The mesh fence lifted up easily – it wasn't supposed to, Jennie knew, but it always had. She squatted down and slipped underneath.

Then she paused and looked back at the house. If her mother saw her on the other side of the fence she would *scream*, and she'd call the highway department and have the fence fixed, and Jennie would be grounded for weeks. As it was, her mother was always worrying about a truck missing the curve and rolling down into their yard, and her father had been writing letters demanding that a proper sound-barrier wall be built.

There was no sign of her mother.

She began to climb the embankment; it was steep enough that she had to go up on all fours, hanging onto the clumps of grass and the tough brown weeds.

She could hear engines running, and tires hissing on pavement, and men shouting to one another. Something was dripping down from the shoulder, something brown, trickling down into the grass, just a foot or so away; she leaned over and sniffed at it.

It had a funny smell – not oil or gasoline or anything she recognized. She reached out a finger and poked at the dirt, deflecting the stream.

A drop splashed onto her finger, and she quickly wiped it on the grass. Most of the stuff came off, and it wasn't hot, it didn't sting or anything. She looked critically at her finger, then shrugged and resumed her climb.

A moment later she peered up over the edge of the embankment and saw the accident.

A big silver and red tank truck had turned over, impaling itself on the guard rail just a few yards from where she crouched. The brown stuff had leaked from the tank; there was a pool of it half on the pavement, half on the shoulder.

All around it was a broad empty space; the highway had been closed off, with flares and sawhorses and blinkers making a big ring around the overturned truck. Around the markers was another ring, of vehicles and uniformed men – police cars, fire trucks, rescue trucks, tow trucks.

None of them ventured near the wreck, though; they all hung back. Then, as Jennie watched, she saw two men in baggy protective suits and soft helmets emerging from one of the surrounding trucks, carrying some sort of fancy equipment that they held out in front of them, as if to ward off danger, as they stepped into the circle.

Jennie wondered what was going on; she followed the curve of the marked-off area around, and realized she was well inside the circle it would have formed had the arc been continued. The circle was not complete, though, because nobody had extended it down the steep slope of the embankment.

This, she knew, was not the usual way of handling overturned trucks; she felt a twinge of fear, and took another look at the tanker.

There was a yellow stripe down the side; a guardrail post had punched into it. There were big black letters on the stripe, but she couldn't read them because of the angle.

There were two diamond-shaped signs on the back of the truck, the end nearest her; those she could make out more clearly. One had scraped on something. That one bore a design of interlocked rings and a word starting with BI and ending in ZARD; the middle portion was illegible.

The other warning sign was still clear – sideways, but clear and legible.

It said HAZMAT.

Jennie blinked. What did "hazmat" mean?

Whatever it meant, it sounded dangerous, and she didn't like the look of any of this, and her mother would be waiting for her. Besides, the rain was picking up. She had been looking for a little excitement, but this was scary, not exciting. It was no fun at all.

She turned and began half-climbing, half-sliding back down to the ditch. She ducked under the fence and scampered up to her own yard, then ran across, out the driveway, and back around to the front door.

"Was the bus late?" her mother asked, when she stepped in.

"No," she said, "I just walked slow."

"In the rain?" Her mother looked up from the newspaper.

"Well, it wasn't raining, mostly," Jennie explained. "It just now started again."

Her mother glanced at the fat drops rattling against the windows. "Oh," she said. "How was practice?"

"Okay," Jennie said.

"Good," her mother answered. Then she returned her attention to the paper.

Jennie threw her bag and jacket in the hall closet and hurried up the two flights of stairs to her room in the attic. She threw herself on the bed and stared out her window.

The lights were still flashing, and she could see the overturned truck and all the surrounding equipment; people were running back and forth, hunched against the rain. No one entered that inner circle without a protective suit, but there were at least a dozen people in suits now, some of them with shovels and buckets, some hauling a big tank on wheels. A group of three was applying a patch to the hole in the tank's side; she couldn't see how they were fastening it. Most of the rest seemed to be trying to collect the brown stuff that had leaked out, scooping it into buckets, shoveling up the dirt that had partially absorbed it, working quickly before the rain could dilute and spread it.

There were even more police cars than before, and traffic had backed up as far as she could see – the southbound side of the highway was completely blocked, and the police were setting up barricades on the northbound side, as well.

Jennie looked at her finger, a bit worried, but it seemed all right. The brown stuff was gone; there was just the faintest little red spot where it had been.

She'd wiped it off in time, she was sure.

She forgot about it and watched as the clean-up continued.

#

The rain had stopped. The southbound lanes were still blocked, but traffic was being directed across the median; one of the northbound lanes had been separated out and was carrying southbound traffic for a few hundred yards, until it could cut back across the median beyond the accident.

Some of the emergency vehicles were gone. A crane had arrived, righted the tank truck, and departed. The men in protective suits had finished their clean-up – but only after a team had carried in a jackhammer and torn up the pavement where the spill had been. Jennie's parents had heard the hammer while eating supper, and her father had gone into another of his tirades about how he hated living so close to the highway.

Jennie had eaten her dinner, watched TV, played a few videogames, and now she was getting into her nightgown, watching out the window as she did.

Her right forefinger was itching; the skin was reddish from the first knuckle to the tip, and was starting to peel in one spot – the spot where the brown stuff had touched her. It didn't actually *hurt*, but she wasn't happy about it.

9

"Hazmat," the warning sign had said, and there had been that thing like four circles arranged in a triangle.

She settled the hem of her nightgown into place and started toward the bathroom to brush her teeth. Then she changed direction and bounced down the stairs.

Her father was in his room, grumbling to himself as he pawed through a bureau drawer looking for something.

"Daddy?" she called.

He looked up. "Yes, Jennie?"

"What's hazmat?"

He straightened up and turned to face her. "What's *what*?"

"Hazmat," she said. "I saw it on the side of a truck."

"Spell it."

"H, A, Z, M, A, T."

"Oh!" he said. "That's not a word; it's an abbreviation."

"What's it stand for?"

"Hazardous Material," he said. "What kind of a truck was it?"

"A tank truck. Like the one that tipped over on the highway."

Her father glanced in the direction of the highway. "Is that what all the fuss was about over there?"

She nodded. "You can see from my window," she said.

He grunted. "Well, you stay away from anything that says Haz Mat on it," he told her, pronouncing it as two separate words.

"Yes, Daddy. There was another sign on it with a funny symbol."

"What'd it look like?"

"Like... like three circles in a triangle, except where the corners of the triangle would be there were breaks in the circles, and they were thicker in the middle, and there was a fourth circle on top, in the middle."

Her father needed a moment to puzzle this out, but after a few seconds he said, "I think that's the biohazard symbol." He anticipated her next question. "Biological hazard. Germs, or something."

"Oh," she said, unhappily. She looked down at her finger and bit her lip.

"Something wrong?" her father asked.

She remembered what he had said last time he'd seen her playing near the highway. "No, Daddy," she said. "I think I'll wash my hands."

"All right," he said. "And don't forget to brush your teeth."

"I won't. Good night, Daddy."

"Good night, sweetheart."

She washed her hands. She washed them thoroughly, with two different kinds of soap, and she scrubbed hard with the scratchy old washcloth that she didn't like but which generally got things cleaner.

Then she went to bed, but her finger still itched, and the redness was spreading to the rest of her hand.

#

There were brown spots on the sheets, ugly brown stains, and Jennie knew they were where her right hand had rested during the night. The whole hand was red and swollen now, the red reaching halfway to her elbow, and the skin of her forefinger was peeling away in thick white flakes. Pale fluid was starting to ooze from the flesh beneath. The hand throbbed with dull pain; the finger itself had gone completely numb.

She no longer worried about getting in trouble for where she had been; she screamed, "Mommy!"

Someone called something downstairs, but Jennie couldn't make it out. She ran to the door and leaned out over the stairwell, shrieking, "Mommy!"

She heard a rattle, and footsteps, and then her mother was there on the stairs, looking up at her. "What is it?" she asked.

Jennie held out her hand, wordlessly.

Her mother sucked in air, shocked. "You need a doctor," she said. "Get dressed, while I call." She turned away.

Jennie nodded and tried to obey, but when she pulled a sleeve over her right hand she screamed at the pain, and she couldn't bring herself to fasten the buttons.

When she had her clothes more or less on, and her nightgown was a puddle of fabric on the carpet, she started to throw herself on the bed – and then stopped at the sight of the brown stains.

They were spreading.

She backed away from the bed, whimpering, and started down the steps. She couldn't hold the railing, which was on the right.

At the bottom, in the second floor hall, she could hear her mother's voice talking on the phone downstairs. She sounded upset.

That made Jennie even more frightened; if her *mother* was worried, then it was serious, not just some normal childhood thing like chicken pox.

She looked at her hand; brownish stuff was starting to seep from her finger where the skin had peeled away, where the pale fluid had been just a moment before. It looked uncomfortably like the brown stuff that had come from the truck. She gave a small, terrified squeak and hurried on down the next flight of stairs.

#

"I've never seen anything like it," the emergency room doctor, Dr. Williams, said, staring at Jennie's hand – or rather, at what had been Jennie's hand just hours ago. Now it was an oozing, misshapen mass of brownish-red flesh, most of it

12

covered with a thick layer of brown goo. Bone protruded from the five lumps that had once been fingers; the flesh had been eaten away.

Jennie could no longer move her hand or her fingers, could no longer feel anything more than a few inches below the shoulder. She couldn't stand to look at her right arm at all; mostly she just kept her eyes shut, squeezing out tears of terror and pain.

Her shoulder ached, and her chest and face felt hot, and there was a faint, dull throbbing where Dr. Williams had, within minutes of seeing her, shot her arm full of every antibiotic he had available.

They had asked her how it started, and she'd told them about the tank truck, but they hadn't done anything about it; Dr. Williams had been too busy with his needles and salves, trying to slow down the spreading damage.

They had not been able to get Jennie's shirt off; the sleeve's fabric was stuck to her arm, and any attempt to tear it free resulted in screaming agony.

"I'm going to see if I can find out what was in that truck," Dr. Williams said, "but unless they've got some kind of miracle, I think the whole arm will have to come off."

Jennie's mother sucked in her breath, but Jennie pursed her lips, took a glance at the ruin of her hand, and nodded.

"Hurry," she said.

#

They were going to cut off her arm.

This wasn't some TV show, like "Agents of SHIELD," or like the end of "The Empire Strikes Back," where they would just put on a robot one and she'd be as good as new. This was real life, and her arm was going to be *gone*, she'd just have an empty sleeve pinned up to her shoulder like that man she saw on the bus once, or the guy on "Dancing with the Stars." She'd be like that for the rest of her life.

But if they didn't cut it off, she was going to be *dead*, like that cat that got run over, or the squirrels on the highway. Sometimes people talked about dead kids going to Heaven, but Jennie didn't think she believed that stuff, and wasn't in any hurry to find out. Dying was *scary*, even scarier than letting them cut off her arm... if cutting off her arm would work.

The way that stuff spread, just that one little tiny spot turning into *this* – wouldn't it already be all over, inside her? Wasn't it already too late?

She whimpered. She was going to *die*, she knew it.

Her mother was standing there watching, and *not* saying it would all be okay, and that was as frightening as anything else, because her mother *always* said it would be all right, even when Jennie couldn't see how – but this time she wasn't saying it; when Jennie whimpered she just bit her lip and stared at her daughter.

And she wasn't picking Jennie up, wasn't hugging her, and Jennie knew why – she didn't want to touch the brown goo. Jennie looked down at the shirt she had never managed to button all the way up because her right hand had hurt too much.

She could see her chest, the pale skin damp with sweat – and the little brown spots that seemed to be spreading as she watched.

Cutting off her arm wouldn't help. It was too late.

"Mommy?" she said.

Her mother looked at her, followed her gaze down to those spots on her chest, and gasped. "Jennie," she said helplessly.

Then Dr. Williams was standing in the door, but not entering the room.

"It's a failed bio-weapon," he said. "There are scientists on the way, experts on the stuff." He stared at Jennie. "Be brave, honey."

"I'm going to die, aren't I?" she asked. Her breath seemed to hurt her throat, and her chest felt tight.

"I don't know," Dr. Williams said. He turned to her mother. "Is there anyone else we should call? Was there anyone else in the house this morning?"

"Her father – he had just left for work when we... when..."

"Brothers? Sisters? School?"

"She's in third grade."

"The scientists," Jennie said. "Can they fix it?"

Dr. Williams started to say something, then stopped. He shook his head. When he spoke again he sounded angry, as if he was trying to control himself and couldn't quite do it.

"They want to see what it looks like," he said. "What it does. But they have no idea how to stop it."

"So I'm going to die." It was not a question this time, but Dr. Williams nodded.

"I'm sorry," he said.

"They want to watch me die."

He nodded again.

"I'm so sorry, baby," her mother said. Jennie could see tears on her cheeks. She looked as if she was trying to control herself and not doing it, too, but where Dr. Williams looked angry, Jennie's mother looked sad.

Jennie felt tears on her own cheeks, mixing with sweat. She held out her arms, the left still normal, the right a misshapen horror. "Mommy!" she cried.

And without thinking, her mother came forward and hugged her.

Jennie closed her eyes as they embraced, then opened them to see brown goo on her mother's jaw where Jennie's right arm had touched.

Jennie saw her mother's eyes widen with horror as she realized what they had done.

Jennie thought she should probably say she was sorry, but the words would not come.

She was going to die, she didn't need to be sorry for anything anymore. She was going to die.

But at least she wouldn't die alone.

end

~~~~~

The Worst Part

Sometimes he tried to tell himself that the wait at the gate was the worst part. Why they called it a gate at all, he wasn't sure – the damn thing wasn't a gate, it was a tunnel, and the combination made him think of the gates of Hell.

That was all too appropriate an image--a tunnel down into the Hell of an airliner's cabin, with its sadistically-narrow seats, its fetid pressurized air, the hard, ugly plastic everywhere.

The wait wasn't really the worst part at all. It was bad, it was very bad, but the *worst* part...

Well, it just kept on getting worse. The long, horrible wait in that dreary holding pen, strewn with other people's newspapers, and then the march down the tunnel like prisoners into their cells, squeezing through that right-angle right turn where the crew greeted everyone with their phony smiles and where, off to the left, he could see into the cockpit, could see all that ominous black machinery with its colored lights, obviously too complex for anyone to actually understand and control properly.

And then down the aisle, waiting while people stuffed heavy luggage into the overhead compartments, standing there sweating and stinking of fear while those idiots blithely tried to jam in as much as possible, so that it could all fall down on him later, and then they'd bend themselves into their horrid little seats and let him past, so that he could find his own horrid little seat and squeeze himself into it.

Grope for the seatbelt, near panic for a moment when one side seems to be missing, visions of bouncing around the cabin, head battering against the reading lights and attendant call buttons, as the plane veers and swoops. Then find the belt, buckle in, and worry about whether he'll be able to get it open again, ever, or whether he'll sit there, trapped and struggling, while the cabin fills with smoke, with flame, with water, while the other passengers all slide out to safety and he sits there, strapped down and waiting, and they don't hear his screams over their own relieved laughter...

And his knees hit the seat in front of him, his head doesn't fit comfortably on the headrest, half the time they're flying the attendants block the aisle with their silly drink cart so he can't reach the lavatory or the exit if there's an emergency.

And the take-off, the engines screaming so that it hurts to think, the wing deforming itself as he watches out the window, what if those flaps come loose, can those little metal struts really hold it all together at six hundred miles an hour, my God, *six hundred miles an hour*, how can *anything* hold together, how can anyone control it, at that speed?

Six hundred miles an hour, thirty thousand feet up, that's *six miles up*, six miles with nothing but empty air below them, nothing holding them up but those bits of metal, those hydraulic struts that hold the wings together, the wings he can see bouncing and shimmying like diving boards that someone's just used for that six-mile plunge, the wings that could tear off or fall to pieces at any moment, and the plane would turn and plummet earthward, falling six miles out of the sky, six miles would give him time to watch, to think, to see that he was going to die, he'd have all the time he needed to think it over, he'd be able to see the ground screaming up at him, and he wouldn't be able to do a thing, he'd be strapped in his seat while the plane was in freefall, like the biggest damn roller coaster you ever saw going down a six-mile drop, only there's no curved rail to swoop him back up, he'll go down and down and *down* until he hits the hard earth, and his neck snaps and his bones break and his blood sprays across several counties, they'll be picking pieces of him out of cornfields and hedges, and everyone will read the newspapers and see just another statistic and they'll never think of the shock of impact, the incredible pain, the burned black flesh when the jet fuel ignites.

And if the wings hold up, if the pilot doesn't go mad and dive just to see how big a crater he can make, if the pilot doesn't die of a stroke and send them diving, if the engines don't explode, if the fuel doesn't spill away into the air as a toxic cloud settling over the countryside and leaving them powerless, if the whole thing doesn't catch fire from the friction of that incredible six-hundred-mile-an-hour speed and smother them all in smoke, if the pressurization doesn't fail and leave them all gasping in unbreathably thin air, eyes bugging out and hands clutching throats as they suck at air that isn't there, drowning in near-vacuum like fish out of water... if none of that happens, then they'll reach the airport where they're to land, and they'll drop down out of the sky *deliberately*, falling down through those six miles of nothing and trusting the plane and the pilot to catch them at the last minute and land them safely on the runway, not to plow into a building somewhere; they'll hit the ground still traveling two hundred miles an hour, and those engines that have been screaming for hours will suddenly roar into reverse, sucking in everything as they try to stop the plane's headlong rush to disaster, and the tires will squeal and shudder as they scrape along the tarmac, and he'll sit helplessly in his seat, his life in the pilot's hands, waiting for the impact with the terminal, with another plane that's on the runway by mistake; waiting for a tire to blow, a strut to fail, for the plane to buckle sideways and drive wreckage in through the window at him.

And *that* was the worst; after that, it would be over, the panic would subside, his stomach would relax--he might need to vomit, he had once or twice--and he would get off the plane only shaking slightly, and he'd tell himself that there, it wasn't really all that bad, he'd tell his friends that he was okay, he didn't like flying but it was no big deal, there was nothing to be scared of. He knew all the statistics, the facts, the reasonable, rational attitudes, and he would convince himself that he believed them, that they applied to him, that he could fight down his fear and control it.

He knew that his fear wasn't rational, not really, and he was a rational man. He'd relax and he'd *forget* how awful it was, he'd forget and he'd agree to do it *again*, he'd buy a ticket to fly somewhere else, and then when it was too late to back out he'd start remembering again, the panic would start to gnaw at his belly, his throat would dry and tighten, and rationality would fall away, he'd *know* that he was going to die this time, that *this* would be the plane that fell flaming from the sky, and it would be worse than ever before, every time it was worse, every time he told himself he was over his fear and every time it was *worse*.

But every time he *forgot* that, forgot what it was like and agreed to fly again, and that brought him back here, right where he was, sitting at that gate to Hell, Gate C3 for Flight 1108, his palms sweaty and his fingers shaking as he tried to control his fear. He looked down at them, tried to will them to be still, to be steady and calm and brave.

"Jack?"

He looked up, startled, and his eyes wouldn't focus at first.

"Jack Hartman? Is that you?"

"Sharon?" The neatly-attired young woman in the dark-green skirt and jacket stood in front of him, looking down at him, a purse hung from one shoulder and an overnight bag held in front of her; he blinked up at the heart-shaped face with its uncertain smile.

"It *is* you!" she said, and the smile became steadier. "Jack, it's been years!"

"Yeah," he said, vaguely aware that he should smile back, that he should have said something clever, or at least semi-intelligent, rather than the single stupid monosyllable. He should have given some sign that he recognized her and remembered her and was glad to see her.

He couldn't; he was too full of fear, too busy worrying about his impending death, his certainty that his plane would crash.

"Are you all right?" she asked, the smile vanishing; she dropped the overnight bag and sat down in the seat beside him, leaning toward him.

"I'm okay," he said.

"You're pale," she said. "I mean, *white*."

"I'm okay," he insisted. "I just don't like flying, and I get nervous waiting."

"Oh," she said, and the tone of her voice wasn't the derision he feared, but it wasn't comforting, either, it was simply puzzled. He started to turn away, then stopped himself; that would be unforgivably rude. She was trying to be helpful, she was concerned about him; it wasn't her fault if she didn't understand something as irrational as his fear of flying.

"So what are... how are you?" he managed to say.

"Oh, I'm fine. Are you sure you're okay?"

"I'm fine, really – just don't like flying."

"But you – you were never scared of anything, Jack; you're afraid of flying?"

The look her in eyes took him back a dozen years, to high school, when he and Sharon's older brother Greg had been pals, teasing Greg's kid sister at every opportunity, but she'd still hung around, staring at Jack with admiring eyes.

That admiration was still there.

He stared at her, amazed and glorified; if he'd ever thought about it at all he'd thought it was just a little-girl crush, that she must have outgrown it long ago, but here she was, a grown woman, looking at him with that same wide-eyed intensity.

No one had looked at him like that in years.

"It's been a long time," he said.

"Oh, I *know*," she said, "It's been *too* long! I kept asking Greg to write to you, or call you, you know, just to keep in touch, I didn't think I should do it myself, you know how that is..." Was she blushing slightly? He almost thought she was.

"I should've written myself," Jack said.

He didn't really mean it; he and Greg had drifted apart, and neither of them had been much interested in staying in touch once Jack moved away. Some friendships lasted, some didn't, and his friendship with Greg had been one he outgrew.

But Sharon obviously hadn't outgrown her interest.

He started to ask what she was doing here, then stopped himself. What *else* would she be doing at an airport gate with an overnight bag? She was waiting for a plane – for the same plane he would be riding.

They would be flying together – maybe they could arrange to sit together. That would be...

That would be horrible. He would be white-faced and gasping for air, and she would be laughing at him. She'd see him for the coward he was, and that admiration would leave her eyes forever, his goddamned phobia would do what years of separation had not.

But maybe her presence would help. Maybe he could hide it, fight down his fear; after all, for several seconds, while he looked at her face, he had managed to forget that he was waiting to board the airplane that would carry him to some horrible humiliating death.

And maybe...

"So you don't mind flying?" he asked.

"Oh, I *love* flying!" she said. "Watching the ground fall away, sailing through the sky – I *love* it!"

Hardly a fellow sufferer, he told himself mockingly. "I don't," he said. "Bad food, cramped seats – I hate it."

"Oh, that's silly, it's not so bad," she said. She blinked. "Oh, is *that* what you meant, about not liking it? I thought it *scared* you!"

He forced a smile, and said nothing.

"I should've known you weren't scared," she said. "You were never scared of anything. What are you doing now, anyway? Are you married?"

She blushed again, he was almost certain – she must have realized just how blatant her interest was.

"No," he said. "Not at the moment. What about you?"

"Never," she said.

"I remember you worked at that drugstore; you still there?"

"Of course not! I have a *real* job now!"

They chatted, and for first seconds, then minutes at a time he forgot his fear. Color came back to his face; his hands didn't shake as he adjusted himself in his seat, as he patted her hand. While she told him about decorating her apartment on the cheap he found himself thinking that maybe this time, maybe *this* time, he could hide his fear, maybe if he had her beside him to talk to he could forget about fire and smoke and falling and asphyxiation.

And maybe when they landed he could ask her out somewhere, if he hadn't made a fool of himself on the flight.

"Now boarding, rows 16 through 23," the PA announced, and Jack groped reluctantly for his briefcase; Sharon snatched her overnight bag out of his way.

Together they walked toward the entrance to the jetway, still talking; at the door she stopped, and he stopped as well, assuming that she must be sitting in one of the rows further forward, the rows that hadn't been called yet. A momentary surge of panic flooded through him at the thought that they would be separated on the plane, that she would not be there beside him to help him stay calm, but would see him when he burst out screaming in terror.

Surely, though, they could trade seats around somehow. He knew that if she was beside him, the flight wouldn't be so bad.

At least, not until the crash.

"All seats, now boarding," came the call.

"I guess I'd better say goodbye," she said, stepping back, away from the gate.

He stared at her, thunderstruck. "Aren't you coming?" he croaked.

"Oh, no!" she said. "I wish I was." She giggled. "I'm sorry, I guess I didn't explain. I'm just here to meet Greg – his plane's delayed, it'll be arriving over there in another twenty minutes or so." She pointed at another gate, Gate C5.

"But the overnight bag..."

"This?" She hefted it. "Oh, this is Greg's; it got checked onto an earlier flight by mistake. I'm sorry, I should have explained. Goodbye, Jack; write sometime, why don't you?" She was receding, somehow, backing away from him, and he was drifting down into the jetway, down through the gates of Hell, toward the plane that would carry him to fiery destruction, and he could not turn back, could not reveal himself to be a coward to her as he watched her carried away from him, lost forever. He could feel the blood draining from his face, could feel his hands trembling more than ever. His last hope was walking away.

She turned and waved.

"Have a good flight!" she called, smiling.

And that was the very worst part of all.

end

HAZMAT

~~~~~

Playing for Keeps

Carefully, Jason leaned out the open window and peered about. The moon was half full, providing him with plenty of light to see that the side lawn was smooth and empty, the hedge dark and unbroken. Nothing moved, nothing was out of place.

He pulled his head back in and listened for a moment. He heard nothing but crickets and his own breathing; his parents and his kid sister were, he was sure, sound asleep.

The coast was clear.

Cautiously, he climbed headfirst out the window onto the porch roof, then pulled himself down the sloping asphalt shingles on his belly. At the edge he reached down and grasped the corner pillar, then gradually worked his feet around, crab-fashion, until he was able to swing his left leg down onto a foothold in the gingerbread.

From there it was easy; he slid the other leg around and shinnied quickly down the pole to the railing, and dropped from there down behind the bushes.

The bushes rustled more than he liked, and he froze for a moment, staring out at the vacant lawn gleaming silver in the moonlight.

The way was still clear. He was out of the house, free to roam. He could slip down to the pond and catch himself a frog without his parents knowing a thing about it.

He gazed critically at the wide back yard, and decided that it was too open, too visible. He would find another route, rather than cutting straight across all that lawn.

The hedge that ran along the boundary with the McPhersons' yard would provide cover. He could follow it to the back corner, then make a short dash to the trees, and from there to the pond it was all woods.

A dash across the side yard, the long creep down the hedge, another dash, and the woods. It would be easy. It would be fun, too, as if he were a soldier dodging bullets or something. He crept out from behind the bush, looked quickly to either side, and ran.

A dozen steps and he was across the lawn, diving for the shelter of the hedge's shadow. He landed on his knees and elbows with his nose inches from the leaves, leaves that looked dead black in the pale light.

He glanced back at the lawn just in time to see the shadow stretch out across the grass.

Horrified, he looked up.

A figure loomed over him, shadowy black, tall, taller than seemed possible, its head bloated and misshapen. He gaped up in surprise. He fought down the urge to cry or scream as a gaunt hand reached down toward him.

The hand grabbed him by the back of his collar and hauled him upright, then yanked him clean off his feet. He dangled helplessly.

"Guess what, kid," a deep, deep voice said. "I'm the boogey man."

He wanted to say something smart, something scathing, in reply to this terrifying stranger, but all he could manage was, "No, you're not; there isn't any boogey man."

Teeth glinted as his captor smiled. "Maybe you're right, boy; maybe I'm not. But I might as well be. Now, you must be Jason Price; why don't we go see hat your parents think about you being out at this hour?" He casually lifted the struggling boy over the hedge and marched up the street, Jason still dangling from his hand.

From his altered angle Jason could see his foe more clearly; he was no longer a mass of empty shadow. The weird bloating of the head was really just a battered wide-brimmed felt hat; the teeth were flat human teeth, the eyes dark and smiling, the hands large, but just hands, with only five fingers apiece. He was just a man, whoever he was.

They reached the street and turned left, toward Jason's house, and Jason demanded, "Put me down; I'll walk from here."

"I don't think so," the other replied; he marched on.

"You're ruining my shirt," Jason complained.

His captor shrugged. "That's too bad."

He turned and marched up the front walk, strode smoothly up the porch steps, and with the boy still dangling from his right hand, rang the bell with his left.

There was a long moment's wait, and Jason heard banging and voices within. The porch light flashed on and his father opened the door, wearing his old bathrobe.

"What is it?" he said, blinking.

"Mr. Price?" the self-proclaimed boogey man said. "I believe this belongs to you." He held Jason up to the light.

"Jason?" Price gaped, then remembered himself. "Oh, of course. Thank you, Mr. Crowley. Where'd you catch him?"

"Oh, I happened to be behind the hedge next door when he climbed down the porch."

"Oh. Well, thank you; put him down, I'll take care of him now."

"All right." Crowley lowered Jason roughly, not quite dropping him. "He's all yours for now, Mr. Price."

"Thank you, Mr. Crowley."

"Just remember," Crowley said with a broad smile, "the third time I keep him."

Price managed a feeble reflection of the other's grin. "Of course." He grabbed Jason's arm and hauled him into the house. "Good night, Mr. Crowley; thanks again."

Crowley tipped his hat and stood, smiling, as Price closed the door.

As soon as the latch clicked into place, Jason demanded, "Who's that guy? What was he doin' back there?"

"Never mind who that is, Jason; what the Hell were you doing outside at this hour?"

"Aw, Jesus, Dad, I just wanted to go down to the pond and catch some frogs when there wasn't anybody else around to scare 'em off!"

"Well, you'll have to find some better time to do it than the middle of the night! Don't you know it's dangerous running around in the dark? You could get arrested, or attacked. You're lucky it was Mr. Crowley who found you, and not some pervert!"

"How do you know *Crowley's* not a pervert?" Jason countered.

"Well, if you must know, he's the new security patrolman for the block; the Neighborhood Council hired him last month."

"So what business is it of his if I go catch frogs?"

"That's one of the things we're paying him for, to make sure you kids don't go running around at all hours, so we don't have teenagers screwing in the woods back there."

"What's that got to do with me? I'm only eleven!"

"And that's too damn young to be running around at two in the morning!" Price bellowed.

Jason sensed he wasn't going to get anywhere by arguing his right to roam free at night. "I still think Crowley's a pervert!" he said, trying a different tack.

"We checked him out, boy, don't you think we didn't – and if he *is* a pervert, that's all the more reason for you to stay in at night the way you're supposed to, so he won't catch you again!"

Jason couldn't think of an answer to that; he shut up and stared at his father in silence defiance.

He wasn't actually punished, just sent back to bed. He watched his father close and lock the window, then stamp out and close the door. He sat in bed, thinking, and it was a long hour before he finally slid down and fell asleep.

The following night he stayed inside, but spent two hours crouched at the window, watching the yard, watching the MacPhersons' yard, studying every detail of the hedge in between, leaning over to stare at the woods far off to the right.

He saw no sign of Crowley, but he didn't risk climbing out; he had seen no sign of Crowley before he was caught, either.

The next day, at school, one of the kids mentioned "the boogey man," and Jason was surprised to hear that half a dozen of his friends knew about Crowley's presence. In fact, some knew considerably more than he did.

"He's six foot five, my dad says," Bill Jenkins told him. "Six foot five, and he weighs a hunnerd and sixty-five pounds, but he's strong enough to pick a kid up and carry him like he weighs nuthin'."

Jason nodded agreement. "He's strong, all right."

"He lives in the top floor apartment at that place on Elm, the one with that tower on the corner, and he sleeps all day and only comes out at night. He was like that anyway, that's why they hired him."

31

"Maybe there's something wrong with him, so he can't stand the sun," Sam Hessen suggested.

"Maybe he's really the boogey man, like he says," Jim Fairleigh said.

"There ain't any boogey man!" Jason said.

"How d'you know?" Jim countered.

"There just ain't," Jason insisted. "He's like Santa Claus or the Easter Bunny, something the grown-ups use to get kids to behave."

"Well, this Crowley guy sure is strange, whether he's the boogey man or not," Bill said. "He *tells* everybody he's the boogey man."

"I think he's a pervert," Jason said.

"Naw," Bill said. "They wouldn't hire a perv!"

"How would they know?"

"Well, he ain't never been arrested, I heard my dad tell my mom that. Clean record, he says."

"If he's really the boogey man they wouldn't have caught him," Jim pointed out.

"There ain't any boogey man," Jason insisted.

"Where'd they find him?" Sam asked.

"*I* don't know," Bill replied. Nobody else volunteered any more information.

Jason mulled it all over, and after he had given it sufficient thought he announced to his friends, "I'm not gonna take it."

"What aren't you gonna take?" Sam asked.

"I'm not gonna take this Crowley character or any of his boogey man crap. It's a free country, ain't it? Who's he to tell me I can't take a walk in the middle of the night if I want?"

"He's just doin' what our parents want, that's all," Joe Kimball said. "I don't think it's his idea. I kinda think he likes kids, from what I seen; he's always makin' jokes and smilin', talkin' about how he'd like to keep 'em."

"Well, I'm not gonna take it," Jason insisted.

"Suit yourself," Bill said with a shrug, "but *I'm* not gonna argue with him."

The bell rang, putting an end to the conversation.

That night Jason watched out his window again, very carefully, starting the moment his bedroom door was closed. He saw no sign of Crowley anywhere. He waited and watched.

The moon was two-thirds full, the sky was clear, and Jason saw no sign of Crowley. He heard the crickets chirping, an occasional frog calling faintly to him from the pond.

Finally, at half past two, he slid out the window onto the porch roof and made his way to the ground.

From the bushes by the porch he stared critically at the hedge. That had been his mistake, he decided, going to the hedge. Crowley might be lurking there right now, and even if he weren't he could sneak along the other side and Jason wouldn't be able to spot him.

If he were to go straight across the back lawn, though, Crowley wouldn't have anywhere to hide, and Jason didn't think he was the sort who would chase a kid halfway across town. No, Jason told himself, Crowley was an ambusher; it went with the calm smiling style.

With that in mind, he slipped out from behind the bushes and headed straight back toward the trees, across the open expanse of lawn.

As he passed the back corner of the house something grabbed the back of his shirt, and he was snatched up into the air.

"Guess what, Jason," that deep voice said. "It's the boogey man, and I've got you again."

Jason was furious; how could he have been caught so easily? He thrashed, kicking, and tried to drive his elbow back into Crowley's chest.

Crowley did not bother with subtlety; his left hand flashed out as his right twisted, and his long bony fingers clamped around Jason's throat.

"Stop it, boy," he said.

Jason struggled for another few seconds, then stopped as his air supply ran out. The grip loosened.

"Listen to me, Jason," Crowley said. "I don't want any of this from you. I caught you where you had no business being, outside at this hour; now you behave yourself, or you'll get a lot worse than anything you've got from me yet."

The voice was flat and deadly, and Jason believed it completely. He put up no further resistance as the rest of the scene was acted out much as before. He was carried helplessly to his front porch, the doorbell brought his father, and Price and Crowley exchanged polite words, Crowley smiling all the time. He was then left in his father's custody.

This time he didn't talk back or argue; the memory of that grip on his throat was too fresh. He nodded quietly and went back to bed when his father had finished yelling.

The next day, however, the pain and fright had faded, and his indignation had begun to mount. How had Crowley dared to treat him like that? He was an innocent child, not some kind of axe-murderer trying to escape. His parents were paying their fake boogey man to protect them, not to manhandle their children. What if his larynx had collapsed? He'd seen that happen on a doctor show on TV, and the person had almost died, and they had had to cut her throat open and stick tubes in.

He told himself that he should have complained, should have said something to his father. Why hadn't he?

Well, he decided, it wasn't Dad's business; this was between him and Crowley. He'd handle it on his own. He was almost twelve now, old enough to take care of himself.

Besides, he wasn't sure that his father would believe him. A glance in the mirror showed no bruises or other marks on his neck.

He thought about it for the rest of the day, making plans, and that afternoon, while he was at Sam's house and Sam was in the bathroom, he snuck into Sam's older brother Al's room. He knew that Al had what he wanted; he'd seen him show it off once, and had seen where he put it afterward.

It was right where he had seen it before. He stuck it in his pocket and hurried back out of the room before he was caught.

That night it rained, and Jason stayed inside. He woke up briefly around three and glanced out the window, and thought he saw something tall and dark moving across the lawn. Before he could focus on it it was gone; he stared futilely for a few minutes, then went back to bed.

The rain lingered through the following day and night, but the day after that was sunny and warm, a lovely spring day.

Night arrived, and Jason watched television disinterestedly as he pretended to do his math homework. Finally, at ten-thirty, his mother turned off the set and shooed him upstairs.

He lay awake in bed, waiting.

At one, he rose and dressed silently, then fished his stolen prize from its hiding place in his bureau drawer. With it safe in his pocket he crossed to the window and opened it.

The night air was cool and fresh, the singing of the crickets soothing, but Jason wasn't concerned with that. He stared out at the lawn, studied every foot of the hedge, peered at the back corner of the house.

He didn't see Crowley, but he had no doubt that the tall dark man was out there, waiting.

He hoped he was out there. He intended to show this Mr. Crowley that Jason Price wasn't just a rag doll you could throw around as you pleased.

He climbed out onto the porch roof, made his way to the ground, and without preamble marched boldly out across the lawn.

Crowley reared up from behind the hedge, his shadow falling across Jason so suddenly that the boy started. Jason's hand dove into his pocket.

Crowley stepped through the hedge with a hissing of branches against cloth, and strode purposefully toward Jason.

"Not this time, Mr. Boogey Man!" Jason said as he whipped out the switchblade and pressed the button.

Crowley didn't say a word; he just kept coming, one slow deliberate step at a time.

That wasn't in the plan; Jason had thought that Crowley would stop at the sight of the knife shining silver in the moonlight, would stand back frightened, and Jason had planned out a little speech, telling him that he couldn't bully Jason Price. But Crowley wasn't stopping.

He finally came to a halt one step away from Jason, staring down at the boy from the black shadows of his decrepit hat.

"Get away from me!" Jason said, brandishing the knife.

Crowley reached out with both hands, reached out and hooked his fingers into the front of Jason's shirt. He hooked his fingers into the fabric and clenched them into fists, and started to pick Jason up off the ground.

"No!" Jason shouted; he stabbed wildly.

Crowley gave a little grunt as the knife was jammed into his belly, and the world froze for the two of them.

Jason stared in utter horror at his hand, at the short little slit he had cut in Crowley's flannel shirt, and at the gleaming steel blade that joined the two, the blade that was sunk three inches into Crowley's flesh.

He hadn't meant for this to happen. He had just committed murder. He had stabbed a human being, stuck a knife into a man.

All he had wanted to do was scare the man, the way the man had scared him. He hadn't meant to hurt anyone. He was a good boy, not a trouble-maker or a delinquent.

He was going to jail, and the other prisoners, the *real* murderers, would beat him and do whatever the terrible things were that men did to each other, and he might be stabbed himself, might feel the steel biting into him and his blood spilling out hot and red. He stared in fascinated revulsion at the knife, at the gleaming steel blade embedded in Mr. Crowley's belly.

He realized, at last, that the blade was clean. There was no blood.

The hands tightened on his shirt and yanked upward, and the moment of frozen time was broken and gone. The knife pulled out of the flesh, and still no blood flowed. Instead Jason smelled burning, hot and metallic, and saw a wisp of black smoke curling up. The tip of the switchblade was black where it had gone in.

His eyes moved up across Crowley's chest to his face, a face that was somehow changed from what it had been, as if a mask had come off. The tall figure grinned, and a dusky red glow showed between jagged teeth. His eyes gleamed dark green around slit pupils.

"Guess what, Jason," that deep and terrible voice said. "I really *am* the boogey man." The grin widened, the red glow brightened.

"And the third time, I keep you."

end

HAZMAT

~~~~~

Back to the Land

The house stood alone on the side of the hill, shaded by great oaks, a thousand feet back from the road at the end of a long driveway that had once been graveled, but was now just mud. The roof and the porch sagged, like swaybacked horses; the shutters, most of them still functional, were closed and latched across every visible window but two, one upstairs and one down, that Matthew placed as the front bedroom and the parlor.

Here and there clapboards hung by one end, or had fallen away completely, and no paint remained anywhere, only the bare gray wood.

The yard was mostly weeds and kudzu now where the lawn had once been; the forsythia, untrimmed, had grown into great twiggy arches on either side of the porch.

Matthew stared at the place through the autumn drizzle that misted the windshield, and wondered how his mother could stand living there.

Of course, she had never lived anywhere else; perhaps she didn't realize how badly off she was. She had been born in that house, in the front bedroom where she now slept, and where she intended to die. She had borne her children in that same room, in the same bed where she now lay; she had refused to tell her husband when she went into labor, lest he insist on taking her to the hospital in town. Even her wedding had taken place in that house, downstairs in the parlor, the room behind one of those still-unshuttered windows, because she had insisted upon it. Her husband, his father, had wanted a church wedding, where he could show off his bride, but she had refused. She had made a home wedding a condition of their engagement.

Matthew had grown up in that house, with his sisters, but he had had no compunction about leaving it. He had loved it, but not the way his mother had, and he had left it, as she would not, so long as she still lived. He'd been delighted to move away, first to college, and then to his job in Atlanta.

This was the first time he had been back in almost five years, and he was horrified at how much the place had deteriorated.

It had needed paint the last time he saw it, and the roof had been sagging, but he didn't remember it being anywhere near as bad as this. Could five years make such a difference in a house that had stood for over a century?

Behind the house he pulled his Dodge onto the sparse grass beside Mary's aging Toyota; beyond it sat Becky's Chevy pick-up. Mother's ancient black Ford occupied the end of the driveway by the shed, where the barn had once stood.

They were all here, then, all of them together for the first time since his father's funeral.

He sat for a moment, hoping the rain would stop completely, but it continued to fall; he opened the door and climbed out.

The rain was so thin that it wasn't worth hurrying; if he did he might slip in the mud and fall, so he just walked briskly across the driveway to the kitchen door. As he did he noticed there was a third unshuttered window back here, the one over the sink. It hadn't been visible from the drive.

He opened the screen door and knocked, then stood, avoiding the familiar drip from the low spot on the eaves, and waited.

When nobody responded, he knocked again.

This time he heard footsteps, and when they had marched across the bare wood of the kitchen floor he heard the knob rattle. The door swung open and he stepped in.

It was Becky who had admitted him.

"Hello, Matthew," she said, stepping back to make room for him, "Come on into the parlor, we've got a fire in the stove."

"Thanks, Becky." He stamped his feet to loosen the mud, then wiped them on the threadbare mat before following his sister.

Mary was there waiting in the shadowy dimness, perched on the faded velvet of the antique settee, leaning toward the heat of the Franklin stove.

She couldn't be cold, though, Matthew thought; the room was stifling hot, the air thick with the moisture that seeped in through every crack.

He wondered if the roof was actually leaking anywhere yet.

"How is she?" he asked.

"Dying," Mary snapped. "What did you *think?*"

Matthew glared at her. "I mean, how bad is she?" he said. "I know she's dying, but how is she right now? Conscious? Will it be hours, days, weeks?"

"I'm no doctor," Mary said angrily, sitting up straight.

"She drifts in and out," Becky said, still standing. "She'll be conscious one minute, asleep the next. The doctor said it could be any time, but he'd be surprised if she lasted another week."

Matthew nodded. A lump had formed in his throat.

41

"Would you like to see her?" Becky asked.

Matthew nodded again. "Yeah," he said.

Becky led him upstairs, to where the frail old woman lay in her bed beneath a mound of lace-trimmed quilts and comforters, wrapped up despite the heat.

Matthew shuddered at the thought that the cold they were trying to keep out wasn't any ordinary chill; it was the chill of the grave.

He stepped up close to the bedside, while Becky hung back.

The face on the pillow was pale, not a normal pallor, but as if all the colors had faded away, as if the face were an overexposed image, a bleached-out copy and not really his mother at all. The skin was drawn tight across the bone, and her breath rattled in and out unevenly.

"Mamma?" Matthew said.

The half-closed eyes opened and stared, unfocused, at the ceiling. Matthew leaned over the bed.

"It's me, Matthew," he said.

The dry lips worked, regaining a trace of color as she moistened them with her tongue.

"Mattie," she said, her eyes almost focusing now.

"Is there anything we can do for you?" he asked. "Anything at all?"

"'m fine," she said.

"Would you like to go to the hospital in town, Mamma? I'm sure they could make you comfortable there..."

"No." She took a deep, rattling breath, then said, "No hospital. Born here, lived my whole life in this house, by God I'll die here and be buried in my own land!"

"No, Mother, the county won't allow that, but we'll bury you in the cemetery in town next to Dad..."

"No!" She lifted her head, eyes wide and staring. "You bury me *here!* This land's been my life, given me everything, and I'm going to stay right here!"

"But..."

Becky came up behind him and put a hand on his shoulder. "Don't worry, Mamma," she said, "whatever you want. Matthew's just got here, he don't know what we got planned."

Their mother's breath came out in a rush, and she dropped back onto the pillow. "Good," she rasped.

Matthew stood staring at her for a moment, groping for words, but then he felt Becky tugging at his arm. He turned and let her lead him out of the room and back down the stairs to the front hall, beside the locked, never-used front door with its two panels of frosted and etched glass.

"Don't argue with her," Becky whispered.

"But we can't bury her here..." Matthew began.

Becky shook her head. "I didn't say we would – but why tell *her* that? Let her die thinking she'll stay here; let her be happy about it."

Matthew frowned, unhappy at the idea of lying to his mother, but then he glanced up the stairs and remembered how pitiful she was, how weak. He felt tears starting.

Becky was right.

"Okay," he said. "I won't argue with her."

"Good."

"Can I go up and look at her again?"

"If you want. Sit with her as long as you like; just don't upset her. I thought you could sleep in your old room at the back; you just go tuck yourself in there when you're ready."

Matthew nodded, and climbed slowly back up the stairs, afraid that by the time he got back to his mother's bedside it would be too late, that she would already be dead and his last words to her would have been an argument.

When he entered the room she was so still that he stopped, certain his fears had been realized – but then her eyes opened. She turned her head and looked at him.

"The land won't *let* you take me away," she said clearly.

"All right, Mamma," he said.

She closed her eyes again.

He fetched a chair and sat at the bedside; after awhile she raised a bony hand from beneath the coverings, and he took it in his own hand. Neither of them spoke.

They didn't need to talk. He was tired from the long drive, and she was tired from her long illness, and they didn't need to talk.

They sat there as the last light faded from the sky outside. A small bedside lamp was on, but the room was dim, the corners lost in shadows. The only sound was his mother's uneven, rasping breath.

He sat silently, thinking and remembering, hoping that she wasn't in pain, wishing that she could be healed, could be young and strong again. He remembered her as the absolute authority when he was a little boy, the loving figure whose word was law; he remembered her moving about her kitchen with deliberate efficiency, never hurrying but somehow always having the family dinner ready sooner than expected. He remembered her lack of interest in his schooling – until *he* became interested in learning, whereupon she devoted herself to seeing that he studied, that he got into college.

He thought of other mothers he had known, none of them like her.

He thought of the women he had dated, tried to imagine them raising children, and for the most part failed.

And he remembered his mother tending the land – weeding the garden, pruning the fruit trees, directing the men who bushhogged the back ten, working in the cornfields. That was the one thing that could take her away from her children, the one thing she did only for *herself*.

The surest sign of how sick she had been, he thought, was how overgrown the lawn had become.

And then he woke up, suddenly aware that he had dozed off and that something had startled him awake. He blinked and sat up.

Nothing seemed wrong. No one else was in the room; his mother was still lying peacefully in the bed, and he was still holding her hand. The sky outside the window was as black and empty as if nothing beyond the house existed at all. Everything was still.

Too still. She wasn't breathing.

And, he realized, her hand was already cold.

He pulled his fingers away and felt her cheek and forehead.

He couldn't define exactly how he knew so certainly, exactly what the difference was, but she was unmistakably dead. Whatever had made her his mother, a person, and not just an object, was gone.

"Becky?" he called. He got to his feet, stiff from sleeping sitting up, and realized he had no idea how long he had been there, or what time it was. He glanced at his watch.

3:34 a.m.

He debated with himself as to whether he should wake his sisters. They would want to know that their mother was gone, but in the middle of the night like this? Couldn't the news wait until morning?

He hadn't been here when their father died – that had been a much quicker thing, and he hadn't made it home in time. Was there anything that had to be done right away, anyone who had to be notified?

He couldn't think who or what might matter at this hour.

The best thing to do, he thought, was to go get some rest. Nothing he did would matter to his mother any more; she didn't need anything now.

Becky had said to use the bed in his old room. His suitcase, with his pajamas and clean clothes, was in the trunk of his car – it wasn't worth fetching it at this point, he could do that in the morning.

He leaned over and kissed his mother's cool, dead cheek.

"Goodbye, Mamma," he said.

He straightened up and looked down at her.

He might never see her again; in the morning there would probably be people from the funeral home, maybe some doctor to make it official, and then they'd take her away, and he'd never see her again.

Something creaked, somewhere downstairs.

He glanced at the door, startled. "Becky?" he called.

No answer.

It must have just been the house settling, he thought. There had been creaks sometimes when he was a boy. His concrete and steel apartment in the city didn't creak, but this place was tired old wood. Of course it made sounds sometimes; he'd forgotten, that was all.

Wood creaked again, a long, drawn-out sound, and Matthew looked about uneasily. Surely, the house hadn't made noises like *that* when he was a boy?

Was there someone downstairs?

Moving as quietly as he could, he crossed to the bedroom door and peered out into the hall.

It was dark, the only light coming from behind him; he could faintly see the floral pattern in the wallpaper as black splotches on dark grey, and he found himself thinking it looked unhealthy, like bloodstains or mold, as if the house, too, was sick or dying.

Something rumbled. Thunder?

But he heard no wind or rain, and the sound had seemed to come from below him somewhere.

This was all too much for him – waking up in the middle of the night to find his mother dead, and the house making strange noises. He didn't want to deal with it.

But he couldn't just go to bed. And he couldn't bring himself to wake up Mary or Becky – what if the noises were just his imagination, just the normal settling sounds, maybe distant heat lightning, magnified by the late-night silence?

He would go downstairs, he told himself, and sit for awhile. Maybe he could figure out where the sounds were coming from.

The stairs were dark; the light switch was down the far end of the passage, at the head of the stairs. He shuffled forward into the darkness, moving slowly in case there were some old toy or forgotten shoe lying in his path; he didn't want to trip.

Wood groaned, the low, painful sound of heavy timbers under massive pressure, and he stopped dead in his tracks.

"Becky?" he said again, quietly. He stood still and listened intently.

He heard a faint susurration, a shifting, sliding, brushing sound, like wind-tossed leaves scraping the clapboards. Wood creaked again

The house almost sounded as it might during a storm – but there was no storm. He heard no wind in the eaves, no rain on the roof – only the house.

This was ridiculous, he told himself. He forced himself to march briskly forward into the gloom, and groped for the light switch.

He found it, and warm yellow light burst from the blackened brass bowl above the stairs. The dark stains on the walls were transformed to faded red flowers and dull green leaves, and the steps appeared at his feet, solid wood beneath worn green carpet.

A drink, he thought. He needed a drink. His mother had just died; didn't he need a drink?

He marched down the stairs and through the darkened parlor – his mother had always kept the liquor in the cupboard above the silver.

He was on the kitchen threshold when the loudest, longest sound yet came, one that combined a deep rumble with the groaning of wood and a series of sharp snapping sounds; the floor shifted under his feet, and he caught himself against the doorframe.

Earthquake!

It had to be that. He had never felt a real earthquake, but what else could it be? The floor had moved beneath him!

An earthquake here, in the Kentucky hills?

There'd been the Maysville quake back in the '80s, when he was away at college, and there was that big one back in the early nineteenth century, but now?

Well, why not? At least that would make sure everyone around here remembered the night Esther Kittridge died.

"Matthew?" someone called.

"Down here," he replied. He decided his drink could wait; the quake must have wakened Becky, and she'd want to know what was going on. He headed back through the parlor.

The floor jerked, and he almost lost his balance again.

Aftershock?

Except it seemed to continue; after the initial jerk there was a steady vibration, and he could hear a dull grinding noise from beneath the floor.

He met both his sisters at the foot of the stairs.

"What's happening?" Becky asked.

"What about Mother?" Mary demanded.

"Mamma's gone – I don't know exactly when, I'd fallen asleep, but... well, she's gone." He glanced up at the door of the front bedroom.

Mary tightened her lips, and Matthew thought he saw the gleam of tears in her eyes, but she said nothing.

"What's that noise?" Becky asked.

"I don't know," Matthew replied. "I thought maybe it was an earthquake."

Becky's eyes widened. "Shouldn't we get outside, then?"

Wood creaked and popped somewhere.

"You're right," Matthew said, turning to look at the front door.

"But what about Mother?" Mary said, an edge of hysteria in her voice. "We can't leave her in here alone!"

Matthew turned and stared at his sister.

"Mary," he said gently, "Mother is *dead*."

"I'm not leaving her."

Matthew glanced helplessly at Becky, who shrugged.

Then the floor shifted under them all, and Matthew barely caught himself against the wall. Becky grabbed the newel post, and Mary the bannister.

Wood groaned, something cracked, and plaster dust sifted down from somewhere above.

"Come on," Matthew said. He lurched over to the front door and grabbed at the knob.

It wouldn't turn.

He found the bolt and slid it open, looked for another lock and found none, but still the knob would not turn. He looked the door up and down, but could see no obstruction. He heard a faint scratching, but could not see how that might have anything to do with the door's reluctance.

"It won't open," he said. "It must be rusted solid from disuse."

"Then we'll go out the back," Becky said. "That's where the cars are, anyway."

Matthew nodded, and he and Becky hurried through the parlor and into the kitchen. Becky flipped on the light; Matthew grabbed the doorknob, turned it, and pulled.

The door didn't move.

Startled, Matthew looked at it, and saw that the frame had twisted and broken from the house's movements, wedging the door solidly in place. "Damn," he said. He turned to the window over the sink.

There he stopped, staring in astonishment.

Becky came up beside him and stared as well.

The light from the kitchen was not spilling out through the glass to be lost in the darkness of the yard; instead it shone on rich black earth, packed against the windowpane, and sliding slowly upward.

"Is that mud?" Matthew asked. "How can it move *up* like that?"

"It's not mud," Becky said. "It's earth. And it isn't moving up. We're sinking."

"What?"

She didn't bother to answer; she didn't have to. He could see it for himself. He could feel it, as well, now that she had pointed it out.

The house was sinking, slipping down into the earth.

"The earthquake did that?"

"If it *was* an earthquake," Mary said from behind them, startling them both. Matthew whirled to face her.

"What else could it be?" he demanded.

"It could just be the house sinking," Mary said. "Maybe nothing else shook; maybe it's just the house. I saw it in the parlor window, the same as you see it here – it's sinking."

"It must have been built on a fault or something," Matthew said.

"Or maybe it's the land, claiming us all," Mary said. "Maybe it's the land making sure we don't take Mother away. She spent her whole life here, and it wants her to stay."

"That's ridiculous," Becky said. "You make it sound like the land's *alive*, Mary."

"Mother thought it was."

"It's the earthquake," Matthew insisted. "That's all."

"Whatever it is," Becky said, "shouldn't we get outside?"

Matthew looked at the window; the soil now covered its full height, and was still moving upward. "How?" he asked, his voice unsteady. "Dig?"

"Upstairs," Becky said, pointing.

Matthew felt suddenly stupid for having missed the obvious. "Come on," he said, trying to cover his idiocy.

Together, walking quickly, the three siblings made their way back through the parlor and up the stairs. Around them the house continued to creak and groan, the earth outside to scrape and hiss against the clapboards. At the top of the stairs Matthew hesitated.

"The shutters are closed everywhere but Mamma's room," Becky reminded him.

"Right," Matthew agreed. He led the way down the passage to the front bedroom.

As they approached, though, he slowed with every step. His mother was still in there, he realized, and irrational childhood terrors stirred in the back of his mind. A dark house at night, a dead body...

What was waiting in the room at the end of the passage? He looked through the open door and saw the great rearing shadows thrown by the little bedside lamp, black smears of darkness across the warm golden light.

Would there be flies crawling on their mother's face? He wasn't sure he could take that. Would she have begun to decay, to turn from his mother into something bloated and dark and horrible?

But she hadn't moved, hadn't changed; at first glance she might still have been asleep. Had her mouth fallen open a little further? Had her color worsened?

Maybe – but there were no vermin, no gruesome discolorations, no foul odors. She lay undisturbed, and the room smelled of dust and old fabric.

"Mother," Mary said, almost whimpering. She pushed past Matthew and walked to the bedside, moving with a strange, jerky step, an apparent unwillingness, almost as if something were dragging her across the room. She bent over the body.

Becky followed her, and stood behind Mary for a moment, looking over Mary's shoulder.

Matthew watched for a moment as his sisters paid their respects, then turned to the window. He blinked in surprise, then stepped closer, to make sure the poor light wasn't playing tricks on him.

The shutters were closed.

This had been the only upstairs window that was *not* shuttered; he had seen it from the outside as he drove up, and again from inside.

They must have come unhooked and swung shut, he told himself. The vibration had done it, the shaking from the earthquake. Nothing else made any sense.

They wouldn't be latched, though, and they must swing freely. He knew some of the shutters on the house were jammed, latches and hinges rusted; the shutters on the back storeroom had been *nailed* shut, twenty years before.

But these shutters had been open a few minutes earlier, he was certain.

He hurried across and pried at the latch on the window sash; it wouldn't move.

"Oh, *shit*," he said – then glanced guiltily at his mother, as if she might come back from the dead to chastise her son for using such language.

"What's the matter?" Becky asking.

"It's stuck," he said.

Before Becky could say anything more, for once acting on his own without her advice, he picked up a heavy silver-backed hand mirror from atop the dresser and swung it at the window like a hammer.

Glass shattered spectacularly; Mary looked up, shocked.

"What are you *doing*?" she demanded.

"Getting us out of here while we still can," Matthew replied, as he swung the mirror back and forth like a duellist's sword, smashing away shards of glass and crumbling century-old window putty. The hot, stuffy air of the bedroom rushed out, and cool, moist night air spilled in through the opening – along with the smell of damp earth.

The wooden divider between the panes of the lower sash did not break when he whacked at it with the mirror, so he stepped back and kicked at it, snapping it.

"Stop it! Stop it!" Mary shrieked. "Can't you... this is *Mamma's bedroom!* Stop it!"

Matthew looked at her, startled. The fact that she had slipped and said "Mamma" instead of "Mother" told him how upset she was.

"Sorry," he said, a bit shamefaced. He dropped the battered mirror back on the dresser, then crunched across the broken glass to the window. He reached out and pushed at the shutters. They opened only slightly before scraping to a stop. Matthew peered out through the inch-wide crack between them.

He was looking out at ground level, as if from a basement; the shutters were blocked at the bottom by thick turf. As he looked, a small clod of dirt rolled in through the crack, tumbling onto the windowsill. An earthworm followed it.

The ground rumbled, and wood creaked; the shutters twisted slightly under the upward pressure of the earth, so that the crack between them widened at the top.

"If we're going out this way we're going to have to hurry," he said.

"What about Mother?" Mary asked, her calm restored.

"I don't know," Matthew said. "Should we try to bring her out? It won't be easy."

"No," Becky said, "what good would it do?"

"We can't just *leave* her here, to be buried alive!" Mary said, horrified.

"She's not alive, Mare," Matthew said gently.

"She always *wanted* to be buried here at home," Becky said.

"But we can't just *leave* her!" Mary repeated.

"Why not? We have to get *out* of here! Come on!"

Wood cracked loudly, and one of the shutters snapped back into its closed position, forced by the rising earth. Matthew jumped at the sound, and turned to stare at the ruined window.

Becky stepped up beside him. "I'm not sure we can get out that way anyway," she said.

"We'll have to smash the shutters," Matthew agreed.

"And then dig." The level of the ground, which had been perhaps three or four inches above the sill when Matthew first tried to force the shutters open, was now halfway up the lower sash and still rising.

"This is insane," Matthew said. "How can this be happening? I never heard of an earthquake going on and on like this. And how can the house just be sinking straight down? It hasn't even tilted!"

"I think maybe we better find another way out," Becky said, as the other shutter was pushed firmly back into place.

"What, up the chimney? The flue can't be more than eight or nine inches across."

"The attic, maybe?"

"There aren't any windows in the attic."

"Can't we just smash a hole somewhere?"

Matthew nodded. "I guess," he said. "Where's the splitting maul?"

Becky grimaced. "In the shed out back."

Wood groaned. A trickle of black earth spilled in through the shutters onto the broken glass that littered the floor.

"I think we better just get up there and try, even if we have to use our bare hands," Matthew said.

Together, the two of them hurried down the passageway to the unlit back bedroom. There, one shadowy wall held two identical doors – one that led to a closet, the other to a steep, narrow stairway to the attic, steps of bare wood between walls of ancient wooden lath.

They both knew what it looked like; both had been up there countless times. Matthew remembered the hot, dry air of the attic, the summer sunlight seeping dimly in under the eaves and through cracks in the gable walls, turning everything brown and warm...

But the sun wasn't up yet. The stairwell was utterly black.

It occurred to Matthew that it was a miracle the power hadn't gone out; the lights in the hallway and the front bedroom were still working.

The attic didn't have any lights.

"Is there a flashlight or a candle somewhere?" he asked.

"I think so," Becky said. She opened the top drawer of the bureau that stood between the attic door and the closet, and fumbled through old handkerchiefs before bringing out a thick stump of candle and a book of matches. She lit the candle and held it high.

Matthew's shadow, huge and black, preceded him up the attic stairs.

The place was smaller than he remembered, and the smell had changed; now it reeked of damp decay, of mildew and rot. The old steamer trunks that lined either side were black and gray, with ugly stains discoloring them. He had to duck under the tie-beams; the roof was only high enough for him to stand upright in the center portion.

That roof looked distressingly solid, though. The wood was old, and blackened with tar; here and there metal points projected through where roofers had used unusually long nails.

"Look!" Becky said, pointing.

Matthew looked and saw it, up near the central roofbeam, at the roof's highest part – a wooden square.

A trap door – their way out. It was meant, perhaps, for clearing snow off, not that it snowed much around here, or for cleaning the gutters; whatever its purpose, it was their way out.

The house shook.

Matthew could reach up and touch the lower part of the trap door, but he couldn't just push it open; together, he and Becky hauled one of the steamer trunks over. He climbed atop it, braced both hands against the trap, and shoved.

It didn't yield.

"It's stuck," he said. "Maybe they shingled over it – I don't remember ever seeing it from the outside."

Becky looked around for a tool, and spotted an old plank, perhaps eight feet long, that lay on the floor behind where the steamer trunk had stood. She set the candle down on another trunk, then slid the plank free and passed it up to Matthew.

He hefted it, then drove it up at the trap, using it as a battering ram.

The trap gave slightly, and Matthew heard the sound of tar paper tearing; the trap *was* shingled over. Fortunately, the shingles were in sorry shape. "Give me a hand," he said.

He held the plank near the middle of its length, while Becky put both hands under its lower and, and together they drove it upward again.

"Keep pushing!" Matthew shouted, as he felt the shingles move.

They both stumbled, and Becky fell across the trunk, when the trap door finally burst open. Cool air poured in. They could hear the dislodged hatch cover skidding down across the sloping roof.

Matthew boosted Becky up and out, then jumped up, catching himself on the lower edge of the opening. Becky grabbed at his shirt and pulled, and one of his flailing feet managed to catch the nearest tiebeam to provide a further impetus.

In a moment he was clambering out onto the roof, looking around in amazement. The clouds had dispersed and the moon was up, shedding a faint glow across the yard that allowed him to see what was happening.

He and Becky were kneeling on the roof of the house, on the gritty asphalt shingles, but they were only a few feet above ground level – and sinking, even as he watched. The house was vanishing into the ground beneath them.

Nothing else was disturbed at all. The cars were just where they had been left, the shed stood where it always had. The one odd feature, other than the house's absence, was the electric line – it came in from a pole in the back yard, and had always hung in a graceful black curve between the pole and the corner of the house.

Now the wire was stretched taut, a straight line from the top of the pole down to corner of the house, a corner that had dropped about twenty feet.

"Where's Mary?" Becky asked suddenly.

Just then the electric line snapped; the wire whipped up, spraying yellow sparks wildly for a moment, then fell lifelessly to the ground.

Matthew turned back to the trap door and shouted, "Mary! Are you in there?"

The candle was still burning, and he could see the attic clearly, but the lights would be out in the rest of the house now. He tried to imagine Mary down there, alone in the dark with their mother's corpse, and shuddered.

"Mary, the attic!" he bellowed. "We're outside! Hurry!"

"Hurry!" Becky shrieked.

Startled, Matthew turned and saw why Becky sounded so desperate – the eaves had reached the ground, and the first scatter of black earth was spilling into the gutters and onto the shingles of the roof.

He heard movement below – not just the steady grinding and rumbling, not the groaning of straining wood, but a human sound, footsteps or something dropped.

"*Mary!*" he shouted into the hatchway.

"I'm coming," his sister's voice replied unsteadily.

And then she was in the attic, he could see her. She climbed up on the steamer trunk, and a moment later he and Becky were pulling her up and out.

Together, the three of them ran for the cars. They jumped from rooftop to solid ground, across a yard-wide expanse of churning black earth.

"That was no earthquake," Becky said, as they watched the house vanish completely beneath the seething black soil.

"Mamma's still in there," Mary said, dazed.

"She wanted to be buried here," Matthew said. "Now she is."

"We aren't going to dig her out?" Becky asked.

A heavy rumble sounded.

Matthew shook his head. "I don't think the land will *let* us," he said.

Becky nodded, and Mary let out a little moan.

Matthew stared at the emptiness where his childhood home had stood, then grimaced. "At least this way we won't be fighting over the furniture," he said. "I guess I'll be taking a room at the motel on Route 12; anyone care to join me there for coffee?"

Then he turned away, and climbed into his car.

In the east, the first traces of dawn were beginning to show.

end

HAZMAT

For Value Received

A cloud of dust arose as Nathan carefully opened the ancient book. He trembled with fear and anticipation as he turned the crumbling pages, searching for the spell he wanted.

He had spent long years in careful study before determining exactly which book of the thousands of grimoires and arcana held the genuine formulae for summoning the Devil, but at last he had that one nameless, blasphemous volume in his unsteady hands.

This was the moment of decision – did he really want to do this? Did he want to give up his soul to an eternity of Hell in exchange for earthly pleasures?

Yes, he decided, he did. All those years of being pushed around, of watching the big bastards around him enjoying life while he had nothing but pain – he wanted some payback. He wanted to be healthy. He wanted to be rich enough that his size and looks didn't matter. He wanted to live long enough to see his tormentors buried. He didn't particularly want to *hurt* anyone – just to gloat over them a little.

And as for losing his soul, while he'd always been a loser, he hadn't exactly been an angel; the chances were good he'd be damned anyway, in the end. He turned his attention to the page and read through the detailed instructions – written, he knew, in the blood of murdered virgins by an insane monk of the seventh century. He pored over them, memorizing every warning, every hint, as well as the ritual itself.

At last, when he was sure he hadn't missed anything important, Nathan removed his clothes, drew the elaborate diagram in chalk on the floor of his rented room, lit the seven black candles at the appropriate points, and recited the long, almost unpronounceable incantation while performing the unmentionable rites the book described.

At first it seemed that the results were all that he might have asked for. The temperature in the room dropped to well below freezing, but before he had seen more than a single breath emerge white and frosty it soared to sauna heat; the thin twists of smoke from the candles thickened to a swirling funnel cloud that filled the chalk diagram from floor to ceiling; the room grew dim, and eerie laughter echoed uncannily from the walls. A towering, misshapen form appeared amid the smoke, standing in the center of the pentagram.

Nathan stared.

The apparition stood nine feet tall, and was covered with matted red-brown hair; a pair of nasty-looking horns scraped the ceiling, and its eyes glowed golden. It was vaguely human, vaguely goatlike in form; it stood on two crooked legs, and spoke in tones that made Nathan think of steam engines at full throttle.

"See my secretary," it said.

Then it vanished, much more abruptly than it had appeared, and was instantly replaced by an attractive young blonde, standing nude in the pentagram, her hair tied back in a bun, wire-frame glasses on her nose, a pad and pencil in her hands.

"May I help you?" she asked.

Nathan stared, at least as disconcerted by this second apparition as he had been by the first, but in response to an impatient glare he finally stammered out, "I was trying to summon the devil."

She nodded briskly. "Yes, you have the correct formula, though it's one we don't use much any more, but I'm afraid Lucifer is a very busy entity, and you don't seem to have an appointment; just what was it you wished to speak to him about?"

"I... I wanted to sell my soul, like in the stories, and be rich and famous and live for centuries..."

"Oh, you want Sales," she said. "Could you hold, please?"

Then she was gone, and Nathan stared at the empty pentagram. The candles were still burning, the smoke still swirling, and she had said to hold, so he stood, staring foolishly, uncomfortably aware that he was naked himself.

This was not how he had pictured it. This wasn't like anything from the old stories; this was more like his everyday life, wading through red tape and spending hours on hold. This was what he had hoped to get *away* from by selling his soul – he wanted to be rich and powerful enough that no one would ever *dare* put him on hold.

He was tired of being small and scared and sick, tired of being pushed around, tired of growing old, and he'd been desperate enough to try anything.

Well, if this worked, it would be *worth* one more runaround.

A man appeared in the pentagram, a tall man in a pinstripe suit; he smiled a huge, toothy smile, and Nathan thought the teeth looked more numerous and more pointed than human teeth ought to.

But then, who said he was human?

"I'm sorry to keep you waiting," the apparition said. "How may I help you?"

"I wanted to sell my soul," Nathan said, a little more confidently this time.

HAZMAT

"Ah, yes." He nodded sagely. "Lilith mentioned that, I think. Well, you've come to the right place; that's my business. We can give you the best deal you'll find anywhere." He smiled again, and even essayed a small laugh. Nathan managed a rather sickly grin in return; if anyone else were in the business of buying souls, Nathan didn't suppose he'd be dealing with these... people?

Whatever they were, they had a reputation for swindling their clients; he needed to be very careful.

"I want a long life," he began, "a hundred years or more of perfect health, and vast wealth, and all the women I want..."

The salesman, his smile replaced by a somber expression, held up a hand; Nathan stopped.

"Mr., ah..."

"Nathan Runkel."

"Thank you. Mr. Runkel, while we do want to keep our customers happy for as long as they live..." He paused significantly and flashed another quick grin. "While we do want to please our customers, I say, we're running a business, not a television giveaway show. Unless there's something very unusual about this soul you're offering, I doubt very much that we'll be able to meet those terms."

"Um... I thought a human soul was supposed to be infinitely precious..."

The salesman smirked. "Really, Mr. Runkel – take a look at the world around you."

Nathan had done plenty of that over the past forty years; he didn't have to ask what the salesman meant.

He should have expected this, he told himself bitterly.

"All right," he said, "What *can* I get for my soul, then?"

The salesman pursed his lips thoughtfully. "Well, I don't know exactly, offhand; you see, we don't really pay for your *soul* exactly, it's really more in the nature of a mortgage, a

64

guarantee that we'll wind up with possession of it upon your eventual, um... termination. So the value of that guarantee of title depends not only on the intrinsic strength and worth of the soul in question, but also upon how much equity we may already hold in it, and how long we'll have to wait for delivery. Quite frankly, our equity in most souls is already fairly extensive – every time you benefit from any of our services, we acquire additional shares. Hardly anyone bothers to deal direct any more, yet our income is at almost unprecedented heights."

Nathan blinked. This did not sound good at all. "All right," he said again. "So how much... um... how much is the remaining equity in my soul worth, then?"

"Well, I'm afraid I'm not familiar with your particular case, Mr. Runkel – you're not one of my regular clients. But if you could hold on a moment, I'll connect you to Accounting."

Before Nathan could protest, the salesman had vanished.

The wait was quite brief this time; Nathan had hardly had time to start cursing when a troll appeared, stooped, ugly, and holding a huge, old-fashioned ledger. It wore a flowered vest and a filthy beard that dragged on the floor.

"Name?" it demanded.

"Nathan Runkel," Nathan answered.

The troll muttered, dropped the ledger with a crash, then squatted and hauled the massive volume open. It pulled a pair of pince-nez from its vest pocket, perched them on its gigantic nose, and began turning pages.

Nathan stood, waiting apprehensively.

Maybe he would settle for living to ninety or so, and just being rich enough that he never had to work again, and maybe a small harem.

"Any relation to the Grossmeyer-Runyons?" the troll demanded.

"I don't think so," Nathan replied, jarred out of his hopeful calculations.

"Too bad."

Another moment passed in near-silence, the only sounds the rustle of turning pages and the creak of floorboards as the troll shifted its weight.

"Runkel," the troll muttered. "Silly sort of name." It paused, studying a page, and asked, "Ever live in Zimbabwe?"

"No."

"Too bad." A lumpy finger ran down a page. "Nathan Runkel, you say?"

"That's right."

"Middle name?"

"Barnaby."

The troll glowered at him. "You might have said so earlier." It flipped back several pages, then asked, "Born?"

"July twentieth..."

"'Yes' will do." It jabbed a finger at the page. "Got it. Did you want record to date, net value, or prospectus?"

"Uh... net value, I guess."

"In what?"

"Um... dollars?"

"What kind of dollars?"

"U.S."

The troll muttered to itself for a moment, then announced, "Seventy-eight dollars and eleven cents."

Nathan's mouth fell open. "Is that *all*?"

"Yep." The troll grinned horribly. "You want it in anything else? Lifespan, personal favors, what-have-you?"

That sounded promising. "Lifespan?" Nathan asked.

"Seventeen hours, thirteen minutes – we can triple that if you're comatose."

"What good is that?" Nathan asked bitterly.

The troll shrugged. "Day might come when you'll appreciate living an extra seventeen hours," it said.

"What about women?" Nathan asked hopelessly.

The troll considered that. "Well," it said, "We can arrange for an under-age girl of ordinary looks to develop a crush on you for three weeks, or get you a one-night stand with a slightly-drunk housewife."

"Don't bother," Nathan said in disgust. "Is that *really* all my soul's worth?"

"It's a tough world," the troll said with a shrug. "And hey, you've got no complaint; lots of folks out there we wouldn't pay more than about ten bucks."

"I can believe that," Nathan said. "You mean like some of those bastards I work with."

The troll nodded. "The ones who aren't already working for us," it said.

Nathan blinked.

"Working for you?" he said.

"Well, sure," said the troll. "The money's never in the production end, you know; it's always the middlemen who get rich."

"Middlemen?"

"Sure. The people who drive *other* people to Hell." The troll shrugged. "A lot of them are volunteers, working for nothing, but we have plenty on staff, too – at thirty percent commission you can do all right."

"Thirty percent." Nathan stared, thinking.

All those bastards who had abused him over the years, driven him to anger and despair – some of them got *paid* for it. They got money, and longer lives, and women...

No wonder it was always the brutes who got the girls. No wonder nice guys finished last.

"That everything?" the troll asked. "You want me to give you back to Sales?"

"No," Nathan said slowly. He chewed his lip, then asked, "These people who work for you – is there any kind of training program or anything?"

"Sure." The troll waited.

"All right, then," Nathan said, "give me Personnel."

end

~~~~~

The Cat Came Back

Michael's throat felt tight and heavy, and he tried to swallow but couldn't quite manage it. His eyes were wet with tears as his father lowered the cardboard box into the hole by the back fence.

His two younger sisters were crying and not trying to hide it, but Michael was eleven and he didn't want to cry like a little kid. He kept his mouth tightly closed.

He still couldn't stop a couple of drops from rolling down his cheeks.

"Goodbye, Bootsie," Ashley said. "You were a good cat."

Michael wasn't sure about that, really. He had liked Bootsie, and the cat had been a part of the family, but he wasn't sure he would have called Bootsie a *good* cat. Right up to the end, Bootsie had sometimes mistaken people's legs for scratching posts; he had ruined expensive furniture, knocked glassware off shelves, and left dead squirrels and chipmunks on the front porch.

But he had also been a big, friendly cat, with a purr you could hear clear across the family room. He was always ready to curl up on your lap and be petted. His fur was soft and sleek, and stroking it felt wonderful. He was black, with white feet and a white patch on his face, and could look elegant and noble when he wanted to.

"That was one reason we originally named him after an emperor," their mother had mentioned once, when Michael had commented on how regal Bootsie looked.

"You mean his name wasn't always Bootsie?" Michael had asked, startled.

"No," his mother had said, "we translated it from Latin to English when you were little, because you couldn't pronounce Caligula. Caligula is Latin for Bootsie."

"There was a Roman emperor called Bootsie?" Michael had asked.

His mother had nodded. "One of the very worst," she told him. "And that was another reason we named him that -- when he was a kitten he was the worst nuisance I ever saw. A real little monster."

Michael could believe it -- but he couldn't remember it. Bootsie had been a full-grown cat by the time Michael was born.

And now he was dead.

It wasn't all that surprising for a thirteen-year-old cat to die, but Bootsie hadn't even been sick. He'd just slowed down enough that after years of trying, Brutus, the dog next door, had finally caught him.

Brutus was supposed to be kept chained up in the backyard, but he got loose fairly often, and terrorized all the cats in the vicinity.

The cats had good reason to be frightened. Michael swallowed again at the memory of finding poor Bootsie dead on the lawn, with the dog still standing over him.

Michael's father straightened up and picked up the shovel.

For a moment they all stood, not moving, not saying anything. Then, with a sigh, their father started filling in the hole, and Michael and the girls shuffled away, drying their tears.

It was going to be strange, not having Bootsie around.

Well, Michael corrected himself, maybe it wouldn't be *that* strange. After all, Bootsie had wandered off a few times.

But he had always come back after a few days, his tail held high and the tip waving back and forth.

This time he wouldn't be coming back.

#

Michael lay awake in bed until almost midnight that night staring at the ceiling. He was tired, but he couldn't get to sleep. The wind was blowing hard, rustling the trees and groaning around the eaves, and he kept thinking he heard Bootsie out there, meowing to be let in.

At last, he fell asleep.

He slept late the next day -- school wouldn't start for another week, but the summer activities program had ended the previous Friday, so there was no reason to get up at any particular time.

He was still eating breakfast when the doorbell rang. His mother answered it, and talked quietly to whoever was there. Michael poked at his cereal, thinking about Bootsie, and paid no attention to anything else until he heard his name called. He looked up. His mother was standing in the doorway.

"What?" he asked.

"I said, have you seen the Marstons' dog this morning?"

"No," Michael said. "Why?"

"Mrs. Marston says he's missing." She turned away again.

Michael resisted the temptation to say, "Good."

A moment later his mother closed the door and said, "When they got up this morning the doghouse out back was empty, but they just thought he'd gotten loose again."

"The way he did when he killed Bootsie," Michael said.

"Yes," his mother answered. "And they thought he would come home again after a couple of hours, but he hasn't turned up yet, and they're getting worried."

"I haven't seen him," Michael said. He turned back to his cereal, hoping that the dog was gone for good.

"Well, he'll probably turn up soon," his mother said to no one in particular. "I hope he doesn't hurt any other cats."

That last comment made Michael feel guilty about not wanting the dog to come home. He didn't care about the stupid old dog, especially after what he did to Bootsie, but Michael didn't want any other cats to be hurt.

He finished his breakfast and wandered outside, with no particular plans. He sort of hoped he would find Brutus somewhere, so he could stop worrying about the neighborhood cats, but he had no idea where to look. He peered up the street, and down, and didn't see any dogs.

He noticed the spot on the lawn where Bootsie had died -- the grass was a bit torn up. His throat tightened. He turned away and walked off, not really thinking about where he was going.

The next thing he knew he was in the back yard, walking toward Bootsie's grave.

It was easy to see where the cat had been buried; Michael's father had tried to get the grass back in place, but hadn't quite managed it, and a lot of loose brown dirt had been left scattered around the site.

This morning, though, it seemed even messier than Michael remembered, and he went to take a closer look.

There was more of a hump than there should be. Michael remembered his father smoothing it all down, but now there was a big bulge in the lawn. And the sod was partly rolled back.

Something had been digging there.

Michael felt a hot anger boiling up inside him as he realized what must have happened. Brutus had got loose and had come over here to dig at poor Bootsie's grave! Even after Bootsie was dead, that horrible dog wouldn't leave him alone!

Michael was furious as he ran to the grave. He pulled up the strip of sod and tried to straighten it.

Then he looked down, and dropped the sod.

He stared for a moment, then ran back inside to get his mother.

She came to look; so did Mrs. Marston.

But it wasn't until Michael's father got home that night that anyone touched the grave again.

Michael's mother had explained what happened, how Michael had found Brutus dead under the strip of sod.

"He must have been digging there, and the hole fell in on him," she said, not really sounding as if she believed it.

Michael's father looked puzzled. "I don't see how that could kill him," he said.

But he got the shovel, and everyone went out into the backyard to see.

Michael's father lifted away the sod, then used the shovel to dig away the dirt on either side and uncover Brutus' body. Then he reached down to pick up the dead dog.

He heaved, but the body didn't come, and Michael's father blinked in surprise. "Something's holding him," he said. "He must have got trapped somehow, and smothered."

He let go of the dog and cleared away more earth. Michael heard cardboard tearing -- the dog must have gotten down as far as the box Bootsie was buried in. He shuddered at the thought.

Michael's father picked the dog up again, but something was dangling from its neck. Then his father lifted the dog higher, and everyone could see what had caught and held

Brutus, what had killed him. Michael's eyes widened with shock.

Bootsie's dead body hung from the dog's throat. The cat's teeth were locked in Brutus' neck, and the dog's blood was smeared on Bootsie's fur.

end

~~~~~

Dead Babies

Allie's baby was coming, wasn't any doubt of it as her water had broke, so I put her in the truck and jumped in myself. My hands was trembling so hard I could hardly turn the key, but I got it started somehow and backed it out the driveway so as not to take the time to turn it around, and I clipped one of the posts at the end of the driveway but I didn't stop. I got us out on the road and put 'er in first and tore across the ford so fast the water was spraying twenty feet on each side.

"Bill, take it easy," Allie said as I upshifted. "Won't do us no good to hurry if you put us in a ditch somewheres."

I saw that she was right, so I tried to slow down and watch the road as we passed Miller's Grocery and turned onto the pavement, but every so often she'd breathe funny, give a little gasp or something, and every time she did that I'd look over at her and my foot would just tromp down a bit more on the gas.

About halfway to town I remembered that I should've called the doctor and told him to meet us at the hospital in Lexington, but I wan't about to go back to do that, and there weren't exactly a lot of pay phones on Becket's Fork Road, so I figured I'd stop by Doc Everett's house in Dawsonville and tell him in person, as it wasn't more than a mile or two out of our way.

But by the time we hit the blinker at the south end of Main Street in Dawsonville Allie was gasping and sort of heaving up from the seat every minute or so, and I wasn't any too sure we were going to make it to the hospital anyways – that was a good twenty-five miles yet, and the interstate didn't cover but half of it. So when we stopped in front of the Everetts' house I went around to her side and got her down out of the truck and I walked her up to the door of the house and rung the bell.

A woman answered, and I asked her where the doc was, and she said, "Why, he's still in bed."

It was gone seven by then, but some folks do sleep in late, so I didn't wonder too much, I just asked, polite as I could, "Could you wake him, please? I think it's an emergency."

"Of course," she said. "Wait right here."

And she closed the door.

Allie sat down right there on the porch, gasping.

A moment later the door opened again, and the woman said, "You just come right on in." She showed us in and turned us sharp right in the foyer there, into a smallish room like an old-fashioned parlor, and sat us down on a fancy couch, then went to fetch the doctor. We sat there, and I noticed this weird nasty smell, and I hoped it was from the house, all the medicines and stuff, and not from something wrong with the baby.

A minute later Doc Everett came in in his bathrobe with his doctor's bag. He took one look at Allie and shooed the woman and me out and closed the door behind us.

So there we were in the foyer, and I looked around and saw a telephone on a little table and a big fancy mirror on the wall, but there wasn't nowhere to sit except maybe the stairs. There was a big sliding door across from that little parlor, and I sort of looked at it hopefully, I guess, because the woman looked at it, too, and said, "We can't go in there, I'm afraid; the baby's asleep and I don't want to wake him."

Well, right then I wouldn't have minded playing with a baby, what with our own about to be born by the look of it, but

I didn't want to be rude, and besides, the woman seemed a little on edge, sorta, so I didn't say that. I said, "How old is he, Mrs. Everett?"

"Oh, it's *Miss* Everett," she said, all flustered. "Laura Everett. I'm Doctor Everett's sister."

"Bill Sellers," I said, holding out a hand. I figured it might not be a real good idea to inquire as to just whose baby it was that was sleeping, if Miss Everett weren't married, and besides, there was something about her made me think I didn't want to have too much to do with her, so after we shook I just leaned against the wall a little and waited.

I waited for what seemed like hours. We didn't talk; Miss Everett seemed sort of caught up in herself, the way some people get, and not much interested in me, and I didn't see any call to bother her.

That nasty smell was still there, so I knew it was the house. I wondered what it was, but I didn't ask; I figured it wouldn't be polite to mention it.

I could hear Doc Everett's voice from the parlor, too low to make out the words, and sometimes I could hear Allie answering him, or making sounds. I waited for the sound of the baby crying.

It didn't come. Instead, finally, I heard Allie scream.

I jumped up off that wall, and took a look at Miss Everett, but she wan't doing a thing, she was just standing there.

I knocked on the door. "What's going on in there?" I called.

I could hear Allie crying, and I opened the door without waiting for any by your leave.

Allie was sitting on the couch with her dress all rucked up, and there were bloody towels piled on the floor, and... and other things. Before I got a good look Allie wailed, "The baby's dead! Bill, our baby's dead!"

"I'm afraid so," Doc Everett said. "Listen, I really think we had better get your wife to the hospital; would you tell my sister to call an ambulance?"

I sort of froze for a moment, trying to take it in, but then I turned and went back out to the foyer, and there was Miss Everett dialing the phone.

"I heard what he said," she told me.

And then it was just waiting, and trying to comfort Allie and not to look at the poor little dead thing there on the towels, until the ambulance came. I rode in the back with Allie, and Doc Everett followed in his car.

They kept Allie for observation, they called it, and sent her home with me the next morning.

Somewhere in there, I don't remember when, I asked Doc Everett what had happened, and he told me that the baby had got tangled in the cord and strangled while it was being born, that it happens sometimes and there wasn't anything he could do, it was too late by the time he saw what was happening.

It wasn't until after I brought Allie home that she asked what had happened to the baby's body, and I realized I didn't know.

Wasn't an easy question to ask anyone, neither.

Finally, though, I called Doc Everett, and he told me he'd sent the body to Tuchman's Funeral Home, seeing as that's the only one in town and he didn't figure we'd be wanting to go to Lexington for it.

Allie wanted to see it, before she made any plans for the burying, so I called up Tuchman's and asked if that'd be possible, and Henry Tuchman, on the other end of the line, sorta cleared his throat and said how it would be *possible*, all right, but he sure wouldn't advise it, as the baby didn't look too good, what with being strangled.

I'd gotten a look at it back at Doc Everett's place, and I hadn't thought it looked so bad as all that, but I told Allie what he'd said, and she broke out crying again, and I don't know what I told Henry but I got off the phone and tried to comfort her, which didn't do either of us a damn bit of good.

That afternoon Henry called back, and asked if we'd want to make the funeral arrangements or whether he should just take care of it, as he figured we were pretty broke up. Allie overheard, and she said we'd be right there to look at the baby and make the plans.

That didn't sound good to me, but she wan't taking any argument on it, so off we went.

At the funeral home, there was Henry Tuchman with his mournin' face on, which made him look more like a pompous asshole of a salesman than like anything decent, and he showed us to a room where this little coffin was set up on a table that Henry called a bier, and there were a few flowers around it.

I asked Henry, "Who picked it?" 'Cause I'd always heard that funeral homes are practically like auto showrooms, with a dozen different models of coffins and all that shit.

"Doc Everett chose it; he's volunteered to cover some of the costs for you, seein' as he knows the two of you han't got all that much set aside."

Now, I knew I ought to be grateful at that, but I wan't, as it seemed damn pushy to have put up that money and picked out that box without asking us first. I was trying to think of something to say about it that wouldn't sound too bad when Allie said, "Open it."

Henry blinked at us and said, like some goddamn Englishman on TV, "I beg your pardon?"

"Open the box, Henry," I said. "We want to see our baby."

Henry got all upset at that. "You really don't want to, Bill," he said.

"The hell we don't."

"The coffin has been sealed," he said.

"That's bullshit. Unseal it."

"I can't."

I was beginning to lose my temper. I'd been standing around feeling helpless while other people did everything, at the doc's house and the hospital and all, and it wan't goin' down well.

"Henry," I said, "you told me on the phone this mornin' that we could see our baby, and now we want to *see* our damn *baby*."

"If you insist," Henry said, "I can have the coffin unsealed for a private viewing. If you could come back in an hour?"

I'd had enough. "Open the damn thing *now*, Henry," I said.

"I can't, Bill," he said. "Honest."

I might've cooled down at that, 'cause he looked as if he meant it, but Allie wasn't having it.

'Bout two years back, after that idiot Jim Bryce raped the Miller girl down on Greenman's Creek, Allie got worried about crazies, so she got herself a .38 revolver and I showed her how to use it, and after that she'd carry it in her purse as a regular thing. I hadn't given it a thought in months – until she pulled it out and stuck the barrel under Henry Tuchman's nose.

"I am not leaving this room," she said, "until I see my baby. If you don't open that coffin right now, Bill's gonna get a wrecking bar from the truck and bust it to flinders."

Henry just sort of stared, and wan't saying anything sensible, and I figured maybe I could save us all some trouble. I didn't know just what all this talk of "sealing" was, so I went and took a look and it looked to me like that coffin just would open right up if you pushed the latch.

So I did, and it did.

Son of a bitch was empty.

I sort of stared at it for a moment, trying to figure it out, and I was still doing that when Allie came up beside me and saw it was empty and pointed the gun at Henry again and shrieked, *"Where is she?"*

Henry threw his hands in the air like Allie was trying to rob him. "I don't know," he said, "I swear I don't! Doc Everett never brought her, told me to fake it, same as he does any time a baby dies."

I stared at him and said, "And you *do* it?"

"He pays me," Henry said. "Pays good."

"Jesus God, Henry," I said, "you mean Doc Everett's been stealing dead babies?"

Henry nodded. "Been doin' it for years."

"What *for*?" I asked.

Henry shrugged and started to say he didn't know, but he didn't have the words out when Allie asked, "Did he kill my baby? So he could take her?"

Henry blinked at her like a startled owl.

"I don't know," he said. "I never thought about it."

I hadn't thought about it either, never would have thought of it, but once Allie asked that I saw how it might be, the doc wanting dead babies for God knows what, and there's our baby right in his own house, no one around to see if he just loops the cord over and tugs...

I felt sick.

"Come on," I told Allie, "we're gonna go see the sheriff."

"No, we aren't," she said.

"Why the hell *not*?" I wanted to know. "Stealing dead babies is a crime!"

"Of course it is," she said, "but who do you think the sheriff's gonna believe, a nineteen-year-old farm kid and his hysterical wife, or the doctor who's been lookin' after this town for the past twenty years?"

I could see how she had a point, but I wan't too sure it was that important – there'd be evidence, wouldn't there?

"So what do *you* want to do about it?" I asked.

"We're going to Doc Everett's house, and we're going to get our baby back," she said. "And Henry, I swear to God, if you call to warn him we're coming, I'm going to shoot you dead if it's the last thing I ever do."

I was beginning to regret ever teaching Allie how to shoot, about then, but it was done, and she was the one with the gun, and I hadn't even left my .22 in the pick-up's gun rack.

"Nobody's gonna do any shooting," I said. "We'll get this straightened out. Come on."

She headed for the door, and I paused just long enough to tell Henry, "All the same, don't you call that son of a bitch."

I drove, and Allie sat there with the .38 in her lap. I wished she'd put it away, but she didn't and I wan't about to argue with her. We'd been married long enough that I knew better than to mess with her when she was in a mood like that.

The whole way down Main Street I was thinking about what Doc Everett might want with dead babies. Did he do some sort of experiments on them? Did he sell 'em for parts? I'd heard there was cosmetics made out of unborn babies; maybe newborns were close enough.

It made me feel sick again, thinking about it.

It was getting on to five o'clock when we pulled up in front of the Everett house, but I saw there wasn't a car in the driveway.

"He's not home yet," I said, pointing.

"Then we wait," Allie said.

I was almost ready to argue about it when I heard a car coming, slow, and I looked up and there was Doc Everett's blue Olds coming down Main Street.

The doc saw us there and waved, and when he pulled into the driveway he got out and came over toward us. Allie kept the gun down out of sight, and we tried to look like nothing was troubling us.

Then when he was about to lean in the window, when he was saying, "What can I do for you folks?" Allie stuck the gun in his face.

"You can give me back my baby, you bastard," she said.

He got this astonished look on his face and took a step back. "Your baby's dead, Mrs. Sellers," he said. He turned to me. "You tell her, Bill."

"We know the baby's dead, Doc," I said, "but we want the body."

"Well, it's at Tuchman's Funeral Home..."

"No, t'ain't," Allie said, pulling back the hammer on the revolver. "You kept her. And if you don't start telling us why, I might just think you *killed* her."

Doc Everett threw up his hands – guess that's something everyone's picked up from TV or something. "I didn't kill her!" he said.

"Then why'd you take the body?"

"For my sister!"

Allie lowered the gun a little. "What?" she said. She sounded mighty puzzled, which was about how I felt.

Doc Everett took that as a good sign, that she'd lowered the gun, though to me all it meant was she was pointing at his gut instead of between his eyes and I wan't sure I wouldn't rather have it over quick than get gut-shot, but he lowered his hands a bit, too. "For my sister," he said.

"What the hell are you talking about?" I asked. "What the hell would your sister want with our baby? She's got her own, don't she? And alive?"

Allie threw me a surprised glance at that, and the doc shook his head. "No," he said. "She don't. Doesn't."

"Bill, Miss Everett ain't married," Allie said, "and I never heard tell she had a baby."

I was beginning to wonder if I was going crazy. This was all so weird. "She *said* she did," I insisted.

Doc Everett nodded. "She thinks she does," he said. "Laura... Laura's not right."

"First I've heard of it," Allie said.

"Well, it's true," Doc said. "Not for five years. Not since the baby died."

"So there *was* a baby?" I asked.

He nodded.

"There was?" Allie was pretty startled by that. She'd been keeping up on the gossip around Dawsonville since she was thirteen, but I guess she'd never heard *this* one.

"Stillborn," Doc said. "Never had a chance. Probably just as well. But Laura couldn't take it."

I glanced at Allie, but if she thought Doc was saying anything about her, she didn't pay any mind to it.

"We'd managed to keep it all quiet – she never went out much, and she carried small, and I performed the delivery right here at home, so no one ever knew," Doc explained. "When he was born dead, I figured it was a blessing, and I buried him in the back yard and thought that was an end to it."

"It wasn't?"

He shook his head. "Laura dug him up," he said.

Allie's mouth came open at that, and the gun drooped a bit further.

"She brought the body back in the house and treated it like a live baby, and I didn't know how to make her stop," Doc went on. "I tried to talk sense to her, but she wouldn't listen, and if I tried to take it away she'd throw a screaming fit until I gave it back."

"Couldn't... didn't *anyone* else know?" I asked. "Couldn't you take her to a psychiatrist or something?"

"Didn't dare," he said. "If it came out that there'd been a baby and I'd kept it quiet, and who the father was..."

"Who *was* the father?"

He looked startled, as if he thought we'd figured that out already. "I was," he said.

Maybe I *had* figured it out, because I wan't really surprised, but Allie was.

"Your *sister*?" she said.

"Two lonely people alone in the house together," Doc said. "Yes, my sister."

"What's this got to do with *our* baby?" I demanded.

"Well, hell, son, dead bodies don't keep," he said. "When the baby got too far gone, Laura said it was sick and told me to make it better – I was a doctor, couldn't I fix it up? Nagged at me day and night, and 'bout then Mrs. Kelliher's little Josie died – crib death, what they're calling SIDS now. So I got an idea and I talked to Henry Tuchman and switched ours for Josie Kelliher. Been doing it ever since." He shrugged. "After all, one dead baby's a lot like another."

"So... but then why isn't there another one in our girl's coffin?"

The doc grimaced. "Last one was too far gone," he said. "It's buried out back. Told Laura it was sleeping, managed to keep her away for three days – don't know *what* I'd have done if you poor folks hadn't come along."

"You killed my baby," Allie said, and the gun came up again. "You killed her so you could give her to your sister."

"No, Mrs. Sellers," he said, "I swear I didn't. I'd never do that. I took an oath, and I meant it."

The gun wavered some.

"Come on," I said, getting out of the truck. "We're getting our daughter back. I feel sorry for your sister, Doc, but that's our baby's body, and we're taking it."

"Right," Allie said, opening her own door.

Together, we marched up the porch steps, right past Doc Everett, and on into the house – front door wasn't locked, not in Dawsonville.

The doc ran after us, shouting, "No, wait! Wait! I didn't tell you... you can't... let me explain!"

I reckoned we'd heard enough; we didn't stop, marched right into the house. I pointed to the big sliding door. "In there," I said.

Allie tried to open it, but it wouldn't move.

"It's locked," she said.

I turned to Doc Everett. "Open it," I said.

"No," he said. "Listen, you can't just barge in here. I'll give you back your baby, I'll give Laura a doll or something, but don't..."

"Open it, or we'll shoot the fucking lock off!" I shouted.

He hesitated, and Allie took the revolver two-handed and pointed it, but then the door opened by itself, and there was Miss Everett, asking, "What's all the noise? You're disturbing the baby!"

She had a bundle in her arms, wrapped up in a white-and-pink baby blanket. It wasn't moving, didn't make a sound.

Allie started to grab for it, then realized she still had the gun in her hand, and got confused.

"Miss Everett," I said, "could we see him? Just for a moment?" I held out my arms.

She looked at me strangely, then smiled, and gave me the bundle.

It was cold and dead, like a bundle of laundry, but I took a look under a flap of blanket.

It was our baby, all right.

"There," Doc said, "you've got what you want. Take it out for some air."

I nodded. I thought that was the end of it.

Then I looked in through the sliding door, into the old drawing room, and saw them, lined up on shelves, on the mantelpiece, on the couch, dried-out little things, skin stretched tight over bone, a dozen or more, all mummified.

"Oh, my God," I said.

Allie screamed.

And Doc Everett, standing in the front door, seemed to slump down into himself.

"Laura always wanted a big family," he said.

end

HAZMAT

~~~~~

Upstairs

They're so damn loud up there. Yelling and fighting, and then that thumping – I guess it must be folk dances or something.

They could show a little consideration, couldn't they?

And then there was the time they left the water running and it leaked through the bathroom ceiling and damn near flooded the place, and of course it was the weekend and we couldn't get hold of the landlord until Monday – no, Tuesday, it was a long weekend! And there was wet plaster falling all over the sink and the floor. And stains everywhere.

I tell you, if we could find a decent apartment we'd have been out of this rathole years ago.

And they won't talk to us when we see them in the halls, when I shout at them they just walk right on by like they didn't even hear me. I went up there once to complain, but they wouldn't answer the door.

Maybe they were busy; I think their refrigerator must have broken down or something, because even with the door closed I could smell something rotten.

They can't be very clean.

Anyway, tonight was the last straw, more yelling, and singing this awful high-pitched song, like something the Arabs sing in one of those old movies, and then thumping about and I swear I heard the furniture breaking.

"I've had enough," Jack said, and I agreed and said he should call the cops, and he said no, he'd settle it himself, and he went up there.

There was more yelling then, and banging, but then it stopped. I guess he talked some sense into them.

I wish he'd get back, though. There's something dripping through the ceiling again.

It's not water, though, it must be paint.

It's bright red.

end

~~~~~

Parade

As usual, Jack Handley was the first out of the elevator, striding quickly across the lobby.

Megan Fausel was next, chatting quietly with Amy Drinkwater. Claude Charette followed them, listening, while Tom Petilli held the DOOR OPEN button and studied the elevator's control panel.

Tom wondered why the buttons for the different floors were arranged in two rows, rather than three or four. One would obviously have been too long, but why settle for two? A child might have trouble reaching the top few, as it was; why hadn't they made it three rows?

"Tom!" Megan called, "Are you coming?"

"Sure!" he said. He forgot about the buttons and hurried after his office-mates.

Jack was already at the street door, waiting impatiently.

"Come *on*, dammit," he said.

"What's your hurry, Jack?" Megan answered. "I mean, we're just going to lunch, and then coming back here, so what's the rush?"

"The *rush*, Megan, is that I'm hungry and I want to eat, and I've got a shitload of work on my desk that I want to get back to." Jack turned and shoved the door open; the roar of the street spilled into the lobby, washing over the five of them.

Amy sighed; Claude glanced at her, then turned quickly away. Tom noticed, and wondered why – he saw nothing repulsive about Amy, nothing that would make a man look away like that.

Jack was out the door already, Megan close behind him.

Tom heard Jack's voice clearly, despite the noise, as it said, "Damn!"

"What is it?" he asked, stepping forward; Claude moved aside to let him through, but he bumped against Amy.

Jack didn't answer. Tom made his way out onto the sidewalk, Amy beside him, Claude close behind.

The sidewalk was jammed with people – not hurrying along, as they usually did, nor standing and talking as groups might sometimes, but lined up in rows, staring out at the street.

"What is it?" Tom called, "What's going on?" He rose up on his toes, trying to see.

A wave of cheering swept over him, coming from up the street, and he craned his neck, trying to spot the reason.

Jack was more direct; he had shoved his way through the crowd to the curb. Megan was close behind, peering over his shoulder.

Amy stood in the entry to the building, looking about in bewilderment, and Claude pressed himself flat against the grey stone wall, staying back where no one would step on his feet.

The cheering was spreading, coming nearer; it drowned out the more ordinary noise of the city. The hum of engines and ventilators and voices, the distant sirens and the jets high overhead, the rainfall tapping of a million hard-soled shoes on concrete, the rumble of subways and all the buzzing and hissing and whining of the city, all were lost in the wordless bellow of the happy crowd.

Megan turned and called to the others, "It's a parade!" She had to shout to be heard over the noise.

"And they've got a police line up," Jack announced at the top of his lungs, "So we can't get across the street to the restaurant until it's passed!"

"Why is there a parade today?" Tom asked, puzzled. "It's not a holiday."

"Perhaps it's a local festival? Something the city sponsors?" Claude suggested.

"Or a march of some kind," Megan said. "A demonstration or a protest, maybe. I haven't marched like that in twenty years."

"I can't see anything," Amy said worriedly, "and I *love* parades!"

Claude turned to look at her, then looked at the crowd, judging them.

"Oh, here," Megan said, "Jack will let you in front – won't you, Jack?"

"What?" Jack said, turning. "I was trying to see if I could spot any banners."

"I said you'd let Amy in front," Megan told him.

Jack glanced sourly at Megan, then at Amy, and then turned back to the street. "Sure," he said.

Uncertainly, Amy slipped from the door, between Tom and Claude, and ducked under first Megan's arm, and then Jack's.

The cheering was almost upon them; Amy turned and looked, and the parade was only a block away.

The vanguard was a line of mounted police, half a dozen men on horseback strung across the street. Behind them marched a row of young women in a uniform Amy didn't recognize – not quite a cheerleader costume, but something similar, with short, tight black skirts, white blouses, blue vests with badges she couldn't read pinned to them. There were twenty or thirty of them, carrying a white banner with blue and gold writing on it, but as the women strutted their knees struck the cloth from behind, sending it bouncing and rippling and making it impossible to read.

That struck Amy as very odd; hadn't anyone told them to hold the banner up a little higher? She almost called out herself, but lost her nerve.

Behind the women the parade seemed to be just a big crowd of ordinary people.

"That's this damn city for you," Jack snarled in her ear. "It's always some damn thing making life difficult, keeping people from getting on with their lives. I mean, who needs a goddamn parade?"

"Oh, Jack," Amy said reproachfully, "I *love* parades!"

"Well, this doesn't look like much of one," Megan said from her spot just behind Jack. "No music that I can see, no one carrying signs. I wonder what it's about?"

"Oh, who cares?" Amy said. "Let's just enjoy it! Nobody will mind if we're a little late getting back from lunch."

"They probably won't even know," Megan said. "Because probably everyone else is out here somewhere watching, too."

"*I* care," Jack said, "but I don't see there's a blasted thing I can do about it."

Tom was beside Megan now, looking over Jack's other shoulder as the horsemen passed. "What kind of a parade is it?" he asked.

"I don't know," Megan replied.

"It's a *long* one, that's what kind it is," Jack added a moment later, as the banner-bearing women marched on past the corner. "Look!"

He pointed uptown, at a blue-mirrored skyscraper a good twenty blocks away; Tom stared.

Then he saw what Jack meant; the reflective sides of the building acted as a mirror, and while it mostly reflected the blue sky and the surrounding towers, the angled portion at the nearest corner gave them a view of the street below it.

The parade was still passing, twenty blocks uptown.

Tom turned to face the street again.

The marchers were ordinary citizens, in ordinary clothes – business suits, blue jeans, summer dresses. Mixed in were a relative handful of people, both men and women, in glittering costumes of red sequins, with red-sequined top hats on their heads or held aloft, whirling through the crowd.

"Join us!" these red-garbed dancers called, "Everybody join in!"

The throng on the sidewalks cheered, and some of them spilled off into the street, past the white-painted police sawhorses, joining the parade.

Amy glanced up at Jack's face, which was set in a frown.

Tom stared, open-mouthed, over Jack's right shoulder; Megan leaned lazily on his left.

Claude remained pressed against the granite, uninvolved and quietly waiting.

Still frowning, Jack looked at the blue glass skyscraper again, then back at the jammed street, and then at the buildings up the block on the far side – particularly the one with the red-and-gold sign announcing PIERRE'S.

"Listen," he said, "This damn parade's going to take forever to get past – see, they aren't even up to Sixtieth Street yet, I can't even see the end. How about if we just cross now, through the parade? Join in, march for a block or two until we can work our way across, and then come back uptown on the other side? I want my lunch."

Megan considered, then nodded. "Good idea," she said.

"Maybe we can make it three or four blocks?" Amy suggested wistfully.

Tom studied the crowd. "It might take that far," he said. "The street's packed pretty tight, but they're moving along at a fast walk all the same."

"Hey, Claude!" Megan called. "Join us! We're going to cut across!"

Reluctantly, Claude left his place by the wall and stepped up close behind Tom.

"We don't want to get separated," Jack cautioned, "so stay close here."

He eyed the marchers – thousands of them, grinning and smiling as they walked past, all the endless hordes of them, the glittering red figures in their midst still calling, "Join us!"

Fools, Jack thought, wasting their time – *everybody's* time – like that.

"All right," he said, pushing Amy forward. "Now!"

Amy stumbled, and a man in a dark gray overcoat caught her before she could fall.

"Hey, little lady," he said, "Watch your step! And step along, join the parade!"

Amy smiled up at him, found her footing, and joined the march.

Jack was close behind her. "Come on," he said. "Come on."

Megan was there, too, making a place for herself in the crowd, pushing aside elbows as she pressed forward.

Behind them Tom was swept up in the march.

And finally, reluctantly, Claude allowed himself to be sucked into the crowd, pressed in among the cheering throngs.

It seemed to Amy that she had scarcely taken a step, and she was a block from the office already, passing a second cross street. She felt as light and airy as a milkweed blossom, and almost danced along amid the marchers.

"I *love* parades," she said, to no one in particular.

One of the men in red sequins smiled at her and tipped his hat. "Glad to hear it, miss," he said.

The others around her smiled, as well – a man in a tweed jacket, a woman in evening dress and pearls, a teenaged girl in jeans and a "Just Say No" T-shirt.

Amy looked for Jack and Tom and Megan, and realized she'd somehow become separated from them in the crowd, in what was surely just a few seconds. For a moment, she worried, her mouth turned down, her forehead creased.

Then she shrugged. It didn't matter. She could find them later. And she wanted to enjoy the parade.

For a moment, then, she glimpsed Megan, off to her left; she waved and called, "Megan! Megan! Go on without me! I don't want any lunch; I'm going to march in the parade. I'll meet you back at the office later!"

Megan smiled, waved, and nodded.

Just like Amy, she thought, silly little Amy who would never get anywhere because she never worried about tomorrow, never planned ahead, got hung up on every little detail. Let the poor child enjoy her parade.

She turned her own attention to working her way methodically through the crowd, but despite her efforts she found herself carried at least three steps downtown for every step she moved toward the far sidewalk.

She looked around for Jack, trying to spot his familiar frown in the forest of smiling faces. She wanted to ask his help in bulling through the moving mass of people, but she couldn't spot him.

Probably already across, she thought with a mix of admiration and resentment. Jack was someone who knew how to get what he wanted.

It was a shame he never knew how to enjoy it once he had it, and that he sometimes chose the wrong things to want. Like that Sheila from Accounting – why had he wanted *her*? Or any of the others he'd gone after over the years?

And why didn't he want *her*, Megan Fausel?

And, she asked herself, where was he, anyway?

In point of fact, at that moment Jack wasn't sure himself just where he was.

He prided himself on knowing his way around, and certainly he ought to know every block on the very avenue he worked on, but he had stumbled somewhere, and been swept along with the crowd, and now the buildings on either side looked unfamiliar. He couldn't see Pierre's; the Warner tower ought to be right *there*, but there was another building in the way, one he didn't know. Had the parade gone around a corner without his even noticing it?

He cursed under his breath and began shoving his way through the moving crowd.

"Hey, there," called one of the men in red, "what's your hurry? Come on along, Jack! Join the fun!"

Jack turned and almost snarled. He hated it when people called strangers "Jack" that way – the fool had no way of knowing it was the right name. The man in red was just using it as a generic form of address, and Jack *hated* that.

He pushed toward the sidewalk.

"Not that way," the man in red called, shoving his top hat tightly onto his head and somehow moving easily through the crowd toward Jack.

That was all he needed, some idiot in spangles telling him what to do. He looked around, and saw two other parade marshals, or whatever they were, watching.

He was outnumbered, just himself against the three of them, it seemed.

Where were Tom and Claude? They weren't much, but they might do to back him up against these clowns.

Where had they got to?

As it happened, Claude hadn't gotten to much of anywhere; from the moment he stepped off the curb he had been swept along, carried downtown by the crowd, unable to make his way across or to resist the steady march without an undignified struggle.

He didn't struggle; he just let the crowd carry him. Sooner or later he'd find a way across.

It was always easiest to go along with the crowd, and Claude always had – though usually not quite so literally. He'd never been one to make waves. If he just did what he was told, things would eventually work out, he was sure. They always had.

So he marched downtown only a yard or so from the sidewalk he'd started from, his feet moving not because he wanted to march, but simply to keep from falling.

Tom had done better, had gotten out into the thick of it, out toward the middle of the street, where he looked about in wonder.

There were people everywhere; when he looked down he could barely see the asphalt for all the marching feet. To his right strode a plump Hispanic woman in a halter top and Bermuda shorts; to his left was an old man with a cane, stepping briskly along, stick swinging but somehow not hitting anyone. A boy in a sailor suit was ahead of him, perhaps ten years old, and Tom marveled at that; he hadn't thought boys that age still wore sailor suits.

One of the women in red sequins was nearby, and Tom called to her, "What's the parade for? What's the occasion?"

"Join in!" she called. "March with us!"

That was hardly an answer; Tom pushed his way toward her as they both marched, but somehow she seemed to effortlessly move farther away, so that he drew no closer.

"Hey!" he called after her. "What's the occasion?"

She was facing away, toward the sidewalk. She called, "Join the parade!"

Tom shrugged, and looked around again.

Now his neighbors were a black man in a trenchcoat, a shirtless kid with a bright blue mohawk and black leather pants, and an Asian girl, perhaps eight years old, in a nightgown, clutching a teddy bear.

What was she doing out here in her pajamas, Tom wondered. He leaned over to ask, but bumped against someone's elbow, and by the time he had straightened that out the girl was gone, lost in the surrounding mob.

He turned to the kid with the mohawk.

"Hey," he asked, "D'you know what this parade's all about?"

The kid turned and gave him a glassy stare – Tom could see that the youth's pupils were hugely dilated, his eyes black and bottomless.

"No, man," he said. "Do you?"

"No," Tom replied, "I just got caught up in it by accident."

"Me, too, man," the kid said, nodding. His blue hair waved gently with the motion. "I figured I'd just walk a couple of blocks." He smiled, showing yellowing teeth.

Tom smiled back. "Thanks," he said. He looked around.

Men in suits, women in dresses, a tall blond man in a leather skullcap, a woman in a velvet hood, three boys in street-gang colors over there, and half a dozen of the figures in red sequins, and beyond them all the sidewalks lined with watching crowds, behind them the blank, eyeless facades of the buildings, concrete and glass and brick, and inside the buildings more people, and beyond them more streets, more buildings, more people.

The weight of the city and all its complexity seemed to be pushing at him suddenly, and he shook his head, almost stumbled.

When he had recovered he looked about.

To the left, that was the sidewalk he wanted to reach. Just get to the sidewalk, turn in behind the watchers and make his way back uptown to Pierre's, eat lunch while the rest of the parade goes by, and then back to the office and away from this teeming mass of humanity, back where he could pretend that he was more than just one of the millions of faceless human ants that made up the city.

All he had to do was reach the lefthand sidewalk. He could find out later what the parade was for; it would be in the papers, surely, or on the evening news.

Where had the others gone, anyway? Were they already at Pierre's, waiting for him?

He began to push his way to the side.

"No need to shove!" called a woman in red sequins. "No need for that!"

He looked up, startled, to find her no more than ten feet away.

"Hey," he called, "I wanted to ask, what's the occasion for the parade?"

She smiled at him, showing brilliant white teeth. "What do you think?" she said.

Then she slipped away through the crowd before he could reply.

What did he think? He had no idea!

He didn't *want* to think about it. All he wanted to do was get over to that sidewalk.

Where was Jack, anyway? If they'd told *him* not to shove, they might have had a riot on their hands.

"Not that way," the man in red told Jack.

"You can't tell me where to go," Jack said. "You can't tell me what to do!" He shoved aside a girl in a yellow party dress and made his way one step further toward the sidewalk, even as the crowd pulled him three steps downtown.

Then the man in red was right there in front of him, pushing him back toward the center of the street.

"This way, friend, this way," the parade marshal, or whatever the man was, told him cheerfully.

"You can't push me around!" Jack shouted. "What right have you got to treat me like that? Let me through!" He lowered his head and tried to force his way past the marshal, between the red-sequined frock coat and a man in a stained white apron.

The marshal blocked him and pushed him back.

"Hey!" Jack shouted. "Hey, you can't do that! You can't walk all over me! I have rights!"

The marshal shoved him again, harder, and he staggered back.

Another marcher, a woman in a black lace slip, pushed him while he was off-balance, and he stumbled, and another, a man in a grey suit, shoved him, and then there was an opening behind him and he fell.

His head hit the asphalt hard, and the pain fountained up from the back of his skull, and his neck seemed to vibrate with the impact, but before he could think about that the first foot hit his belly and knocked the wind out of him.

He gasped for breath, and a boot came down on his throat and closed his windpipe, leaving him airless and drowning for an endless handful of seconds.

Then the boot had moved on, but a woman's spike heel was digging into his thigh, and a dirty sneaker pressed his shoulder down against the pavement. He waved his hands, struggling to find a grip somewhere; a woolen skirt slid through his fingers as a heavy black Oxford rammed down on his arm, slamming his elbow into the pavement and sending shooting pain out in all directions.

He had his breath back for an instant and wanted to yell, but a shoe caught him in the mouth, and another in the groin, and the weight of a fat man hit his foot and twisted it so that he thought his ankle would break.

And then he lost track of the individual blows, as the pain spread everywhere and the feet struck him everywhere and the parade marched on, oblivious, marched on across him, trampling him.

The last sound he heard, over the cheering of the crowds on the sidewalks, was a high-pitched giggle, as sunlight glittered on red sequins above him.

Amy giggled.

"I do love parades," she told the man beside her, as the two of them watched a juggler ahead. The performer was having a hard time of it in the tightly-packed throng, but he was gamely continuing, tossing his glittering gold balls up in intricate patterns, catching each as it came down and tossing it back up – most of the time. He missed fairly often, because of the crowd, and when he did someone else would catch the ball and throw it back to him.

Sometimes he caught it, sometimes he didn't; if he didn't, someone else would, and they'd try again.

The man at Amy's side smiled.

She smiled back, then stumbled over something, and he caught her before she could fall.

"Thank you," she said.

"You folks okay?" asked a voice nearby; Amy turned and found herself face to face with the white-painted face of a clown in full regalia.

"Just fine, thanks," she answered, grinning.

"Better watch where you step; we've a good long ways to go yet before this parade's over."

"Oh, do we?" Amy asked. "Oh, good! I love a parade. I always want them to last forever."

The clown nodded. "Me, too," he said.

"Yes," Amy said. "It's always such a let-down when you get to the end and have nothing to show for it but sore feet."

"I know what you mean," the clown agreed, "but maybe this time it'll be different."

"Oh, that's silly," Amy said. "How could it be different?"

"Well, look around you," he replied.

She looked.

The crowd seemed to have thinned somewhat. The juggler ahead was tossing handkerchiefs now; a man on stilts, dressed as Uncle Sam, was striding along nearby. Someone was passing out cotton candy, though Amy couldn't see where it had come from.

"It's like a circus," she said.

"Not the parade," the clown said, "I mean the city."

Amy looked up, puzzled, at gleaming white spires, like fairy castles, that had replaced the brick and concrete to either side.

"Oh," she said, not questioning. "Oh!"

"Oh!" said Megan, as she stumbled over something, "Damn it!" She glanced down, not to see what she had tripped on, but to make sure her shoes still had their heels. They seemed intact.

She looked up at the buildings nearby.

"Where the hell are we, anyway?" she asked nobody in particular. "Is this Thirty-fifth Street? I don't see any signs."

No one answered.

She looked about.

The man to her right wore a greasy T-shirt and a black denim vest; she wanted nothing to do with him. On the left, though, was a tall, thin man with a greying mustache, clad in an impeccable blue suit.

"Excuse me," she said, tugging at his sleeve, "but where are we? I don't think I know this part of the city."

She had meant that to be a lie, but looking up again she realized it wasn't. The buildings and streets were unfamiliar.

The man in the blue suit brushed her hand away, then looked her over appraisingly – it struck her as an unusually impolite look for a man of his obvious breeding.

"Ah, my dear," he said, taking up the hand he had just knocked away. "What were you saying?"

"Do you know where we are?" she asked. "I seem to have lost my bearings."

He didn't so much as glance away from her face. "No, I'm afraid not," he said.

"Do you know the parade route?" she asked. "I mean, where we'll come out?"

"Oh, I think it's headed straight downtown," he said, with a smile.

"Thank you," she said, smiling back. She started to withdraw her hand.

He didn't let it go.

"Do you have your ticket?" he asked.

She blinked at him, startled, then snatched her hand away. "What ticket?" she asked.

He frowned at her. "Should have known," he said to himself, as if he had forgotten she was listening. "Well, it should be quite a show."

"What should be?" she snapped. "What's that supposed to mean?"

"Oh, nothing," he said, "Nothing at all."

Claude could see nothing at all that he recognized. The buildings to either side were strange – not just unfamiliar, but unnatural, alien. As the parade swept him downtown they seemed to merge, from separate buildings with their own personalities into a single unbroken facade of concrete and stone, one with few windows, and those small and high and oddly placed.

He could see no doors.

And the sidewalks had narrowed, almost vanished. There were no watching crowds any more; the parade surged up over the curbs and filled the street from side to side, an unbroken mass of humanity, himself trapped in its midst. It was as if the entire population of the city was crowded onto this single thoroughfare.

The air had grown thick and polluted, though the day had been sunny and the air clear when he left the office. It was as if the strange buildings were somehow holding in this foul atmosphere.

He didn't understand how this place could be here, how he could be in it. The parade had made no turns, and yet this was definitely not the familiar avenue; he knew he had never seen any place like this in the city, ever before, and he had driven all through downtown. He had driven past, safe in his car, past the streetwalkers and the old men clutching bottles and the young men with their little plastic packets and vials, very pleased that he was better than they, and he had never seen any place like this, anything like these blank gray walls.

He had driven through rain-slick, gleaming black nights when the streetlights shone from the wet pavement and the police cruisers sprayed red and blue light across the asphalt, watching it all from securely behind the tinted glass of his windshield, and he had seen buildings of concrete and stone and brick and wood, buildings that were rubble and charred timbers, buildings that were steel frame yet unadorned, and he had never seen anything like these featureless barriers to either side.

The people around him had somehow changed, as well — they were gaunt and hollow-eyed, staring straight ahead. No one was cheering any more; all he heard was the shuffling march of thousands of feet. He could see none of the red-dressed marshals; everyone around him, men and women both, wore suits of gray and brown and black, drab and hostile.

Something was clearly very wrong here, something was happening that he didn't understand. He realized he should have followed the others, fought his way across the street instead of allowing himself to be propelled along.

It was too late now, though; there was no longer any sidewalk on either side. Near panic, he watched helplessly as the crowd trudged onward, carrying him with it.

At least, he thought, we'll come to an ending somewhere. This weird parade can't go on forever; they'll have to disperse eventually, and I'll be free, I can find my way out and go back.

He looked ahead, and realized that the street was, indeed, coming to an end. It turned into a ramp, leading upward into a miasmic haze of pollution; the marchers were continuing on up the ramp.

He looked up, rising up on his toes to see over the heads of those in front of him, trying to make out what stood at the top of the ramp.

At first he saw nothing but blank grayness.

Then he saw the ovens.

And the marchers marching on, carrying him with them.

He began screaming, but it made no difference, no difference at all.

Megan had been trying in vain to reach the sidewalks, had tried shouting and pushing, but it made no difference at all; she was still in the same spot in the crowd she had been in for blocks, being carried helplessly forward. And now, ahead, she saw that the parade was reaching its end, marching into a gigantic stadium.

She didn't remember any such stadium being downtown.

"What is this place?" she asked.

"The Arena, of course," the mustached man replied.

"It is?" She tried to remember whether she had ever heard of a city arena, and thought she had; wasn't that where the hockey team played?

"Certainly," the mustached man told her. "Can't you tell?"

"No," Megan replied, defensively, "I've never been here before. I'm not a hockey fan."

"Oh, it's not hockey they play here," he said. "What ever gave you that idea?"

She shrugged. "What is it, then?"

He made no reply, but smiled and looked away.

They were under the arches of the stadium, amid a maze of concrete pillars and chain-link fence, and although the crowd seemed to be thinning Megan had been swept through one gate and was approaching another before she was able to stop her forward motion. "Tickets!" a uniformed man was calling, "Tickets!"

The mustached man had pulled a blue pasteboard from his breast pocket; the greasy fellow dug one out of his jeans. The ticket-taker waved them through.

Megan looked for some way out, but could find none, and then she was at the gate, people behind her forcing her forward.

"Ticket, lady?"

"I'm sorry," she said, "I don't have one. I must be here by mistake. Could you direct me to the exit?"

"No ticket?" The man looked her over critically. He was young and blond and trying unsuccessfully to grow a beard.

"That way," he said, pointing off to the left. "You go down that way and through the red steel door. Any problem, ask the guard."

"Thank you." Megan turned left.

The crowd was suddenly all behind her, she was in the clear, and she found herself in a narrow, shadowy passageway between two tall fences – both of them, she noticed, topped with coils of barbed wire.

She walked on, nervous – this place made her nervous, being alone made her nervous, and she still didn't understand how she had come here. She could hear the crowd roaring in the distance, like a heavy freight passing just out of sight.

She glanced back, thinking she might go back and ask the ticket-taker to repeat his directions, but she could no longer see him; she must have been walking longer than she realized.

Then she saw the red steel door ahead, illuminated by the glow of a sign, the uniformed guard a dark shadow to one side. She tugged her jacket straight, brushed back her hair, and strode forward.

Tom strode forward. If he couldn't get out of the parade to the side, and if the mob behind him wouldn't let him stop, then he would fight his way up to the front, up to those cheerleaders or whatever they were, and the mounted policemen, and he would get out that way.

No one tried to stop or slow him, and he pushed easily through the mass of cheering, marching people.

There were certainly a lot of them, and so varied – it was as if all the world had come out to march.

There was a woman in a black string bikini; he paused for a second to stare. And there was man wearing nothing at all, he realized, a great fat man with short black hair – hadn't anyone else noticed? Tom wondered if the man would he be arrested.

It wasn't any of his business, of course, and he pushed onward, past a boy in a loincloth and a girl in a purple down-filled parka, a young woman in full harlequinade, an old man in blackface, a mime in whiteface.

The clown smiled at Amy. "We're almost there," he said.

She smiled back at him. "And my feet don't hurt at all," she said. She danced a little pirouette to demonstrate. Her fellow marchers applauded, and somewhere overhead a bird whistled appreciatively.

Amy curtsied in response, then looked up.

They were at the end of the street, where the gleaming pavement ran up to broad marble steps, and at the top of the steps glittered immense crystal gates. Faintly, Amy could hear people singing somewhere.

The gates were closed; the marchers were lined up along either side of the steps, waiting.

Amy stopped. "What's everyone waiting for?" she asked, worried.

"For you," the clown told her.

"Me?" Amy shrank back. "But who am *I*?"

"Well," the clown asked, grinning, "Who *are* you?"

The guard smiled at Megan. "Name, please?" he asked.

"No, I just want to get out," she said. "I'm here by mistake."

"I need your name, please," he said.

She frowned, and then decided it didn't matter. "Megan Fausel," she told him.

He glanced at a clipboard on the wall behind him, and nodded.

"Go right out, Ms. Fausel," he said, rolling back the heavy steel door.

"Thank you," Megan answered, stepping through.

It was dark on the other side, not just dim as the passageway had been, but utterly black; that wasn't right. She knew it couldn't be night yet, and besides, the city was never dark, not really.

She was still in the stadium somewhere. She blinked, trying to adjust her eyes, and then light sprang up, blinding her anew. She shielded her face with one arm.

Dimly, through the glare, she could make out the interior of the arena. All around her were tiers of seats, all of them filled, men and women and children, and they were all staring down into the arena, staring at *her*, and she was caught in the spotlight, on the sand floor of the arena.

"There's been a mistake," she said, turning.

The red steel door was closed. She pushed at it, but it didn't move.

The crowd laughed, an immense, overwhelming sound, and she realized they were all laughing at *her*.

She pounded on the door, and her banging was lost in the redoubled laughter of the audience.

She turned, trying to gather her dignity, trying to keep from crying in embarrassment, and marched over to the stands, to find herself at the foot of a sheer concrete wall some nine feet tall.

The spotlight followed her, and the crowd quieted, watching her intently.

She put her hand on the rough concrete and began following the wall.

There had to be an opening, a way out, somewhere.

The crowd seemed to be hushed in anticipation of something, and Megan wondered uncomfortably what it could be. She stumbled along the wall, and found nothing but solid, bare concrete – no doors, no steps, no way up into the stands, no way out.

When she had gone halfway around a circle, she found a door, at last – a black steel door hung from a rail, much like the red one she had entered by.

The crowd was utterly still.

Megan hesitated. She tugged at the door.

It moved slightly, but she released it again, didn't push it open.

Something was wrong here, she knew from the crowd's silence. She put her ear to the black door and listened.

Something growled, a deep, inhuman growl, close behind the door. A terrifying, powerful growl – a *hungry* growl.

Megan shivered at the sound.

The crowd laughed. She looked up at them.

"Open it!" someone called, and amid renewed laughter part of the crowd began to chant.

"Open it!"

"Open it!"

"Open it!"

"Oh, God," Megan said. She sank to her knees on the sand.

"This can't be happening," she said. "This can't be happening to me. I'm just an ordinary person, I never did anything terrible; why am I here?"

No one answered; the chanting died away, and the laughing, and an uneasy, anticipatory silence fell.

A nervous giggle sounded somewhere high above.

And then a rumble sounded, close at hand.

The black door was opening.

"I'm just Amy Drinkwater," Amy told the clown, and the singing grew louder, rising in a triumphant chorus.

"Tell *them*," the clown said, gesturing toward the gates.

Amy turned. "I'm Amy Drinkwater," she said.

The gates trembled. She glanced back, and the clown nodded encouragement.

"I'm Amy Drinkwater!" she called, and the crystal gates swung open before her, the chorus of song welled up on all sides, sweeping her up the steps into paradise.

Tom swept forward through the crowd, past men in armor and bearded dwarfs, past naked women and writhing dancers, and still he could not see the front of the parade.

He could no longer see the sides, either. The avenue had widened, the buildings drawing farther back, until now all he could see, from horizon to horizon, was the marching, dancing throng. The city's buildings were gone; only the street and the people remained, marching on to an unknown destination.

Tom struggled on, trying to find his way out, away from the sweating, singing crowd.

It was several days before he began to wonder why he wasn't tired, and weeks before he began to worry.

end

A Public Hanging

Russ and Ginny and Terry and I all went down to the hanging together, along with Ginny's baby Carol, who was three months old and still pretty ugly, the way young babies are. Not much more than a lump with hands and a face. Couldn't very well leave the little nuisance at home, though, so Ginny hauled her along.

I wasn't sure Russ would be up for it, what with his bad leg, which he'd got at the hanging last year; some of the crowd had got rough with him, and it didn't heal right, so from then on, even once he could walk again, he had to sort of drag his left foot.

So we had a limp and a lump slowing us down, but we were all eager to see it, to work out our aggressions the way we're supposed to. So we went, but we were a little late.

It was a good crowd this year. By the time we arrived there must've been at least a thousand people in the park, laughing and yelling and shoving. I saw folks waving bottles around, and needles, and masks. A man wearing nothing but blue shorts had climbed up a lamppost and was hammering at the white glass globe with his fist, but it wasn't breaking, so he hit it with his head and it shattered, and the glass showered down on the crowd, and everyone there shrieked. He'd cut his forehead open, so that blood spattered on them, too, but nobody seemed to notice that.

It looked like there was a lot of anger being worked off. Terry shouted something, and I yelled, and we all joined in.

There were people holding shards of white glass now, too.

Little Carol whined and started to cry, so Ginny opened her shirt and pulled out her breast, to shut her up. Carol started sucking and quieted right down.

Someone shoved Russ, and he threw a punch, and whoever it was fell back and went down, and I saw a boot hit him on the neck and then we were past and I didn't see any more.

A woman screamed nearby, and I laughed. Ginny smiled, but she looked a little uncertain about it.

The man in the blue shorts fell off the pole somewhere ahead of us; I caught a glimpse of him falling into the crowd, but then he was gone and I didn't see what happened to him.

There was a girl near us with her skirt torn away; I spotted her past someone's elbow and tried to move toward her, but I couldn't get through. Then someone got her blouse off, and she went down, yelling, and there were eight or nine men there in a circle around her, and I looked and decided to move on.

Ginny watched a little, but then she turned away. She'd been there last year, of course, and had Carol to show for it.

I wanted to get up close this year, so I pushed on, and Terry and Russ stayed right behind me. The crowd was thick, and seething, and I got shoved and jostled and I shoved and jostled right back, and I managed to work my way forward, toward the gallows.

I was about halfway to the fence when I stepped on something soft, and I looked down and saw wet blood and pale skin, and I moved aside to better footing. Whoever I'd stepped on wasn't moving, but that was all I could see.

Up ahead someone had started the chant – it seemed early to me, but someone had. I looked back, to see how far we'd come and how far back Ginny was, and someone had pulled

Carol away to get at Ginny's tit. Carol was crying, and Ginny was trying to grab her back, but then whoever held her flung her aside, and someone knocked Ginny down, and I lost sight of them both.

Russ and Terry were right next to me, shoving me forward, so I looked ahead again and pushed on.

The chant was picking up, "*Hang* him, *hang* him!"

It seemed like a path opened up all by itself, then, and the three of us slid through it, and a moment later we were all right at the front, right up against the fence, and in fact the top rail was pressing right into my stomach. I looked back, but I couldn't see Ginny, but I figured she'd be okay. She was fourteen now, old enough to take care of herself.

It was too bad about Carol, and I didn't expect to ever see her again – and I never did – but maybe Ginny would have another one in another nine months. Besides, Carol was just an ugly baby, not really a kid yet.

Russ was chanting now, with the rest, leaning on the fence beside me. On the other side Terry was looking around, trying to spot the hangman, or maybe the victim.

Then a cheer went up, and I looked, and there was the hangman, stepping out from behind the gallows, his black hood in place. When the cheer died away the chanting was louder than ever – "*HANG* him! *HANG* him!"

"Who?" the hangman yelled, though I'm sure most of the crowd couldn't hear him over the chanting, "Hang *who*?"

I braced myself, ready to fight back, but nobody shoved me; instead, about thirty feet to my left, someone shrieked, "Hang *him!*", and a man in a black T-shirt fell sprawling across the fence, his feet waving in the air as he tried to fight his way back. The crowd heaved his legs up and he tumbled over, onto the grass below the gallows. A dozen fingers pointed at him, and the chant was louder than ever. *"HANG HIM! HANG HIM!"*

The man got up, and even before Terry said anything I recognized him.

It was Terry's father.

"Daddy," she shrieked, and someone laughed.

I looked at Terry, and she was staring at her dad, and there the hangman was, taking him by the arm, and he was getting to his feet, dazed, looking back at all of us, and we were all chanting, and even Terry was chanting, a little off the beat and not very loud, but she was chanting with the rest of us.

"This one?" the hangman called.

"Yes!" we yelled back, "Yes!"

"No!" Terry's dad shouted, but hardly anyone could hear him over the crowd, and the hangman was pulling at him, pulling him toward the gallows steps.

He pulled away, but he couldn't go far, with the fence on one side and the gallows on the other, and the crowd reached out across the fence and struck at him, slapping and punching and slashing with those pieces of white streetlight glass, and a bottle whacked him behind the ear and shattered. The hangman stood aside and waited until he went down, and then reached down and grabbed his hand and dragged him upright again.

He got to his feet, and the hangman pulled him along, and as he went along the fence the crowd struck at him, and as he went past I reached out and got him in the mouth, punched him right in the teeth, took the skin off one of my knuckles doing it, but I didn't notice that until later. And Terry spat at him, and punched, but she didn't connect, and then the hangman had him on the steps, and they went up together, one, two, thirteen steps, and he was crying, and beside me Terry was crying, and somewhere in the crowd behind me a woman was sobbing, and another woman somewhere much farther away was screaming, but most of us were yelling wordlessly and cheering and chanting.

And then the rope was around his neck, and the hangman tipped him off the edge of the gallows in front of us, and his hands flew up but not in time, the rope snapped tight around his neck.

And then it was over, too quickly, the way it always was, the corpse hanging there, tongue out, eyes rolled back, and the stains spreading on his pants. The smell reached us a moment later.

The crowd quieted, then, for a moment, but then it burst out in a fresh babble. The people at the edges started to turn away, trickle away home, but we stayed for a little longer, Terry crying and laughing and Russ swearing about some bastard who had stepped on his bad leg, or kicked it, or something.

"It was too quick," someone behind me said.

I tried to turn and see who it was.

"Yeah," someone else answered, "It's been a rough year. We need something more if it's going to calm us down for a whole year. How much frustration can you work off when it's over so fast?"

"I don't care about that," the first voice said, "I just want it to last longer."

"Yeah, well," the second voice said. "Me, too. If we're supposed to work off all our frustrations and aggressions here so we won't be violent the rest of the time, no five minutes is gonna last me all year."

"Not enough!" I called in agreement. "Takes more than that to chill *me* out!" Not that I really thought I was working out any frustrations. I was just there for the fun of it.

Someone laughed.

Maybe, if there's a lot of violence during the year, I mean more than just the regular beatings and gang stuff, they'll start scheduling hangings more often, not just once a year. And maybe they'll find a way to make them last longer.

I'd like that, but it probably won't happen. I've heard some of the smartass sociologists think the hangings aren't working. I've heard they want to stop them.

If they ever tried it, we'd kill them.

Next year I'm gonna get there earlier.

end

~~~~~

Hell for Leather

The odor reached her a few seconds after jingle of the front bell; she wrinkled her nose and, always wary of offending a customer, kept her voice low as she muttered, "What the heck is that *smell*?" She looked up from the invoices and peered over the counter.

Someone was on the other side of the main coat-rack, poking through the wall display of whips, handcuffs, and fetish gear – someone short, as all she could see of him was a rat's nest of hair and the black-gloved hand fondling the merchandise. The smell was almost certainly coming from him, but it wasn't at all any of the usual unwashed-customer odors; it wasn't sweat or cigarettes or poor hygiene, but a horrid stench of decay.

She wondered if the little guy might be seriously ill. That was not a healthy smell.

He was taking down a whip, and she decided the time had come to say hello. She pushed back her chair, rose, and strolled around the end of the counter.

He cracked the whip, and she picked up the pace; an amateur with a whip could do some expensive damage. "Can I help you find..." she began.

Then she rounded the end of the coat rack, and the word "...something" died in her throat as the customer – if he was a customer, after all – looked up at her.

He grinned, an impossibly wide grin full of far too many teeth, all of them pointed. A wisp of smoke curled up from his left nostril, and his immense pointed ears folded back against the sides of his head. He flicked the whip gently, sending a ripple down its four-foot lash.

"Urk," she said.

"Don't need any urk," he said, in a voice like air brakes talking. "This whip's pretty good, though – looks like if you put a barb in it it'd strip the flesh right off." He flicked it again. "And the smell's mostly just brimstone, with maybe a bit of putrescine, a dab of cadaverine in the mix – yes, I heard you, these ears aren't just for show."

"I didn't mean to be rude."

"Don't sweat it." He chuckled. "You aren't *supposed* to like the way I look and smell."

That was obvious.

He stood about five feet tall, and three feet wide, on clawed feet covered in greasy black fur. The dirty tennis shorts that were almost his only clothing did little to conceal that he was grotesquely, disgustingly male. His protruding belly was as furred as his feet, while the sunken chest above showed stringy gray flesh between scattered clumps of black hair. His head was large and misshapen, topped with a tangle of black hair that, she now saw, did not entirely conceal his two stubby horns. His eyes seemed to shift between bilious yellow and reddish-gold, and glowed faintly. His black gloves hid his hands, but she was fairly certain they would have claws.

He was, in short, a demon. He really couldn't be anything else. She had never really believed in demons, but with one right in front of her she was not going to waste time trying to tell herself it was a costume or an illusion or a dream. She believed what she saw, and what she saw now was a demon.

"But I... Right." She swallowed. Demon or not, he was presumably a potential customer. "Was there something I could help you with?"

"Probably a *lot* of things, honey, but let's stick to business for now. This whip, here – you got more of these?"

"I believe we do, yes. How many did you want?"

"About ten thousand. To start."

She closed her eyes and bit her lip, then opened them again. "We don't have anything like that many," she said.

"So how many *do* you have?"

"I'd have to check."

"You do that, chickie."

She hesitated. She was alone in the shop; Bruce had called in sick, and Genevieve couldn't make it until 2:00. Going into the back room to dig out the entire supply of Quick Flick #3 whips would leave the cash register untended, the stock unguarded against shoplifters – and a demon loose in the store.

"I think I'd like to know a little more of what you have in mind first," she said.

"What I have in *mind*, Angela baby, is buying enough whips from your precious little store to pay your rent for the next thousand years. This isn't a *problem*, is it? Don't you like money?"

"Sir, if you don't mind my saying so, that seems a bit silly. If you really need ten thousand whips – well, first, I can't imagine what you could possibly need ten thousand whips *for*, but more importantly, for an order that size, you must realize you could just go to the manufacturer and get a volume discount. If you buy them here at Nice 'n' Knotty, we'll charge you full retail."

"Well, I was hoping we could, y'know, make some sort of deal on that."

Angela stared at his hideous face.

"Sir," she said, "I'm afraid that I'm going to have to ask you to leave."

The somewhat-faded grin vanished completely. "No, please," he said. "Don't do that."

"I'm afraid..."

"No, wait! I can explain everything. Please don't make me leave."

The sensible thing to do would be to order him out of the store, then get to a phone and call the cops and tell them there'd been an attempted hold-up – they wouldn't believe any stories about demons, but they'd come for an ordinary thief. And the sooner she got him out of here, and that whip away from him, the better – eventually he would realize she was alone, and that he could easily overpower her even *without* the whip. He hadn't done anything threatening yet, but the one thing everyone agreed on about demons was that you can't trust them. He might have wanted her to go in back so he could rape her without being seen from the street, after all.

From the look of him, she had serious doubts about surviving such a rape. She swallowed.

But on the other hand, he was almost pleading now, he looked genuinely worried, he still hadn't made any threats or hostile moves, and she was as curious as a kitten as to who he was and what he was doing there.

"I'm listening," she said, stepping back just a bit. "When I stop believing you're telling the truth, out you go."

"Fine, fine," he said. "Okay, first off, my name's Lorifer, and I'm just a supply imp, a Lickspittle Fourth Class. I'm in charge of supplying some of Hell's torturers with certain equipment. I don't do the big cauldrons, the burning sulfur's someone else's turf, but when one of the binders needs a length of rope, or a flogger needs a whip, it's my job to put one in his hand toot sweet."

124

Angela swallowed. "Torturers," she said. She glanced at the fetish wall.

"Yeah, torturers," Lorifer said. "Not the silly games your customers play, the real thing. I mean, I work in Hell, baby, the underworld, the lake of fire, the infernal regions, Satan's sanctuary, Lucifer's domain, the Bad Place. We torture the damned. Ten billion served."

Angela shuddered. "You mean it's real?"

"Well, of *course* it's real! You think someone *made up* all that stuff? What kind of sick mind would do *that*?"

"I don't know."

"No one, that's who. No one human, anyway. God and Satan worked it all out when they made their armistice, back when, after Satan tried a little self-promotion and got his ass kicked out. If you want to blame anyone, blame them – but anyway, that's not the point. The *point* is, my job is providing the torturers with stuff. Mostly it's easy, I can get ropes and chains and blades at any hardware store, but some things get tricky, and one of those is whips."

"You don't make those in Hell?"

He gave a disgusted snort. "No, of *course* not. Don't you get it? Hell doesn't *do* creation. We don't make anything but pain and misery and degradation. That's the deal. Not exactly the greatest bargain I ever heard of, but you know, the boss had just lost a war, pretty much unconditional surrender, and he wasn't really in a position to argue terms, so making *anything* is the other side's prerogative. We have to get all our stuff elsewhere – which is to say, from you guys here on Earth."

"Oh." She glanced at the fetish goods again. "And you use whips?"

"Well, duh. Yes, we use whips."

"You don't just throw everyone in a lake of burning sulfur and leave them there?"

125

"Not *forever* – they'd get used to it eventually, and we can't have that. Gotta break it up, can't ever let them think it's as bad as it can get; we want them to know it can *always* get worse. So we let 'em stew in the brimstone for fifty or sixty years, then pull 'em out and flog 'em to ribbons, then maybe crush them under a millstone, or freeze 'em in ice, or give 'em another turn in the brimstone – we try to vary it, you know, not let it get into a rut where they know what's coming. Whips are a big part of the whole experience, gotta have 'em if only for variety. And while they'll generally give a beating for a long time, they don't last forever."

"Oh," Angela said again, feeling a bit queasy.

"So it's my job to get whips to the torturers. Now, for a long time, that was pretty easy – you guys had whips all over the place, for beating on each other, or on horses, or on oxen, or whatever. But then you went and got civilized, and *then* you went and invented the automobile, and my job got so much harder you wouldn't believe it. I mean, I kept the last couple of buggy-whip manufacturers in business all by myself for a few years, stocking up – I was kind of hoping that this whole car thing was just a passing fad that would blow over in a couple of decades, but I could see it might take awhile, so I built up a good big reserve. Lasted me almost a century, even at the rate we wear the things out, but it's gone now, and your stupid horseless carriages aren't, so I'm back, and places like this are about the best place I can find to buy whips."

"What about tack shops?"

"Most of them, all they have is those wimpy little things, or the longe stuff that's too stiff; I need something flexible with some *reach*. It's you or the rodeo supply guys, and frankly, you're cheaper." He sighed. "You know, I really thought for awhile that when you guys realized how dangerous automobiles are, you'd give them up. *Thousands* dead every year, *tens* of thousands, but no, you keep on driving. Gory movies in driver's ed class didn't do squat; Ralph Nader's scare stories just got you to make the damned things *safer*, not give them up. The Arab oil embargo – when that didn't work, we gave up. Nothing short of divine intervention's gonna get you out of the driver's seat, we see that now, which means buggy whips aren't coming back."

"You wanted us to give up our cars?"

"Well, *I* did," Lorifer said, "and some of the others. The lust guys were all in favor of keeping them; the theft department, too. Upper management kind of seesawed."

"Um." Angela blinked. "So okay, you want whips – why not order them wholesale? Why come to *me*?"

"Because of the terms," Lorifer said. "Because we deal in souls."

"What?"

"We can only make deals with people with souls. That's the rule. Even if we aren't *buying* someone's soul, we aren't allowed to deal with anyone who hasn't got one. Our bargains all require swearing on one's soul to be binding – signatures aren't enough, even when they're signed in blood. No soul, no hellish business."

"You're saying that whip manufacturers don't have souls?"

"Angela, baby, whip manufacturers are *corporations*. Corporations are soulless; everyone knows that. We can't buy from corporations. Gotta stick to sole proprietorships – which is getting harder all the time, even for hardware stores."

"So I... oh."

"Yeah, it wasn't just chance that I walked in here when you had the place to yourself. Nice 'n' Knotty Leather Goods, Angela Christian, sole proprietor and general manager. Sorry for what we did to Bruce, I had to call in a favor from one of the Asmodeus boys, but he'll be fine by Friday, I promise."

"So you're here to barter for my soul?"

The demon's eyes rolled up, and he let out a long, exasperated sigh. "No, I'm here to barter for *whips*. I need as many as you can get me, as fast as you can get them to me – I've got back-orders for about ten thousand, and I'd like to stock up a little. You can keep your soul. I mean, if you *want* to sell it, I could call a broker and get you a pretty fair price, and I won't say I'd turn down the commission, but that is absolutely *not* what I came for."

"I can't get you ten thousand whips. I can maybe get you three or four hundred, and even that is going to get questions."

"Three or four...?" The demon winced. "Well, damn, it's a start, anyway. I'll take it – and when you can get more, you let me know."

"Uh... how were you planning to pay for them?"

"Do you take Visa?"

Angela snorted with involuntary laughter. "From *you?* I don't think so."

Lorifer grimaced. "Smart girl; the card's stolen. Okay, then, how about gold?"

The laughter vanished. "Real gold?"

"Yes, real gold. Come on, don't be petty."

"I'd prefer cash. I'm not a jeweler."

Lorifer sighed again. "Another step. Okay, fine. Good old American dollars. I don't have it on me; when's good?"

Angela glanced back at the calendar over the counter. "Tuesday?"

"Tuesday it is. Ten a.m., say?"

"All right."

"Then I'll be here with the cash and a bill of sale – gotta have the paperwork, management insists. You can bring a needle, or we can use one of my claws."

"Needle?"

"For your signature."

"I thought you said you didn't need it signed in blood."

"No, I said signing in blood wasn't *enough*."

She glanced at his gloves and shuddered. "I'll bring a needle."

"Now, about the price..."

"It's marked." She pointed to the tag.

"Yeah, but can't I get a discount? I mean, four hundred of these babies..."

"You need them fast, you pay a premium."

"Oh, come on. I'm on a budget."

Angela opened her mouth, then stopped, as the reality of her situation hit her.

She was making a deal with the devil.

Well, okay, not *the* Devil, but one of his minions – a Lickspittle Fourth Class had to count as a minion. She'd seen enough old movies and "Twilight Zone" episodes to know that was dangerous. One wrong step could endanger her immortal soul, and condemn her to an eternity of torment!

Half an hour ago she hadn't really thought she *had* an immortal soul, but now its eventual fate was the most important thing she could imagine.

She hesitated; was that really true? The only proof she had was that there was a demon in her shop.

But really, that was enough.

And she was talking about not just having dealings with Hell, but selling this demon instruments of torture. That couldn't be good. Selling people whips and bondage gear as toys was one thing, selling whips to flay poor damned souls was another.

But it was a lot of money, and those people were already in Hell, and the demon would undoubtedly find a source somewhere, and...

Inspiration struck.

"Okay, here's the deal – 15% off if you put a warranty on my soul that I won't ever go to Hell. In writing. In blood."

Lorifer blinked at her.

"I can't do that," he said.

"Why not? If you guys can make contracts saying you *do* get specific souls, then you can make contracts saying you *don't*."

"Well, yeah, I guess, but *I* can't; I'm just a supply imp. You'd need a soul broker."

"So? Get one."

He shook his head, dislodging a large spider. "Not for 15% off – I'd have to pay a back-commission, and I can't..."

"20% off."

"I..." He hesitated. "Thirty?"

"Twenty-five."

"You understand that this would only apply to Hell, right? It wouldn't rule out purgatory; that's a franchise operation, we don't hold sway there."

Angela frowned. "Purgatory's not eternal, though, right?"

"Technically, no, but you could get a few million years even if you don't go all Pol Pot or anything. I mean, if you start eating babies for Sunday dinner you could wind up the last soul in purgatory, a few billion years from now when Earth's a cinder and the sun's gone cold, before you finally get your pass."

She shuddered. "I wasn't planning to eat any babies, thanks."

"Okay, but then I don't quite see why you want a Get Out of Hell Free card, when you're an Episcopalian and all – you've already *got* the whole confession-penance-repentance option for the ordinary stuff."

"Insurance," Angela said. "Just playing it safe. So, twenty-five? That's one-quarter off list, and the soul thing, it's not like you'd have gotten it anyway – after all, now I know you guys are all real..."

"Well, if we had sicced the Temptations Division on you – but yeah, okay, 25% off retail, and we warrant your soul."

"Up front, no contingencies or hidden options."

Lorifer sighed. "Yeah, yeah."

"Then it's a deal. Ten a.m. Tuesday."

Reluctantly, Angela shook a black-gloved hand. Lorifer left, grinning.

It took a day and a half before the stench finally faded.

#

By Tuesday morning Angela had bought up every serious whip from every leather goods warehouse in a three-hundred-mile radius, for a total of three hundred and eighty-six, baffling her suppliers.

"It's a religious thing," she had told them. "Special order."

She had also gone over the conversation with Lorifer a hundred times, trying to remember for certain whether she had ever actually promised him four hundred, and whether the missing fourteen were going to be a problem. She had just concluded that she hadn't ever said four hundred as a definite number when the bell jingled and Lorifer stepped in.

The smell reached her a few seconds later, and she knew she would need to air out the shop all over again.

The transaction went as smoothly as she could reasonably have expected, though she was not happy when she dumped out the contents of the manila envelope and discovered several of the bills had blood on them. Most of it was old and dried brown, but a couple of stains appeared fresh. She looked at Lorifer.

"Don't ask," he said. "You don't want to know."

With anyone else she might have argued, but with Lorifer she knew immediately that she really *didn't* want to know. She counted the money, and made change – after calculating the price for the 386, the promised discount, and the sales tax, the demon got back a small stack of his well-used twenties and $2.54 from the register. She left the payment on the counter, though; the money wasn't hers until everything else was settled. She demanded the agreement she was to sign.

Her chest tightened at the sight of it. Lorifer had called it a bill of sale, and even with the warranty on her soul she had been thinking of a simple little slip of paper; instead the demon thumped a thick wad of parchment on the counter

"I'll have to read it," she said apologetically. "After all, my soul is at stake."

"Your idea, Toots, not mine," Lorifer said.

The document was hand-written in fine uncial calligraphy, and was in blessedly... no, in *damned* large letters, with generous margins, making it easy to read and not as long and complex as she had feared – but then a thought struck her.

"There isn't any fine print hidden in here, is there? Invisible ink, or anything like that? Nothing concealed?"

"Fine print's on the last page. Nothing's hidden – if we're going to cheat, we don't use cheap tricks like *that*. And in this case, for once we aren't trying to cheat – I need you to keep on supplying whips."

Angela grimaced, but kept reading.

Some of the phrasing was unfamiliar and unpleasant – the bit about "This instrument shall survive the mortality of the flesh and the passing of the natural world, unto eternity, and shall remain perpetually binding upon the parties, and upon no others, nor shall it transfer in whole or in part to their heirs, either spiritual or physical, neither shall it bind the fruit of their loins or the children of their blood, nor any person whose seal is not subscribed hereunder," sounded suspicious at first, but upon consideration she could not see any way to twist its meaning into anything she didn't want.

And finally, she reached the end and the dreaded fine print, which read simply, "This agreement shall be interpreted according to the laws of God and Man, as generally accepted in the Infernal Regions, the Celestial Realm, and the State of California."

It *seemed* to be just what she had wanted, delivering a number of whips in excess of three hundred in exchange for an appropriate sum of money and a guarantee that her soul would never gain entry, willingly or otherwise, to the realm of eternal torment popularly known as Hell, with an option – but no requirement – for additional cash-only purchases. It looked right. She could see no loopholes or booby-traps. Even so, it took a ferocious struggle within herself before she could bring herself to thrust the needle into her finger and draw blood for her signature.

Lorifer waited patiently, and when at last the dark red blood welled up he handed her a sharpened goose-quill; she accepted it, dipped it in the oozing fluid, and signed.

Then she dropped the quill and hastily wiped both hands on a paper towel from under the counter, as Lorifer snatched up the document and grinned. "All done," he said. "Now, was that so bad?"

"I guess not," she said. "The boxes are over there." She pointed.

He opened them, pawed quickly through the contents, emitted a satisfied grunt, then dropped the bill of sale in one and picked it up.

"I'm committed now, right?" Angela said.

"Committed to what?" Lorifer asked, as he heaved the first box up on his shoulder.

"To whatever I've agreed to by signing that thing."

He glanced at her, looking puzzled. "You sold me these whips," he said. "You can't back out on that."

"I mean about my soul."

"Oh, sure – you won't go to Hell. Even if you want to."

"Why would I *want* to?"

"Well, we call that the Orpheus clause – we don't want you poking around trying to fetch anyone out." He bent to pick up the second box.

"So it's too late to back out."

"Right."

"So can you tell me now whether there's a catch? Have I been tricked? Is there something I've missed?"

Lorifer shrugged, then had to drop the second box to steady the one already on his shoulder. "Not really," he said. "I mean, I could be cruel and leave you wondering, but I'm going to want as many more whips as you can get me A.S.A.P., so it'd be kind of stupid to piss you off that way. There's no real catch. You're safe from us – though the mere fact that you were willing to deal, instead of going 'retro me, Sathanas,' has probably bought you a few weeks in purgatory's boiling pitch. That's not my department, though, and a good sincere confession may get you out of it."

"That's it?" Weeks bathing in boiling pitch sounded bad, but not *that* bad.

"For *you*. But see, we play the odds – there are billions of you humans, and you're pretty much interchangeable as far as we're concerned, so we're willing to sign you away, because we know from long experience that if we give you a free pass, you're likely to take advantage of it and do some real sinning. And y'see, the great thing about that, Angie, is that one sin leads to another – if you decide to raise a little figurative hell, *you're* safe, but the odds are pretty good you'll put a few other

134

souls on our radar." He gestured at the store's stock – the studded black collars, the lace-front bustiers, the multi-zippered masks and hoods. "Some of this gear is just the sort of thing we love to see you people play with. It's not that there's anything inherently wrong with it, it's just that it makes it easier to push things just a little too far. And now *you* can push things just a little too far, knowing that *you're* safe – but the people you play with don't have any guarantees. Even just spending the extra money you're earning by selling to us might give someone a push in our direction – love of money is the root of our business, after all. We signed away a long-shot chance on you, and in exchange we improve our odds ever so slightly on everyone you mess with from now on. You'll always have the temptation to screw over your enemies, knowing that it can't hurt *you* in the extremely long run, but it might give us *their* business. Works for us." He hoisted the final box into position.

She stared at him in horror.

"But I won't *do* that," she said. "I won't. I'll be good. I mean, now that I know Hell is real, I wouldn't risk sending anyone there! Not even my enemies!"

"That's what you tell yourself now," he said, as he strode toward the door, "but we both know what my road home is paved with."

He kicked the door open and stepped out.

"Have fun," he called back over his shoulder.

She stared silently at the closed door for several seconds before asking quietly, "How?"

end

HAZMAT

~~~~~

The Great Ritual

He scrubbed at the lines painted on the tiles, wishing blood was easier to get up. He really couldn't allow the cleaning woman to see the pentagram, he told himself; she'd probably think he was some sort of Satanist.

He smiled wryly to himself. As a sorcerer he knew better than anyone that Satanism was nonsense, but he wasn't about to attempt to explain to some ignorant drudge the difference between raising demons and the ritual manipulation of natural forces.

He promised himself that next time he did anything here that required a drawn figure he would use a sheet, or a piece of paper the way Gerry did, rather than having to go to all this trouble afterward.

Even as he muttered the promise, though, he knew he wouldn't. Some rituals had to be done *properly*, with everything exactly right, and he would not trust a sheet, either of cloth or paper, to stay as flat and steady as required. One little tear and the pentacle seal would be broken and worthless, unable to contain the forces he wanted to control.

At home he had a pentagram cut into the concrete floor of the basement, grooves ready to be filled with whatever substance might be called for, but he could scarcely set up anything like that in his office.

Perhaps the best and simplest approach would be to do all his conjuring at home, but for most of the year he couldn't be sure of getting home before sunset, and many of the most interesting effects could only be achieved at the moment the sun touched the horizon. His weekends were usually devoted to the really major spells, so these smaller experiments had to be done here.

He looked the floor over critically and decided that it would do. It was not entirely clean, but the remaining traces were not recognizable as blood, and the lines were not complete enough for someone ignorant of magic to recognize them as a pentacle.

Satisfied, he rolled down his sleeves, tossed the rag he had been using into the bucket, then shoved the bucket and mop back in the storeroom where he had found them. He fetched his jacket and briefcase from his desk and strolled out toward the elevators.

When the elevator door opened he saw that someone else was in the car – a young woman he recognized as one of the Circle, a fellow sorcerer. She was not one of his own little group of friends, but he had definitely seen her at the full convocations.

He stepped into the car and looked her over as the doors closed.

She was tall, with shoulder-length brown curls, dark eyes, and skin that was neither tanned nor pale. She was too thin for his liking; if she had come seeking a partner for any of the sexual rites he wasn't particularly interested.

She turned and said, without preamble, "I was sent to fetch you."

That was rather intriguing. "Oh?" he said.

"The Council wants to see you."

He froze. That was not intriguing, that was distressing. The High Council of the Inner Circle did not summon people casually. If they wanted to see him, something was wrong. He had not petitioned for an audience, had done nothing, so far as he knew, that might attract the Council's attention. He had no idea why they should summon him, and he didn't like the idea. It seemed likely that they intended to recruit him for something, or else to reprimand him for some proscribed act he had inadvertantly committed.

Neither prospect was appealing.

"I don't know what you're talking about," he said, stalling. He looked at the lighted number above the door; they were passing the eleventh floor.

The woman shook her head. "Nonsense," she said. "You are Philip Saunders Briley, Adept of the Inner Circle, Sorcerer of the Fifteenth Degree, and I have been sent to bring you to the High Council. You know quite well what I'm talking about."

"You mean the Masons, or something? I..."

She cut off his protest with a raised hand. A glittering something shone in her palm, and he felt the energy of a binding spell. Instinctively, he worked a simple countercharm, and the glow faded.

The woman stood, hand up, staring at him. She didn't have to say anything; no one but a sorcerer could have stopped her binding.

"All right," he said, "you've got me. I'm Philip Briley. What does the Council want with me?"

"I don't know," she said. "They just told me to bring you, they didn't explain why."

"I suppose it's important?"

"Very important, Mr. Briley; they did tell me that much. If you were reluctant, I was given the means to bring you by force." She opened her purse and allowed him a glance at its interior. He recognized the seething greenish thing it held, and asked no further questions; if the Council was desperate enough to give something like that to a mere messenger, he was not inclined to argue.

The elevator reached the garage level and the woman led him to her car. He climbed in, and said nothing as she maneuvered it out onto the city streets. When they were on their way north, however, he eventually grew bored watching the tenements and brownstones roll past, and asked her her name.

She was, she said, Maura Kilgallen, Sorceress of the Sixth Degree. By the time they reached the Council's Connecticut mansion he knew a good bit of her family history.

She turned the car into the driveway, coasted to a stop at the front door, and announced, "Here we are."

He looked out the car window at the blank white doors, then out at the darkness that covered the lawns. He could feel the currents of power that flowed here, and it was not a comfortable feeling. It seemed worse than usual just now.

He wondered whether the neighbors, who didn't believe in magic, could feel anything. Did they avoid the house without knowing why?

"I never liked this place," he remarked.

"Why not?" she asked, startled.

"I don't know; I just don't."

"It makes me nervous sometimes," she admitted, "but it's a lovely house."

He shrugged.

"Go on, then, get out of the car; they're waiting for you," she said, when he showed no signs of moving.

"What about you?"

"Oh, they don't want me," she said with a self-deprecating wave that left a trail of green sparks.

"Oh." He opened the car door and clambered out, then stood irresolute on the pavement. Something out on the lawn seemed to be drawing his attention, and he wondered if that was a summoning he was supposed to respond to.

"Well, go on *in*, silly!" Maura said behind him.

Reluctantly, he marched forward and rang the doorbell.

Almost immediately the door swung open, and a heavily-built grey-haired man in a gray pinstripe suit peered out at him from a dozen feet away.

"Mr. Briley!" the man exclaimed, approaching the open door, "finally! You're the last one; we've been waiting for you."

Briley recognized the man as Kenneth McCary, a member of the High Council, and wondered that he himself should be answering the door.

"Hello, Dr. McCary," he said as he stepped inside. "What's up? Why am I here?"

"Come in, and I'll tell you," McCary said, ushering Briley into a wide marble-floored hallway. "We have a problem here, a very serious problem."

"What is it?" Briley asked impatiently, as he shooed a small blue gremlin away from his pants-leg. The concentration of energy in this place must be really stupendous, he thought, for a gremlin to be so clearly visible to the unaided eye.

"Do you remember Stephen Llewellyn? Our youngest member?" McCary was leading the way across the hall at a brisk pace.

"I think so," Briley answered as he turned down a hallway, following McCary toward the grand dining salon. "Dark hair, mustache, smiles a lot?"

"Well, I'm afraid he's not smiling much any more. He was working on a new conjuration – I'm not sure what it was intended to do, as he wanted to surprise us; he was always doing things like that. Well, anyway, something went wrong. He's gone."

"Gone?" Briley was startled. "Dead?"

"That's hard to say, actually. He just vanished; fell into a hole in reality and was gone."

That was a very disquieting bit of news, and Briley was appropriately uncomfortable as he entered the salon.

"Mr. Briley," McCary said, as he closed the door behind him, shutting the gremlin outside, "let me introduce you to the rest of the High Council, and to your fellow sorcerers."

The room was full; at least twenty people were standing about looking worried. Briley recognized the other Councillors: the ancient, shriveled John des Mondes with the eerie blue aura that flickered fitfully about him; the dark-haired, dark-skinned Anastasia Pettilangro, with the thing perched on her shoulder that Briley could never quite make out; and Catherine Lucey, middle-aged and sturdy, her red hair streaked with gray, and with no unnatural phenomena in attendance.

Or at least, Briley told himself, no visible phenomena. Lucey reminded him of his third-grade teacher. She and McCary could still go out in public among ordinary people; Briley had heard that des Mondes and Pettilangro were so charged with magic that it was visible even to outsiders, so they stayed always in or near the Council mansion.

Some of the others in the room were also familiar. Looking around, Briley realized that gathered together in this room were virtually all of the sorcerers in the Circle who had achieved his own level or higher. He saw one he knew to have reached the Eighteenth Degree, an almost unheard-of eminence for someone not on the Council, and several of the fifteenth and sixteenth degrees.

Ordinarily a group this size would be awash in chatter and idle conversation, but this gathering was deathly silent, and Briley felt more uneasy than ever.

"Ladies and gentlemen!"

Dr. McCary shouted, but that was hardly necessary; he had the rapt attention of everyone present.

"Ladies and gentlemen, we are all here now, and in case any of you are unclear as to the exact situation, allow me to explain."

He paused, cleared his throat, and went on, "This morning, Stephen Llewellyn, Adept of the Inner Circle, Member of the High Council, and Sorcerer of the Twenty-First Degree attempted a new spell, a conjuration whose purpose we do not know. The spell failed, or at any rate did not work as anticipated; it opened a flaw in the structure of our reality, an opening into which Llewellyn was drawn, removing him forever from mortal ken."

Briley would have expected a murmur at that point, but the throng remained as silent as ever.

"Bad as that is, it is not the worst. The serious problem is that, as some of you may have sensed, the hole Llewellyn opened on the front lawn has not closed spontaneously; in fact, it's growing, and threatens to disrupt all of reality if we don't act to prevent it. Therefore, we have gathered together all our most powerful magicians, in order to perform the Great Ritual and thereby heal the fabric of our universe."

That did draw a murmur, and a gasp from Briley. The Great Ritual!

"As some of you may know, there exists a ritual by which the universe can be reshaped, and we can only suppose that whatever Power designed our reality intended it to be used in just such cases as this. It requires the active participation of some twenty-four sorcerers of the higher orders, and therefore has been performed only twice before in all the recorded history of the mystical arts – once to eliminate a group of renegade wizards, and once to consolidate the power of a Persian ruling elite. The exact form of the ritual has, fortunately, been recorded and passed down to us, in the habitual secrecy that has shielded magic from common knowledge all through the centuries, along with several dire warnings pertaining to its use. We have gathered you here to aid us in performing these rites, in order to repair the damage our colleague has caused. Will you help us?"

Various signs of assent were made, a chorus of affirmatives sounded.

"Good. We've photocopied several documents, to teach you all your roles. The ritual must be performed in a single night, between sunset and sunrise, and if there is any error, the records say, the sun will not rise, and our world will be slowly but inevitably replaced by the chaos that legend says the Power first shaped into the comfortable order we all know. I don't know just how much credence to give such a claim, but keep in mind that any error could have truly terrible consequences. Irreversible consequences, at that; our best divinations show that the ritual cannot be repeated in our lifetimes. The spell is such that it binds all the participants to it, and ties them into the structure itself. It cannot be performed again while any of those who have performed it previously still live; not even those same sorcerers can do it again, for to do so they would have to reverse it first, freeing themselves, and no method by which that can be done has ever been known. Therefore, it's absolutely *essential* that the ritual be performed without error. Is that understood?"

Heads nodded.

"Fine," McCary said. "Now, we've been watching the flaw Llewellyn created, and we estimate that it will take a week to do any irreversible damage – but to be on the safe side, we've scheduled the ritual to begin tomorrow at sunset. I trust that meets with approval from all of you."

The assent wasn't quite so immediately unanimous this time, but general assent there was. With that, McCary and a handful of the others began passing out sheaves of paper, explaining just how the ritual was to be conducted.

Briley accepted his and pored over it carefully. With something like this, he knew, no possibility of error could be allowed. The Great Ritual would effectively tear the universe completely apart and then rebuild it anew, without the flaw Llewellyn had caused. Any mistake would be magnified a millionfold.

McCary called for attention again; Briley looked up, annoyed at the interruption of his reading.

"Ladies and gentlemen, in order to save time and avoid any risk of desertions or unfortunate accidents, we hope that you will all be willing to stay here with us until the commencement of the ritual. Accommodations have been arranged – crowded, I'm afraid, but serviceable. In order that you may have as much time as possible for rest and preparation, you will now be shown to your rooms."

Briley nodded. That made sense. He went along willingly when Lucey led him and three others up the stairs to a lush bedchamber where a great canopied bedstead was now accompanied by two simple cots, which looked thoroughly out of place in their luxurious surroundings.

He ignored his roommates and promptly appropriated one of the cots as his own. There he lay, and read through the documents carefully before fighting down his excitement and forcing himself to sleep.

He awoke at dawn, joined the mob of magicians being served a hearty if somewhat bland breakfast, and then found himself a secluded corner where he alternated periods of meditation with further study of the manuscript describing the ritual and his part in it. He ignored the muttering of a nearby television, and around noon the set was turned off, as the others all devoted themselves to preparing for the upcoming ordeal.

As the sun made its way down the western sky the members of the High Council gathered together the sorcerers, Briley among them, on the mansion's front lawn. When everyone was present they arranged themselves around the invisible flaw in space-time in the initial pattern the ritual required. Briley, as one of the juniors of the company, had a relatively unimportant role at the periphery of the elaborate design, but even there he could feel a subtle tug toward the hole, and sense a slight warping of the world around him, a wrongness in the shape of space.

He sat and waited, running over in his mind what he had to do.

The sun touched the horizon and des Mondes, nearest the center of the circle, began to chant in a high, quavering voice. His raised fingers lit with an eerie golden light.

Lucey and McCary joined in, a high clear soprano and a pleasant tenor, and a ring of crimson sparks began to form about the gathered magicians.

Pettilangro's voice, grating and harsh, merged with the sound, and then another voice, and another, as the whole group began the preliminary rites. By the time the sun's upper rim sank from sight the whole group was chanting, Briley among them, and the red sparks had extended into an intricate web of glittering polychrome force, weaving elaborate patterns around the company.

146

Briley raised his hands on cue and joined in the gestures that were needed, clasping hands with those on either side when the ceremony required it, passing the strands of mystic energy, bringing in the lines of arcane force that would bind reality to the combined will of the two dozen wizards. He wore on his belt the silver dagger with which to cut those strands when necessary, and on his fingers were the golden rings with which to bind them when the spell required it.

As the ritual continued he stared outward, never bothering to glance at his compatriots. He studied the patterns that shimmered about him. In them, he knew, lay the secrets of the universe, the structure of reality itself, and he stared out at them, hoping to glimpse something of those secrets, to learn something of that ultimate structure.

He didn't discern any wonderful secrets; the patterns reminded him slightly of the opening of the old television show, "The Outer Limits."

The webs grew brighter and larger and more complex, seeming to extend away forever into the darkness outside the mystic circle. The world beyond the patch of lawn on which he knelt had vanished, to be replaced by the eerie mesh of raw magical energy. Briley was overwhelmed by the beauty and power it evoked.

The ritual wound onward, wrapping the arcane power ever more tightly about the sorcerers, weaving it into ever more complex patterns, and Briley carried out his part by rote, without thought, as he marveled at the glories he beheld.

Hours passed. Briley wielded voice, hands, dagger, and rings, and the other sorcerers did the same, each fitting smoothly into the great pattern.

Midnight approached, and the chanting ceased; the central hour of the ritual required silence, save for the exact instant of midnight, when the sun would be at its nadir beneath their feet.

At that moment, all twenty-four sorcerers were to speak a single ineffable Word, in unison, marking the pivot point of their efforts. For this, the twenty-four sorcerers formed a single great circle, standing hand in hand, facing outward at the glowing walls of magic that surrounded them.

Briley wondered what was happening in the outside world – if it even existed at this point. Was there a world out there, or just a vast magical flux? If the world was still there, what would all the mundane people, the farmers and politicians and insurance salesmen, see or feel of the magic that was reshaping their universe? Would they ever know what had happened here tonight?

The moment approached; the webs of energy seethed and roiled, whipping about now as if caught in some celestial loom running wild. Briley felt the power mounting, felt the forces struggling to escape from the control of the humans who bound them, and reveled in his part in controlling them.

The glow of the meshes brightened, growing ever more vivid, lighting the world in a myriad of unnatural hues, and Briley stared hungrily out at it, feeling the power mounting toward its midnight crescendo. His mouth opened, and he licked his lips in anticipation.

Something was caught on the corner of his mouth, a bit of leaf from one of the nearby trees or an insect, perhaps; he poked at it with his tongue, and succeeded only in knocking it into his mouth. It tasted horrible. He couldn't reach up and pick it out; his hands were firmly clasped in the hands of the sorcerers on either side, and to break the ring would be to destroy the spell. Desperate, knowing that any sound might have catastrophic effects, he struggled to spit it out silently, and finally managed to leave it dribbling down his chin. He swallowed saliva – just as twenty-three voices spoke the Word in a great outpouring of magical power.

The glowing webs reared up in an instant of final triumphant splendor, obscuring everything else, then sank down again.

Briley risked a glance to either side. No one had noticed his dereliction; surely, twenty-three voices were enough. He carried on as if nothing untoward had happened.

The rest of the ritual proceeded as it was supposed to, and with each moment Briley grew more confident. The forces that had been drawn forth and reshaped were now bound and sent back, one by one, to their places in the rebuilt mystical underpinnings of the universe.

Finally, half an hour before sunrise was due, the ritual was completed. The world beyond the circle was restored and visible. Even the red sparks and golden glow with which the ritual had begun had subsided into nothingness.

Exhausted, the sorcerers sank down onto the grass. Someone waved a hand through the air where the flaw had been, and sent a triumphant shower of multicolored sparks skyward to demonstrate that the hole was gone, leaving only normal air.

"It's done," someone said. "For the first time in a thousand years, and the last time in our lives."

"And all those billions of people out there will never know," someone else added.

"It went perfectly!" a woman near Briley remarked.

"Did it?" des Mondes replied. "Something felt wrong toward the end."

"I felt nothing wrong," Lucey said, her tone worried.

"Nothing was wrong," Briley replied, pointing toward the eastern horizon. "You see? The sun is coming up, and if we'd done anything wrong the sun would never rise again. All the books say so."

Most of the magicians, those not too exhausted to move their heads at all, looked where Briley pointed. The eastern sky was awash in red light with the approach of dawn.

Des Mondes peered at Briley uneasily, then looked to the east.

A line of red fire appeared on the horizon, and Briley smiled with relief. Twenty-three voices had been enough. No one would ever know he had been careless.

"The books all agree," des Mondes said slowly, "that the sunrise will be the mark of success."

"Then we've succeeded," Briley said happily, smiling at his companions.

"Have we?" des Mondes asked, his voice bitter.

Worried by the old man's tone, Briley looked back to the east, and his confidence drained away. Something was wrong with the red sliver that showed above the hills. He stared. It was not the smooth symmetrical rim of the sun at all, but something irregular and terrifying.

All the world would know something had happened that night, Briley realized. They might never know what had gone wrong, but they would know something had.

If they lived long enough to see it.

Briley watched with growing horror as the glowing thing rose – not the sun, but a seething tentacular mass of burning red chaos pouring up across the horizon and spilling bloody light across the sky.

end

150

~~~~~

Beneath the Tarmac

The hearing protectors, which looked like headphones without wires, were amazingly effective; they shut out the human world almost entirely. Murphy looked out across the vast expanse of paved ground, and through the fence at the desert beyond, and he didn't hear a single human voice.

Oh, the jet engines penetrated, all right, though they were muffled, but that whine and roar didn't seem like any part of the everyday reality of modern life. It was something alien, something primeval, something that sent shivers through him.

Murphy watched Delta 8806 taxiing out to the runway, its engines growling. Some people compared the big airliners to great silver birds, but he could never see the resemblance. Both had wings, and they both flew, but other than that, where was the similarity? Birds were curved and organically graceful, their wings warped and flapped and folded; the planes were stiff and straight and hard, the wings rigid. If they resembled anything that had ever lived, it wasn't birds; it was pterosaurs.

He had seen those in books, even seen one's skeleton once in a museum, the long, pointed, bony head thrust out like an airliner's nose, the straight, stiff wings, the trailing legs as complex as the tail assembly of a 727.

And pterosaurs were more appropriate out here, anyway – what kind of place was this flat, burning desert for most birds? Distant buzzards and an occasional roadrunner were about it, where birds were concerned.

Pterodactyls and pteranodons – he knew all the names – those belonged. A rhamphorhynchus would look right at home, out there above the parched Texas sand.

People, though – people didn't belong here. Not the ordinary travelers he glimpsed through the windows of the jetways and the planes, not the pilots and flight attendants in their tailored uniforms; they were civilized, in a way this land would never be.

For himself, he was, perhaps, as alien and strange as anything else here, in his dayglo orange coverall, with his two red signal lights in his hands, guiding the great mechanical creatures to their nests, leading them out to fly.

He knew that most of the other traffic crew didn't agree with him about any of this; they didn't see how the land itself was rejecting them. When he shrugged off the bombed airliner and all the other recent disasters as an inevitable part of the land's struggle to rid itself of humanity his co-workers shouted at him, told him he was sick, argued that he should back up his union, that it was all because management was doing something wrong, though none of them could define exactly *what* mistakes management was making. They didn't believe in the land.

He knew better, and even when he wasn't wearing the hearing protectors he could shut out the voices, could look out at the black pavement and the bleached golden desert beyond and know that those people didn't belong here.

Did he belong here himself, with his understanding of the land, and his inhuman appearance?

He wasn't sure.

Continental 3302 was down and coming to the gate, engines whining; he raised the lights and took his place on the tarmac, waving it in.

152

The pavement felt almost soft beneath his feet; the hot spell was in its third week now, sun beating down on the asphalt as the pterosaurian aircraft lumbered across, their wings casting mere instants of shadow, the weight of them pressing hot tires down into pavement.

That asphalt was made of the bones of dinosaurs, in part – oil and tar mixed with gravel, and oil and coal were the compressed and transformed remnants of the ancient fern forests and the beasts that once roamed them. Perhaps that was why it didn't seem like an intrusion on the desert – this was oil country, and the asphalt had come from ground much like this.

He backed up to the gate, arms waving in the come-along gesture, as he watched the giant pterosaur's claws...

No, he corrected himself, as he watched the airliner's wheels. He was letting his fancies run away with him. A little imagination was fine, he told himself, and his theories about what belonged here were all very well, but he mustn't let any of it interfere with his work. Safety first. Guide the plane in, get the jetway hooked on – *then* he could daydream about the desert, and the dinosaurs, and the pavement shimmering in the sun.

He got Continental 3302 in place without difficulty, helped guide the jetway up to the side, then stepped back and glanced at his watch.

Shift was over; Continental 4587 was late, but that was too bad. Jerry would bring it in. He waved a farewell to the man driving the jetway, then turned toward the door in the terminal wall.

Then he blinked, and turned back.

Something had moved somewhere out there, on the broad asphalt-black and concrete-grey plain of the airport. He had seen it from the corner of his eye.

At first he thought that maybe 4587 had come in after all, and he'd just missed the signal, but no, there was no plane on the taxiways. A United DC-9 was lunging down Runway 22, starting its take-off, but that wasn't it.

Had some kid gotten out there, perhaps? Had a cat or dog escaped from a pet carrier in someone's luggage? *Something* had moved, he was sure of it.

Where the hell was Jerry, anyway? Late again, of course.

Well, whatever was out there, it shouldn't be, and safety was his job. He turned off the red-capped flashlights, thrust them into the loops on his coverall, and marched out past 3302, trying to spot whatever he had seen.

There, toward the maintenance area – it had ducked around the corner, out of sight.

Nobody else would see it there, either, he realized; that was a blind area. The main terminal was around the corner, and a blank concrete wall separated the maintenance area from the departure gates – it wouldn't do to have passengers watching as maintenance crews stripped down malfunctioning aircraft.

Except that the way the wall angled around, there was a stretch of empty pavement that couldn't be seen from the maintenance bays, either. It was roughly triangular, bounded on one side by that unnecessary blank wall, on another by an equally-blank wall of the terminal, and on the third by a taxiway.

And whatever he had spotted, out here on the tarmac where it didn't belong, had just gone into that blind area.

He sighed, and headed in that direction.

Probably some lost kid, trying to get away from the noise, he thought. Or maybe there'd been another "accident," and the kid had panicked and run off to find somewhere safe.

Murphy didn't know exactly why there had been so many accidents lately; especially since the bombing it seemed as if safety had gone all to hell around Dry Plains International. Most of his union blamed it on bad management, but Murphy didn't see how management had gotten any worse lately than it had always been.

A few people had said it was some kind of Indian curse, but Murphy didn't buy that. Indians were just people; they didn't cast real curses.

It took something older and more powerful than just *people* to make a curse.

His own theory was that there *was* a curse, of sorts – or really, a rejection. The desert itself was rejecting the intrusions upon it.

Whatever the reason, there *had* been accidents, and Murphy didn't want there to be another, if whatever he had glimpsed turned out to be a scared kid who might panic and run out in front of a plane.

He rounded the end of the wall, into the blind area, and stopped, a little more abruptly than he had intended.

The pavement here had softened in the sun; his foot had sunk in when he took that final step. Carefully, he lifted it free.

Black gunk was stuck to the gum sole.

Murphy cursed quietly, then put his foot back down. It sank in again, but he ignored it; the damage was done. He scanned the triangle of black pavement.

No one was there – but as he watched, the movement came again. This time he saw it plainly.

The pavement itself was moving; it had humped up for a moment, easily a foot or two, and then sunk back down.

Murphy stared. What the hell could make it do *that*?

Forgetting about the softened tarmac, he took two steps forward. Both his feet sank into the asphalt, an inch or so down into the pavement; black goo oozed up around his shoes.

He looked down, and cursed again. Some contractor had decided to save a few bucks, using cheap tar, he guessed – but south Texas was so damn hot that maybe this stuff had been up to spec, and that hadn't been good enough.

That didn't explain that *lump*, though. He looked up, ignoring his ruined shoes for a moment.

The pavement rippled – not like a pond in the breeze, or like any sort of natural effect he could imagine, but as if something was moving beneath it and leaving a raised trail, about six inches high, that took a second or two to sink back. He stared.

What could do *that?*

Had he been out in the sun too long? Was he hallucinating?

Again, the pavement moved. Again, it looked for all the world as if something was *under* it, as if some beast or something was moving below the tarmac, that instead of a hard pavement he was watching something rubbery, something like a black tarp thrown over...

Over what? What was under there?

He pulled his foot up -- it took a real effort to free it from the tar – and took another step forward, watching for movement.

The asphalt obliged him by humping up a mere yard or so away, then flattening again.

Murphy supposed he ought to be terrified, but somehow he wasn't. He had always said this place, this desert, wasn't quite natural. Besides, the whole thing seemed slightly unreal, those silent movements...

Then he realized that they might not be silent; he was still wearing his hearing protectors. He pulled the headset off.

The asphalt moved, a lump rising and crossing a few feet before him, then sinking again, and there *was* a sound, a sort of crunching, hissing sound.

That made it much more real, all of a sudden. He stepped back – or tried to; the tar held him fast at first. He had to pry his shoe free by rocking it back and forth, toe-heel-toe-heel, until it came loose.

He remembered those Indian scare stories, tales of dead savages buried beneath the airport's pavements – was that what was moving around under here? Was this neglected corner the sacred burial ground the rumors talked about?

It didn't seem very likely. And why would dead Indians be heaving up the tarmac in these aimless, random movements?

Another lump arose, and moved so close that the asphalt that held his right shoe twisted beneath him; he waved his arms, regaining his balance.

"Hey," he shouted, "Who's down there?"

For a moment, nothing happened; then, once more, the tarmac swelled upward. A larger mound than any previous arose before him, and this time it didn't immediately sink back down; it stayed, a miniature hill, perhaps ten feet across and four feet high at the center. He could hear the asphalt straining and cracking; he could see seams opening where the hardtop split to reveal soft shiny black tar.

He still didn't see anything of whatever was pushing up the pavement, though.

If anything was.

He remembered his earlier musings about dinosaurs, and the oils and tars that they had become.

Could the *pavement itself* be moving? Could whatever force was responsible for the sightings of dead Indians have also brought back something far older, and far deader?

That was crazy.

He clipped the headset in its place on his coverall and took out, for lack of anything better, one of the directing lights. It was basically just an ordinary flashlight with a long red plastic cone over the top, but it was a foot and a half long, the most suitable thing he had for poking at the mysterious mass of pavement.

The red cap of the light tapped on asphalt.

Maybe the desert was rejecting the whole airport, he thought, trying to throw off the asphalt covering.

Whatever was happening, he decided he didn't like it. Despite the hot sun, a chill ran down his spine. This was unnatural. It was dangerous. He should report it.

He tried to pull up his left foot, to turn around and go, but the sole had settled down even further into the asphalt – the black tar was started to close over the toe.

He reached down and grabbed his ankle with both hands, and tugged.

The shoe didn't move – but the tar did. It surged up, moving slowly, perhaps, but far faster than tar should; it inched up over the instep, up the heel.

Panicking, Murphy yanked his foot right out of the shoe, despite the tight laces; threads caught, and his white gym sock tore open.

He didn't care; he put his left foot atop the empty shoe and quickly untied the right. As he pulled at the laces, he could see a tendril of the black tar creeping up toward his stocking foot.

Then both feet were free, and he turned and realized that he was eight feet from the corner, and that even if he got that far, the asphalt extended well beyond. The entire apron, and the taxiway beyond, were all that same black asphalt – and he could see gentle movements in several spots now.

Why would this weird phenomenon, whatever it was, stay confined to one little corner, when there were acres of asphalt out there in the sun?

He imagined the great jet planes settling into the tarmac and being trapped, like pterosaurs caught in tar.

If he could get around the end of the wall, though, he would be in sight of the gates. He could call for help, he could wave, he could signal.

Where he was now, he could only be seen from planes as they passed by – and who aboard a departing airliner would see that he was in trouble, would be able to tell that anything was wrong? And what could they do if they *did* see?

He jumped, hoping to make it around the corner in a step or two, quickly enough that his feet would not have time to become stuck in the tar, but the instant his right foot, his leading foot, landed, he knew it wasn't going to work.

Because his foot sank right into the asphalt as if it were soft mud; by the time his left foot touched pavement, the right was sunk to mid-calf in sticky black tar. The left fared little better, and he lost his balance, sprawling forward.

The tar adhered to his coverall, from ankle to chest, and he was trapped, like a fly on flypaper – like, he thought, one of those animals long ago that had stumbled into a tar pit, and been trapped there until it sank and fossilized.

And even with his arm outstretched – his left elbow had landed in the tar and been caught, but his right was free – even with his arm outstretched, he could not reach the corner.

For a moment he panicked, thrashing wildly, but it did no good; he stopped himself just short of trapping his right arm, as well.

He tried to calm down and consider his situation rationally – even though there didn't seem to be anything rational about it. Even if the tarmac had melted in the sun, how could he sink so far into it without hitting the ground beneath? And what about the moving asphalt masses?

So his situation wasn't rational, but still, rationality might help him get out of it.

Moving seemed like a bad idea; it seemed as if every time he moved, he sank deeper and got himself into more trouble. If he waited...

His first thought was that he would die of thirst, and his bones would be found years later, but then he drove that thought away. He'd had a drink of water from the cooler not half an hour ago, and the sun was well down in the west; even in the dry heat of the desert, he wouldn't be in any danger of death from dehydration until mid-morning at the very earliest. Hunger was even less of a problem.

Sooner or later, he would be missed – Jerry would show up and want to check himself in, check Murphy out. But would anyone think to look out here?

Probably not. And he couldn't think of any way to attract their attention; if he tried shouting, he wouldn't be heard over the racket of the planes.

But if he waited, it would be dark in a couple of hours, and he had his lights; he could signal. Someone would be bound to notice. He could shine a beam that would reach around the corner. Then they'd come find him.

He wondered if anyone else was having trouble with the pavement, if there were tar pits appearing under planes or jetways, or out in the parking lot. A vision of cars sinking out of sight like trapped dinosaurs, came to him, and despite his predicament he managed a smile. Cars like stegosaurs, airplanes like pteranodons, all caught in the tar pits.

And they'd named this place Dry Plains. Not so dry after all, perhaps.

If such things were happening, the rescue crews would be busy, it might be hours before they came for him; he would have to conserve his flashlight batteries carefully.

Sooner or later, though, if he had his lights, they would find him, and save him.

Perhaps the cool night air would harden the pavement again; perhaps he would be able to chip his way free with the butt end of a flashlight.

It was just tarmac. Even animated by some supernatural force, it was just tarmac, the remains of creatures dead for sixty million years. He could beat it.

All he had to do was wait for nightfall.

The roar of a plane's takeoff faded away into the sky, and he heard a crackling, hissing noise – the sound of whatever lurked beneath the tarmac, moving. He turned, expecting to see the big hill sinking away.

It wasn't; it was growing.

He choked with horror.

Making it till nightfall might be harder than he thought. If that thing fell on him...

Then the hill broke open, like an egg hatching, and the tyrannosaur's head rose up, eyes gleaming red in the setting sun. Its huge mouth gaped, revealing rows of razor-sharp teeth, and its ridiculous little foreclaws reached out in a swimming motion, pulling it forward through the tar.

It never tried to climb out. Murphy never saw most of it. He started screaming even before the jaws closed on his legs, but Delta 9016 was coming in just then, and the sound was lost in the roar of engines.

A hundred feet away, guiding Continental 4587 up to the gate, Jerry Ingels wondered what had happened to Murphy; it wasn't like him to skip the check-in/check-out procedure.

If he wasn't careful, Jerry thought, Murphy could be in trouble.

Through his hearing protectors he heard the howl of 9016's jets – and for a moment he thought he heard something else, like the growl of some big animal.

He shook his head and got back to business; amazing the odd fancies people came up with.

end

~~~~~

What the Cat Dragged In

Amber looked up from her book. She could hear Charlie scratching at the front door, wanting to be let in. He wasn't meowing, though, and that usually meant he had something in his mouth.

She looked around, but no one else was in sight; she supposed her parents were both still out, and her brother was off in some other part of the house or yard, out of earshot.

She sighed, then closed the book and got up out of her chair. She'd been all comfortably curled up, with a self-indulgent snack and the newest Xanth novel, and much as she loved him she wouldn't want to get up just to let Charlie in. If he'd caught something he wasn't supposed to, though, like a squirrel, it might still be alive and she might be able to make him let it go before it was too badly hurt.

And if it was already dead, or if it was something he was *supposed* to catch, like a snake or a rat, it would probably still be a good idea to get it away from him before he got bloodstains on the welcome mat. She left the book on the coffee table and hurried to the door, then paused, holding the knob.

Charlie was still scratching, but not very enthusiastically, and she could hear squeaking, and a sort of fluttering noise – had Charlie caught a *bird*? She hadn't realized he was fast enough. She felt a guilty pride at the idea that good ol' Charlie had managed to catch a live bird.

But of course, the bird might have been sick, or it might just be a baby – if it was really a bird at all.

Whatever he'd caught was still alive, and she didn't want it loose in the house; she knelt by the door, one hand ready to fend Charlie or his unknown prey off, and started to turn the knob with the other.

"Hey, Amber," Jason said from behind her, "Whatcha doin'?"

Startled, she sat down heavily, and turned her head to glare at her kid brother, who had just come down the stairs to find her crouching in the foyer.

"Charlie's caught something," she said. "I want to get it away from him without letting them in the house."

"Can I help?"

Amber considered that, then nodded.

"I'll wait here," she said, arranging herself on her knees, hands held before her ready to ward off Charlie. "You open the door."

"Got it." Jason stepped up beside her, turned the knob, and opened the door.

Charlie lunged for the interior in a flash of sleek black fur, but Amber was ready for him; she got both arms around him and picked him up, holding him against her shoulder.

Sure enough, there was something in his mouth, something with wings, something that was squirming frantically, and squeaking like a frightened guinea pig.

It wasn't a guinea pig, though, and despite the wings it wasn't a bird, either.

Amber didn't get a good look at it; she was too busy keeping Charlie still, and his head was up over her left shoulder, his captive dangling down her back.

She saw the fluttering wings as it went by, though – *transparent* wings. Birds didn't have wings like that, bugs did. And not the nice bugs like butterflies. A dragonfly, maybe?

It was too *big* for a bug, though, wasn't it? Even a dragonfly? And Charlie never bothered bringing bugs into the house, he just ate them out on the lawn.

And bugs didn't *squeal*; the thing was still squeaking, whatever it was.

"Jason," she called, "what's he got? I can't see it."

Jason moved around behind her and stared.

He didn't answer at once, and she was too busy with the struggling cat to have much patience. "Come on, Jason, what's Charlie holding?" she demanded.

"Jesus," Jason said.

Amber turned and looked up at her brother. He wasn't supposed to talk like that; he was only ten. "What *is* it?"

"Ol' Charlie's caught a fairy," Jason said.

"What?"

"He's caught a fairy! With wings an' everything!"

"Oh, come on, Jase..."

"No, really! I swear! I'll hold the cat, you look for yourself!" He reached over and grabbed Charlie by the scruff of his neck.

"Not so rough," Amber said. Charlie couldn't help being a hunter, that was just in a cat's nature; it didn't justify Jason hurting him.

The cat growled angrily, but couldn't do much more than that. Amber slipped out from under, so that Jason was holding the cat in mid-air; then she turned and looked.

Jason hadn't been kidding. It *was* a fairy.

"Wow," Amber breathed.

Then she snatched Charlie away from her brother and started swatting the cat on the back. "Let go!" she shouted. "Drop it, cat!"

A real, live fairy *was* a reason to get rough. With a yowl of protest, Charlie released his prey.

The creature fluttered, trying to fly away, but instead fell to the tile floor.

"Get a box," Amber ordered Jason. She looked at the fairy, then quickly opened the door, tossed the cat out onto the porch, and then slammed the door shut again.

Jason was back with a shoebox in seconds.

"We need a towel or something, too," Amber said. "To line the box. Something soft, like cotton or something."

"*You* get it," Jason said.

"Okay, but don't touch anything!" Amber dashed away, box in hand, and found one of the fluffy white guest towels on the top shelf in the linen closet. That would do.

A moment later the two children knelt on either side of the wounded fairy, staring down at it.

It was shaped exactly like a tiny woman, except for the wings – a very thin woman, but a woman. She wore a sort of over-one-shoulder robe that appeared to be made out of tent-caterpillar tent, but that did little to hide her female figure. Her hair was blonde and incredibly fine, drifting out in a halo about not just her head, but most of her body--Amber judged that if the fairy stood up, her hair would reach to her ankles. From the crown of her head to the tips of her tiny pointed toes she measured no more than three or four inches.

And she had wings. Iridescent, glittering, transparent wings that grew from her back, reaching down to her knees and well above her head, and with a wingspan of perhaps six inches.

Her left wing was broken; Charlie's fangs had punched neat holes right through it, holes that were leaking thin clear fluid, and there was a fold to the wing that shouldn't have been there. The almost-invisible veins and ribs that gave the wing its strength had been bent until they broke.

The fairy had stopped squeaking and fluttering; she was lying still and staring up at the children.

Cautiously, moving very slowly, Amber reached down and slid a hand under the fairy's undamaged right wing, then used her other hand to push the creature's body onto the fingers. Then she quickly lifted the fairy up and placed it gently in the towel-lined box.

"I'll get some paper towels," Jason said, heading for the kitchen.

Amber looked up, startled, then down at the tiles, at the smear of fluid the fairy had left. She made a face. Then she looked down at the fairy again.

The creature was still staring silently up at her.

"Are you okay?" Amber asked.

Hesitantly, the fairy nodded.

That meant she understood English, Amber realized. Somehow, despite all the stories, despite the thing's almost-human appearance, Amber had been thinking of her as an animal.

"Can you talk?" she asked.

"Yes," the tiny thing squeaked.

"Oh, wow," Amber said in a hushed voice.

Jason returned, a wad of paper towels in his hand, and began scrubbing at the smear on the tiles.

"It talks," Amber told him.

Jason looked up at her, startled.

"Go ahead, ask it," Amber said.

Jason looked suspiciously at his sister, then at the creature in the shoebox. "Do you talk?" he demanded.

The fairy nodded.

"A nod isn't talking," Jason told Amber.

"I can speak," the fairy said, before Amber could reply. Her voice was high and squeaky, but very clear and somehow rich.

"I'm sorry the cat got you," Amber said. "And I'm sorry you're hurt. Is there anything we can do to help?"

"Take me home," the fairy answered.

Amber and Jason glanced at one another, then looked back at the fairy.

"How?" Amber said.

"Where?" Jason asked.

"Down behind the garden," the fairy told them.

"What, you mean just in the back yard?" Jason asked.

The fairy nodded.

"I thought it'd be, you know, over the hills and far away, or something," Amber said.

"Behind the garden," the fairy repeated.

Amber and Jason looked at each other; then Amber picked up the shoebox.

"Come on," she said.

Together, the two of them went out the front door and around the house, past the sun porch and the patio, down across the wide back lawn where a rusty croquet wicket still stood even though the slope was far too steep to allow a decent game, to the big old garden where their mother maintained a few patchs of herbs and vegetables and a simple floral border while allowing the brick walks and three-fourths of the old beds to be overgrown with weeds.

Charlie meowed at them from under the back porch as they passed, and Amber told him, "Hush up." She looked down into the box and saw the fairy trembling, and assured her, "Don't worry, we won't let him near you."

At the entrance to the garden, where a white picket gate had once hung but had eventually rotted out and been removed, Amber stopped.

"Now where?" she said. She leaned down to hear the fairy's answer over the buzzing of insects and the rustling of leaves.

"Past the summerhouse," the fairy said.

Jason looked around, puzzled. "You mean the gazebo?" he asked.

The fairy nodded.

Jason and Amber looked at each other. The gazebo at the back of the garden, like the gate, had long since rotted, and two years before their father had finally torn it down and hauled away the wreckage.

"There's as much fungus and bugs here as wood," he'd said as he loaded the fragments into heavy-duty trash bags. Amber and Jason had watched him work, and helped where they could, and neither of them had ever glimpsed any fairies.

Amber shrugged. "Come on," she said.

Together, the pair walked down through the garden, pushing aside weeds that overhung the path. A seedpod burst and Jason sneezed as powdery fluff reached his nose; a thorn scratched Amber's leg and snagged on her sock. At last, though, they reached the site where the gazebo had stood, a wide patch of rich black dirt now thick with green vines and weeds.

They had never played back here much; they hadn't been allowed in the gazebo, as their parents had said it wasn't safe, and there were plenty of other places that weren't so overgrown. It was a very big yard--too big for their parents to maintain properly, especially since it had been left to run wild for years before the family bought the old house at auction.

"Now where?" Amber asked again.

The fairy hauled herself up to peer over the side of the shoebox.

"Straight ahead three steps," she said, "then turn full circle."

Amber blinked. *That* didn't make any sense. She glanced at Jason, who shrugged.

Together, they walked forward, Amber counting the steps aloud.

Three steps brought them right up against the towering, untrimmed hedge across the back of the garden. Amber could see nothing but hedge.

Feeling foolish, she spun around on her toes--and found herself facing a gap in the hedge.

Astonished, she turned and looked back, and saw the rest of the world unchanged--the half-wild garden, their familiar old house at the top of the slope, Charlie watching from under the back porch.

But there was a gap in the hedge that hadn't been there a moment before.

Jason had turned around, as well, and was just as surprised, but trying not to show it. "Come on," he said, stepping into the opening.

Amber followed, the shoebox in her hand, and found herself in a sort of leafy green dome, surrounded on all sides by hedge, sunlight trickling through in drops and speckles. The earth beneath her feet was hard-packed bare black dirt, as if trampled--but who could have trampled it, here in her own back yard?

"Put me down," the fairy said.

Uneasily, Amber lowered the shoebox to the ground.

A breeze rustled the leaves of the hedge, and Amber had a sudden sensation of being watched, as if a thousand tiny eyes were staring at her; she looked quickly around, and thought she saw shapes flitting through the hedge.

Leaves turning in the wind? Sunlight scattered by the leaves?

Or other fairies?

"Thank you," the fairy said. "You saved my life. I owe you a boon."

"You're welcome," Amber said automatically. "Listen, you don't owe us anything; we just want you to be safe. Will you be all right here? I mean..."

"What *is* this place?" Jason demanded.

"This is our home," the fairy answered.

"There are others?" Amber asked.

"Oh, yes," the fairy replied. "We've been here all along, ever since the garden was first laid out."

"Why don't they show themselves?"

"They don't know you."

"I'd like to see them," Amber said.

"Is that the boon you would ask?"

"Boon?" Amber had to think what the strange word meant; she'd seen it in stories, never heard it spoken before this. "You mean, like a reward? Three wishes, or something?"

She would never have believed in wishes ordinarily, but she was talking to a *fairy*, for heaven's sake.

"Our power's not enough in these sad days to grant wishes," the fairy said, "but if you'd have a reward, come to this place at midnight, and we will celebrate, and give you what reward we can." Her voice seemed stronger and more confident, Amber noticed--either she was recovering quickly from her wounds, or this place, whatever it was, gave her courage.

"I don't need any reward," Amber said. "We just wanted to help you." She hesitated. "But I would like to see the others, you know, just to be sure you'll be safe here."

"Return at midnight, and you may see them."

"But I meant... can't I see them now?"

"No. Go now," the fairy ordered. "Return at midnight, if you wish."

Uneasily, Amber backed out of the clearing in the hedge; reluctantly, Jason followed.

Charlie meowed at them from the porch; Amber turned to look at him, and when she turned back the opening in the hedge was gone.

She and Jason spent the better part of an hour exploring, walking up and down the hedge on either side, but they found no sign of an opening, nowhere that the hedge looked wide enough, front to back, to have contained the dome-like clearing she remembered. They turned up nothing on the site of the gazebo but pillbugs. Turning, whirling, pacing, and jumping about did not cause the gap in the hedge to reappear.

Eventually they gave up and returned to the house, but Amber couldn't bring herself to pick up her abandoned book; instead she let Charlie in and sat in the window seat on the stairway landing with the cat on her lap, petting him as she stared out across the back lawn at the garden and hedge.

"I love you, Charlie," she said, looking down at him, "but don't catch any more fairies, okay?"

The cat looked up at her with half-closed eyes and purred.

At supper neither Amber nor Jason mentioned anything of the day's events to their parents; they ate quietly, listening to chat about cars and jobs.

At bedtime that evening, as Amber let Charlie out for the night, Jason asked her, "So, you goin'?"

Amber nodded. "If I can stay awake," she said. "You?"

"Sure," Jason replied.

Amber lay in her bed with the lights out, thinking about the day.

She had always thought that their big old house looked like something out of a storybook, and that the semi-abandoned garden was especially spooky, but fairies? It seemed incredible.

She wasn't sure whether to be grateful that Charlie had caught the fairy, or worried. Charlie was a lovely cat, all sleek and black, and very friendly, but sometimes he could be so stubborn...

She didn't realize she had dozed off until Jason shook her awake. She sat up, startled.

"Come on!" he whispered. "It's only about five minutes till midnight!"

"Oh!" She jumped out of bed and shooed Jason out of the room so she could get dressed.

It was a good thing their parents hadn't stayed up late that night, Amber thought as she crept down the stairs.

Together, she and Jason stumbled down the sloping yard to the garden, tripping over things in the dark. Everything seemed bigger, somehow--the hundred feet of lawn seemed like a thousand. At last, though, they arrived at the brick pillars that had held the garden gate, posts that ordinarily barely reached Amber's waist--and they were over her head.

"Jason?" she said, looking up at the posts, the red brick black in the moonlight.

"We're shrinking," Jason said. "Down to fairy size, I guess--so we can celebrate with them."

Amber nodded.

"Come on," she said.

They made their way cautiously through the garden itself, and that walk was even worse, with the uneven bricks and the trailing vines and the tangled weeds and pricking thorns, all of them seemingly growing larger and larger as they proceeded, until by the time they reached the soft ground where the gazebo had stood it was a veritable jungle.

The hedge loomed over them, black in the darkness--black, solid, and impossibly tall.

"Now what?" Jason asked, staring at it.

"Now we take three steps and turn around," Amber said. "And if it doesn't work, we go back to bed, and I sure hope we grow back to normal size."

"I wish we'd taken a picture of the thing before we let it go," Jason muttered.

"A bit late to think of that," Amber retorted as she took her first step.

Then the second, the third, turn around...

And the hedge was alight with tiny glowing specks, like miniature candle flames, and the opening into the clearing had reappeared, a gigantic leafy archway outlined in flickering golden light.

"'Tis the mortal children!" a voice called. "Make ready the feast! Those who saved Maurienne from the Beast are come!"

And then the fairies appeared on either side, long lines of them, almost as tall now as Amber and Jason, all of them inhumanly beautiful, with gleaming iridescent wings and radiant heart-shaped faces, long hair flowing down their backs. Their clothes were woven of spider-silk and milkweed and a hundred other fine fibers, in shades of white and grey and gold. Two leapt forward and took Amber and Jason by the hand, and led them down between the lines as the fairies cheered wildly.

At the end they found a table, elaborately set with plates made of shining beetle-shell, acorn-cap bowls, thorn knives and carved twig forks.

And on the other side of the table stood three fairies. In the center was the one they had rescued, her injured wing now bandaged with something green and white; to her right was a male fairy taller than any of the others, fully Amber's own shrunken height, while on her left was a female fairy of Jason's current size.

The tall ones wore rings on their heads, like crowns--a simple gold band on the male, while the female's had a diamond chip set in the front--and Amber realized these must be the king and queen; dredging up a memory from an old movie, she curtsied deeply, going down on one knee, wishing as she did so that she had worn a skirt instead of jeans. Jason, after a moment's befuddlement, picked up his cue and bowed.

"It's all like a story," Amber whispered as she rose.

Jason nodded.

"Welcome to our home," the fairy king announced. "We do not ask your true names, as we seek no power over you, but what names shall we call you?"

Amber and Jason exchanged glances.

"Amber, your Majesty," Amber said.

"Bill," Jason said.

Amber glared at him. "Bill?" she asked.

He shrugged and smiled sheepishly.

"Come then, Amber and Bill, and feast with us!" the king proclaimed, "that we might honor you for what you did for our beloved subject, whom you rescued from that foul monster and brought safe home to us!"

Amber started to object that Charlie wasn't a monster, just a cat, *her* cat – but then she stopped herself. To these things, a cat *would* be a monster, and if she admitted Charlie was hers they'd hardly feel kindly toward her, would they?

The king waved a hand, and fairies began to load the table – which, Amber saw, was made of an old clapboard set up on chunks of 2x4 – with food. Nuts, berries, steaming chunks of meat – Amber wondered what sort of meat it was, but decided not to ask. The acorn bowls were filled with golden wine-- probably made from dandelions, Amber guessed.

She remembered stories of fairy feasts, and people being lost for years, or forever, if they ate so much as a bite – but this wasn't a story, this was real, strange as it seemed, and it would be rude not to eat.

Besides, the chance to bite into a strawberry the size of her own head was just too weird to miss. She and Jason, as directed, sat down on chairs made of empty spools and joined in.

As they ate, the fairies sang, and although Amber wasn't usually interested in folk music – she preferred Elastica – she enjoyed it immensely. Their voices were beautiful, and about every third song was a funny one, and she laughed until she cried at those, though the minute each song ended she could never again remember any of the words or jokes.

Everything was delicious, everything was wonderful. Maurienne, if that was her name, stared across the table at Amber and Jason with a look of adoration that made Amber feel ten feet tall; the king and queen smiled proudly at them.

At last the feast was done and the dishes were cleared away; Amber felt full and sleepy and fine. The king and queen arose, and Amber remembered that she was supposed to stand as well; she got to her feet and stood, swaying slightly. Jason followed suit.

"And now," the king said, "the reward you were promised!"

He gestured, and Amber felt something touching her shoulders; she turned, startled, and found that two fairies had come up behind her and draped a cloak across her shoulders.

Two others had done the same for Jason.

"Cool," he said.

Amber, tired as she was, tried to focus on the cloak that covered her shoulder.

It was fur, fine black fur; she stroked it.

It was sleek and soft and smooth.

It felt somehow familiar.

"What kind is it?" Jason asked, as Amber looked up, horrified, at the king's smiling face.

He had canines almost like fangs, she noticed for the first time, and the queen's smile was equally sinister; the two were leering, mocking.

"Why, you said that the reward you asked was to see us all safe," the king replied. "This cloak is the sign of our safety, now and forever, from the Beast that savaged Maurienne. What else would be fitting for your cloaks but the Beast's own hide?"

"What?" Jason said. His face went pale, but Amber didn't notice.

"Charlie!" she shrieked.

And then the fairies and the candles and the table, the king and queen and everything else, vanished, and Amber and Jason were kneeling together in the moonlight in the weeds behind the garden, each of them clutching a scrap of their cat's skin.

end

HAZMAT

~~~~~~

Dead Things Don't Move

The house stood alone at the end of the road, a thousand feet or more from its nearest neighbor, and the big graceful oak trees that had shaded it from the summer sun all day also hid most of it from view. It was a perfect target.

At least, Sid said it was a perfect target. Jack had his doubts.

"So what're you *worried* about?" Sid asked. "There's just the one broad living there, I'm sure of it." He stubbed out his cigarette in the van's overflowing ashtray, ignoring the hot ashes that drifted to the floor.

"I dunno," Jack said, "I just don't like it. How c'n you be so damned sure she's alone?"

Sid sighed, and leaned forward over the steering wheel. "Look, I *told* you," he said, "There's just one name on the mailbox, and it says 'Mudgett,' and I looked up Mudgett in the phone book, and the only one on this road is *Carol* Mudgett, Carol with one R, so it's a woman. If there was a man there, or anybody else, don't you figure he'd have *his* name on the mailbox, too? Or if his name's Mudgett, wouldn't he be in the phone book?"

"I wouldn't be too damn sure," Jack muttered.

"Well, damn it, if you really gotta know, I've been watching the place for three days, and I haven't seen anybody go *near* the place except the one broad and a couple of the neighborhood kids. I even fired off the twelve-gauge, just to

179

see if anybody'd notice, and nobody did – not even Carol goddamn Mudgett. Now, quit *worrying*, will you?"

Jack slumped down in his seat and didn't answer.

The van pulled off the road onto the shoulder and slowed to a stop; Sid turned off the engine and yanked the key from the ignition in one quick gesture, then reached forward and flicked off the headlights.

Darkness engulfed both men; there were no streetlights this far from town. The only light came from an upstairs front window of the house, filtered through the leaves of one of the oaks.

They sat in silence for a moment, contemplating that light; Sid stared out the van's window at it, Jack peering around him.

"You got the gun?" Sid demanded, turning away from the light.

"Of course I got it," Jack answered, annoyed. "I've had it on my goddamn lap for the last five miles."

"'s it loaded?"

"'Course it's loaded."

"Check it."

Jack started to protest, then thought better of it. "Put on the light," he said.

Sid reached up and switched on the overhead light; the darkness vanished, then seemed to seep back around the edges as their eyes readjusted.

Jack broke open the gun and held it up. "See? Shells in both barrels, all set to go."

"Good." Jack slammed the breech shut, and Sid turned off the light. The darkness surged back around them.

"I need a cigarette," Sid said into the night.

"No, you don't. Come on, let's get this over with," Jack replied. He opened his door and climbed out onto the gravel, the gun nestled under his arm.

The driver's door opened as Jack rounded the front of the van, and Sid stepped out.

"Gimme the gun," he said.

"Take it," Jack said, relieved; he thrust it out in both hands. Sid accepted it, weighed it carefully, and held it ready.

"Come on," he said.

Jack followed him up the crumbling concrete walk, stumbling once on the broken surface in the dark. The steps creaked under first Sid's weight, and then his.

"Be a shame if she didn't have anything worth stealing after all this," Jack whispered.

Sid smiled. "Oh, there's always *something*. Worst comes to worst, we can always hock her refrigerator or something."

The porch was narrow; Jack couldn't stand comfortably behind his partner unless he stayed on the steps, so they stood side by side, Jack glancing nervously back at the van perched up by the roadside, while Sid pressed the doorbell button.

They didn't hear it ring; all they heard was the sound of insects chirping in the tall grass. A few seconds passed, and Jack said, "Try it again."

"No, I think I hear footsteps," Sid said.

Jack had not heard any footsteps. He started to say so, but before he could get out the first word the porch light came on. The night was pressed back down the steps and over the railing, and Jack could see that the paint on the old narrow clapboards beside the door had faded and begun to peel.

There was no screen or storm door; when the door opened and the woman leaned out, there was nothing to block Sid's actions. He thrust the shotgun under the woman's chin and pulled the trigger.

That instant seemed to freeze as Jack watched. He saw very clearly every detail of the woman's face. She had a long nose and faded red hair, and was younger than he had expected. Her expression was vaguely worried, and Jack thought she had been starting to speak. Her eyes were shaded by the doorframe and he couldn't make out their color; the hallway behind her was unlit. Her lips were pale – no lipstick, Jack thought. Why should she be wearing any? She hadn't expected company.

She looked like she might have been a nice person, Jack thought; a bit old for him, though, in her late thirties at least, but younger than he had expected. He had been thinking of her as a little old widow, living alone out here, and had been worried, he realized, that she might look like his mother.

She didn't.

The roar of the gun drowned out the crickets and everything else, and the flash was blinding. Jack blinked, twice.

The woman's face was gone, fallen out of his line of sight; he heard the thump of her body hitting first the wall, and then the floor, as she tumbled backward into the dark. He smelled gunsmoke.

"So much for Carol goddamn Mudgett," Sid said. "I think the damn recoil just about broke my wrist." He kicked the door wide open and stepped over the corpse's legs into the hallway. "Come on," he called.

Jack didn't move; he stared at the legs. They stretched across the doorway, full in the light of the bare bulb hanging from the porch roof. They were bare to just above the knee; the woman had been wearing an old blue dress, shapeless and baggy, and the skirt had bunched up as she fell.

They were still a woman's legs, just as they had been. They looked as if their owner might awaken at any moment and reach down to tug her skirt back into place. The blue dress was visible up to the waist; the woman's upper body lay back in the shadow behind the doorframe.

Then Sid found a wall switch, and light poured into the hallway from an adjoining room.

"Oh, my God," Jack said.

Blood had sprayed in a broad, wet stripe down the dirty wallpaper, from eye level down to the floor, and bits of hair, bone, and tissue clung to it. At the baseboard lay the woman's body; her head had rolled forward onto her breast at an angle that would have been utterly impossible had it still been fully attached. Her neck consisted of two blood-drenched strands of ragged flesh; the shotgun had drilled a two-inch hole through the front of her throat and ripped the back of her neck and the base of her skull completely apart. Blood was pooled on the hardwood floor, dripping from where her neck should have been. One pale hand was flung out, the other folded across her breasts, where her almost-severed head stared blindly at the splayed fingers.

"Oh, my God," Jack said again.

"What's wrong with you?" Sid asked from the other room; he came to the door and peered back.

"Jeez, she does look bad, doesn't she? I didn't get a good look at her before," he said.

Jack didn't answer, and Sid cast him a worried look.

"Hey, c'mon, don't stand there staring; you'll be sick. Get in here and give me a hand."

Jack looked up and tried to swallow.

"C'mon, you knew we were going to kill her," Sid said.

"Yeah, but... I mean, my *God*, Sid! What'd you *do*?"

"I shot her, dummy. One barrel, like we said, in case we run into trouble."

"I didn't know it would do *that*!"

"Well, hell, neither did I, but dead is dead. What difference does it make? At least it musta been fast. Now, get in here and give me a hand, willya?"

Jack refused to look at the corpse again. He stepped over the spread legs and hurried across the hallway into the room where Sid waited.

"I think we're gonna do all right," Sid told him, smiling. "Take a look!"

Jack looked. The room was a relic – a relic worth a fortune in antiques. An octagonal clock hung on one wall, ticking loudly with each swing of its gleaming brass pendulum. Dresden china was packed on the mantle like the crowd on the rail at the track, and the mantle itself was an elaborate Victorian construction of carved oak and bevelled mirrors. An honest-to-God velveteen settee stood in one corner between matching cherry end-tables, one holding a bell-jar anniversary clock, the other a huge old music box and a stack of punched copper disks for the box to play.

"It might be hard to sell," he said, not really believing it.

"The hell it will be! We drive up to New York, go to an antique dealer, tell him that our dear sainted mother passed away last month and we need to sell her things to settle her medical bills. We'll get a thousand bucks, easy, for a vanload of this stuff!"

"Yeah, I guess," Jack said. He couldn't work up any real enthusiasm with the image of the dead woman in the front hall still fresh in his mind.

"We'll need the blankets and stuff to wrap everything," Sid said.

Jack remembered the corpse lying across the threshold and said, "You get 'em; I'll look around some." He headed toward a door at the back of the room, wanting to get further away from the body.

"Okay," Sid agreed. He turned back toward the hall, and then froze.

Jack did not notice; he had no intention of looking in that direction.

"Jack," Sid called in a loud whisper, "Something moved."

"What?" Without thinking, Jack turned around, and saw the bloody smear on the hallway wall, framed in the rectangle of light from the parlor. He looked quickly away, before he could see anything worse. "Jesus, Sid, what're you talking about? There's nobody here but us and that woman, and she's dead."

"I know," Sid said, still whispering, "but I swear, I saw something move out there in the hall. Honest to God, Jack." He stared into the shadows.

"My God, Sid, you blew her head off! She's dead; dead things don't move!" Memories of stories he had heard or read as a child, of horribly-mutilated corpses pursuing bloody poetic vengeance, flooded his mind.

"I didn't say *she* moved, I said *something* moved. I don't know what it was."

"Well, so what? Maybe she's got rats." Jack immediately regretted that suggestion as he imagined what rats might do to the body after he and Sid left. "You got the gun; go take a look if you think you saw something. I'm gonna look at the rest of the house." He turned away again.

Sid was not visibly reassured, but he said, "Yeah, you're right; I got the gun." He broke it open, checked the remaining live shell, then snapped it shut. "I'll go look."

"You do that. You just yell if you need me," Jack answered. He fumbled around the far side of the door to the next room, and finally found the light switch.

The switch worked an old hanging lamp with a stained-glass shade; more money, Jack knew. It hung above an oval table strewn with tatted doilies, and lit a glittering collection of

185

china and glassware in matching cabinets along the far wall. Jack went to investigate what looked like Wedgewood.

Sid, too, was investigating. He inched toward the hallway, his gaze fixed on the red ruin of his victim's head. He knew that she was dead. He knew that as Jack had said, dead things don't move. Still, he was certain that he had seen something move, and what else could it have been? The hallway was almost unfurnished; a braided rug lay on the floor, a hat-rack stood at the foot of the stairs, and the corpse was sprawled by the open door, but otherwise, it was empty.

Still staring at the body, the gun clutched tightly in both hands, he stepped through the doorway.

Immediately, before he consciously felt anything, he knew he had made a mistake. He knew that he should have turned on the hall light, should have looked carefully around the corner. He hadn't; he had been too busy watching the corpse. That was his mistake. Dead things don't move; that meant he had seen something alive.

That something, whatever it was, had gotten him; he felt a sudden sharp coldness exploding into his side, beneath his left arm, and sensed something warm running down inside his shirt, and then the pain hit him. He sucked in air, but couldn't find the strength to scream.

"You killed my mother," a voice hissed. Sid looked down and saw a small hand pulling the butcher knife from his side, and then driving it in again. The pain turned to blackness, the gun fell from his hands, and he toppled forward.

In the dining room, Jack heard the crash. "Sid?" he called.

No one answered.

"Sid?" He called more loudly this time, a note of desperation creeping into his voice.

Still no one answered.

"God, Sid, if you're pulling a joke, I swear I'm gonna kill you. You hear me, Sid?"

The house was silent, save for the ticking of the clock in the parlor.

Jack stood in the dining room for a long moment, waiting for some new sound, waiting for something to happen. He could hear the crickets, very faintly, chirping outside the window; he could see nothing but darkness and his own reflected image when he looked at the glass. China gleamed, white and cold, in the light from the lamp; he noticed that one of the little squares of yellow glass in the shade was cracked across.

"Sid?"

Nothing answered.

He had to do something, he knew that. His first thought was to get out, to run, to get away as fast as he possibly could. He would forget about Sid and about the antiques and just leave.

Sid had the keys to the van; without them, he would have to walk, five miles back to town, alone in the dark.

Worse, the corpse lay in the front door. He would have to get past it. Sid had vanished when he went into the front hall to see if the dead thing had moved. To get out of the house, Jack would need to do the same thing.

He couldn't do it; he knew that immediately. He would have to find some other way out of the house.

There would have to be a back door, but to reach it he would have to explore new, still-dark rooms. That did not appeal to him.

He looked at the window. It was certainly large enough to climb through, but he could see immediately that it couldn't be opened; he would have to break it. He could tell by the doubling of his reflection that there was a storm window on the outside, and those could, he knew, be almost unbreakable.

There were other windows, though. He would find a way out. He started back toward the parlor.

"Don't move," a voice said, a small, high-pitched voice, neither man nor woman; visions of freaks and monsters whirled through Jack's mind. He froze.

The voice came from his left. Very slowly, keeping his hands well out from his sides and open flat, he started to turn, to see who had spoken.

Another doorway, one he had not paid attention to, connected the dining room to the hall, and standing in that doorway was a young girl, perhaps nine or ten years old. She was wearing an old flannel nightgown, white with pink flowers. Her face was flushed, and speckled with chicken pox. Her feet were bare. Her hands, and the front of her gown, were smeared with fresh blood.

She held Sid's shotgun awkwardly in both hands.

"I told you not to move," she said conversationally. "And you're moving, but I know how to fix that."

She raised the shotgun and pointed it at Jack's face.

"Dead things don't move," she said as she pulled the trigger.

end

~~~~~

When Hell Froze Over

At the time we all thought it was a really clever idea, one of the best that the boss had ever come up with. It was one of those things that nobody ever thinks of, until someone does, and then it's just so *obvious* that you sit there saying, "Why didn't *I* think of that?"

And really, it was great fun at the time, despite how it all turned out.

It seemed like such a simple thing. For centuries, people had been promising to do this, that, or the other when Hell froze over – so the boss thought, why *not* freeze it over?

I mean, sure, burning's about the most painful thing possible, and we had an obligation to keep all those damned souls suffering, but after ten thousand years you can get used to *anything*, and the older souls were taking it all in stride, getting really complacent about it – "Ho, hum, another flame; how hot is *this* one? Sulphur and napalm – didn't we do that *last* week? White phosphorus was good – when do you think we'll have that again?"

Satan hates it when his people get complacent.

Besides, he's always liked to shake things up – that's how he wound up running Hell in the first place, isn't it? He got thinking about expectations and surprises, and just how nasty a good cold spell can be, and how sometimes something's worse if you get a break from it for awhile. And there were all those thousands and thousands of promises.

So he started planning it all out, in private.

189

Well, of course, in private; he wanted it to be a surprise. Wouldn't do to have people expecting it, as if it were a vacation or something. Pleased anticipation is *not* something the damned are entitled to.

Besides, the technical aspects were tricky. The heat isn't just something we *do*, after all, it's the natural climate down here. And changing that, all at once, everywhere, dropping the temperature a couple of hundred degrees for a week – he figured a week would be about right – and then bringing it back up to normal again, that was quite a challenge.

Sure, the boss has what you might call supernatural talents, but he's not *God*, after all – that's why he's *down* here, instead of running the universe. And he put most of what power he had into seeing that all those old promises were kept – after all, people wouldn't even *know* that Hell had frozen over without a little help.

To this day, I don't know all the details of how he did it. I know the basic technique, which was pretty hard to ignore, but I suppose...

Oh, you don't know how it was done? Basically, the tech crew just blew the entire atmosphere of Hell – everything, air, brimstone, all of it – out into hard vacuum somewhere in interstellar space, to dump most of the heat. That added a nice little twist, as it left everybody strangling for a few hours, until the ice arrived.

I think the ice came from a cometary cloud somewhere – must've been enough raw mass for half a dozen fair-sized planets, all hitting the ground at once. *Hot* ground – the old atmosphere didn't carry off *all* the heat, and vacuum's a good insulator, the best.

So all the slush and ice in the first wave flashed up into steam on impact, and we had air again, after a fashion – and then the next wave hit, and the next, and we had people crushed and splattered all over. If they hadn't already been dead, we'd probably have lost the entire population, one way or another.

I'll tell you, there wasn't *anybody* out there thinking this was a winter vacation! None of them – none of *us*, because we lower-level types hadn't been told yet – had the faintest idea what in Hell was going on. We thought maybe it was Armageddon, and they'd changed the rules on us somehow.

Anyway, after the first three batches of ice, Hell was down below room temperature, with slush and ice water everywhere, and damp fog that was nearly as hard to breathe or see through as the smoke had been.

But it wasn't frozen over – just cold and clammy.

And then, after a day or so, when we were getting used to it, when we had just about everybody dug out – well, I don't know how they did it, but that was when the *real* cold hit. Went down to about eighty below in maybe an hour and a half.

The air was clear and sharp, like nothing I'd ever seen, and it seemed to cut right into you when the wind blew. All that wet ground froze hard as iron, with sheet ice everywhere – all those meltwater pools were slick and smooth as a con-man's pitch, and a lot of the damned were frozen into the ice.

And that was when they broke out the skates. Millions of them. You see, for some people, the saying was, "When they ice skate in Hell."

Or ski; I didn't get skis, but some demons did.

And it was when they brought around the equipment that they finally told us what was going on, and we all admired the idea. We wanted to do our part, so we got out there and we skated and skied, gliding over the ice, and over the frozen souls when we found them handy.

But you know, we hadn't thought it through. All that time, when we were down there skating and skiing and watching those poor damned folks wishing they could freeze to death and get it over with, we were figuring that it meant more business, that we'd be getting more customers as a result.

We were all wrong.

Sure, it's obvious *now*, but it caught us by surprise. We all knew people made promises they said they'd keep when Hell froze over, but we hadn't thought about what *kind* of promises, what sort of prophecies we were fulfilling.

"You won't get your money back until Hell freezes over!"

"They'll ice-skate in Hell before this is fixed!"

"Forgive you? It'll be a cold day in Hell!"

So the boss had delivered a cold day in Hell – and when we saw the reports later, we were flat-out amazed by the wave of forgiveness, of fairness and justice and people doing things they should have done long ago.

Cut our incoming business in half for a good six months.

Old Satan caught on fast enough, and cut the whole thing short, so we only got three days instead of a week, but the damage had been done. Took almost a month to get the fires going again and boil off all that water, and I don't think we've got everything up to its proper temperature even yet.

That about did it for experimentation for the next few millennia. Unless...

Well, while we were out there skating over all that ice, a few of us got talking, and we came up with this idea we've sent up through channels. It's been working its way up through the chain of command for a couple of years now. I don't suppose it'll go over, really, after the way the ice turned out, but I think it could really be great. It'd be right there on Earth, not down here, so it wouldn't disrupt everything here – but it would drive all those rationalists up there buggy. Might do some serious damage to common sense, which is one of our worst enemies when it comes to recruiting. Sure, we'd have a few promises we'd rather not see kept, but nowhere near as many of them, and I, for one, think it'd be worth it.

Ever heard the phrase, "When pigs fly?"

end

HAZMAT

~~~~~

Grandpa's Head

My grandfather was being packed off to the nursing home to die – he knew it, I knew it, we all knew it.

I was doing the packing – most of it, anyway. My friend Susie was helping out with the kitchen stuff and the old man's clothes, and Grandpa packed a few things himself, but I got to take care of about fifty years of accumulated clutter.

It wasn't much fun, but it had to be done if we weren't just going to throw everything away, and it wasn't really all that bad. I was grateful he hadn't had a bigger house, and hadn't been much of a packrat.

A lot of it was just going to go into one of those rent-a-shed storage places and sit there until Grandpa died, when we'd sell it or give it away, and we all knew *that*, too, though we didn't say so, any more than we said aloud that he was going off to die.

There wasn't any point in storing more than we had to, though, so I was sorting through it all, seeing what we could just haul out to the curb with the trash.

I'd finished with most of it, boxing up the newer drapes, trashing the old ones, hauling the broken-down paisley couch to the curb for some poverty-stricken college student to steal for his dorm room, and so on, and had reached the attic, where I found a dozen cardboard boxes and a couple of footlockers.

I figured I'd start with the footlockers, so I found the keys in the collection Grandpa had given me and opened the first one.

And there it was.

There were scrapbooks and newspapers and some old clothes packed around it, so at first all I saw was the lid, which looked like tin or something. I didn't know what it was, but it looked moderately interesting, so I slid my hands down either side of the jar and lifted it up where I could get a good look at it.

I knelt there, staring at it, for a few seconds. Those seconds seemed like an hour – I know that's a cliche, but it really did seem a hell of a lot longer than it was.

I didn't scream or drop it or anything, which is a damn good thing because it would have been a hell of a mess; I just held it, and stared at it, and turned it slightly to get a better look, and then when my hands started to tremble I put it down, very gently, and stared at it some more.

You might think I'd have been confused, that I'd wonder what it was doing there, that I'd want to know *why* my grandfather had a woman's head in a jar in the attic, but I wasn't doing any of that.

I *knew*, right away, what it was doing there.

I could have tried to rationalize it, tried to explain it away, made up theories about medical specimens, all of that, but I didn't bother; what was the point in lying to myself?

Maybe if I hadn't recognized her – but I *did* recognize her, immediately. Even though I'd only seen her face before in old black-and-white photos, I'd looked at it enough that I knew it was the same face.

This was Constance Happerson's head.

And Constance Happerson was the family scandal, the woman Grandpa had been dating who had disappeared in 1945, and whose family had always suspected that Grandpa was somehow involved in her disappearance.

And sitting there in Grandpa's attic with that jar, I knew that her family had been right all along.

What's more, it looked as if it hadn't been some sort of desperate impulse or unfortunate accident. You don't keep a woman's head as a souvenir if you've been overcome by temporary insanity or are trying to cover up a botched abortion – the abortion theory had been the most popular at the time, as I understood it.

If you're a normal man with a dead body on your hands, you don't stick a piece of it in a big jar in the attic.

I'd known for years that Grandpa wasn't exactly a wholesome specimen – I mean, an old man's supposed to have stories about his wild youth, but Grandpa had more than his share of unsavory ones – but it was still a shock to realize that he was apparently a cold-blooded murderer.

And I had some decisions to make. There's no statute of limitations on murder, and I didn't particularly want to be an accessory after the fact, and that's exactly what I would be if I just ignored that jar.

But still, he was my *grandfather*, and he was a sick old man, and what good would it do to turn him in now, after all these years?

I couldn't ignore it, and I couldn't just call the cops, and that left just one thing to do.

Grandpa was downstairs, talking to Susie, having a little tea; he wasn't in any hurry to leave the house he'd lived in for so long and rush off to the nursing home, and he always enjoyed a chance to chat.

I went down the steps, brushing off the attic dust, and on down to the kitchen. The cupboards and cabinets were all standing open and empty, and a few boxes were stacked by the door; one box was open on the floor, waiting for the kettle and cups and the box of tea.

Grandpa and Susie were sitting at the table; she was laughing, and I guessed he was telling her one of his obscene war stories.

"Hi," I said. "Susie, could you do me a favor?"

She looked up, smiling.

"Take the car down to the corner and get it gassed up, okay? We don't want to get stuck anywhere with all Grandpa's stuff."

"Can't we do that on the way?" she asked.

"I'd rather get it out of the way now."

She looked at Grandpa, and he said, "Oh, go on. The boy probably wants to talk some boring family business in private."

Grandpa was always pretty sharp.

Susie looked back at me, then stood up. "Gimme the money, then," she said.

I gave her a twenty, and waited until I heard the car start before I sat down across from Grandpa.

He was looking at me expectantly.

"I found the jar in the footlocker," I said.

"Ah," he said, with a nod. "I thought that might be it. Proves I *am* getting old, that I didn't think of it sooner and keep it away from you – wasn't until I saw the look on your face when you came in here that I remembered I'd left it there."

I was glad I was already sitting down. I'd known it must have been him, there wasn't really any other explanation, but to see him sitting there, calmly admitting it...

"You killed Constance Happerson," I said.

He nodded. "Sure did," he said.

I thought I was going to faint.

"Why?" I asked.

"For fun," he said.

And that was absolutely the worst of it. My mouth dropped open and I stared at him.

"Shut your face, boy, you'll catch flies," he said.

I closed my mouth, but I went right on staring.

He nodded. "Sure, I killed Constance. With a steak knife. Gutted her. Had a fine time doing it, too."

I was beyond shock; I couldn't react any more.

"It was kind of careless, I guess, doing a girl I'd been seen with so much," he said, "but I just couldn't resist. I was young and reckless, and there'd never been any trouble about the others, so I chanced it. And she was such a pretty thing, I couldn't bear to just dump everything when I was done, so I got that jar, and some preservative stuff..." He shrugged. "I used to take her out and look at her sometimes, but I guess it's been fifteen, twenty years since I opened that trunk."

"Others?" I said.

"Sure." He smiled, and for a moment I almost wanted to throw up. "I was... well, nowadays you call 'em serial killers; in my day we were sex maniacs, or thrill killers. I was one."

"I thought... I didn't know there *were* serial killers back then..."

"Oh, crap, boy, don't give me that. Every generation thinks it invented sex, or at least some kind of sex, and there isn't a thing a person can do in that department that wasn't tried back in the caves. You never heard of Jack the Ripper, fer chrissakes?"

"Well..."

He wasn't listening, though; he was on a roll.

"And H.H. Holmes, only his real name was Herman Mudgett – he built himself a house with his own private glass-topped gas chamber so he could watch pretty young women die. Albert Fish used to torture kids to death for fun – mostly black slum kids, and nobody cared till he killed and ate a white girl. Been going on forever, Jim – there've always been men with a twist in the sex drive somewhere, and I happened to be one of 'em. Nowadays they figure maybe it's some kind of brain damage from being walloped too hard as a kid, and maybe it is, because there's no denying my ma used to whale on me pretty good, but whatever it is, I've got it – isn't anything that gives me a bigger kick than killing a girl."

"But it's *murder*," I said.

He shrugged. "Sure it is. But it's fun."

I sat there and stared at him and wondered if I was just having some especially realistic nightmare.

"Who else?" I asked. "How many?"

He leaned back and considered that.

"Well, I got started in Italy, during the war," he said. "I was on leave in Rome, and one of the whores tried to steal my wallet, and I decided to teach the little bitch a lesson, and I got a bit carried away. I figured I'd catch hell, that somebody would report the whole thing and I'd be court-martialed and sit out the rest of the war in Leavenworth – but no one did. No one noticed, near as I could tell. After all, there was a war on – people turned up dead all the time, all over the place. So as time passed I got less and less worried about getting caught, and I remembered more and more how much fun it was, and then I began planning how to do it again – at first it was just sort of an intellectual exercise, y'know, a daydream, but then I got more and more serious about it, and eventually... well, I think there were about half a dozen in Italy, and then the war ended and I was sent home, and I figured that was the end of it."

"Except for Constance Happerson."

Grandpa nodded. "Her, and plenty of others. I said I *figured* that was the end, I didn't say it *was* the end."

"There were others?"

"Sure. The first one back stateside was this girl I picked up in a bar in New York – I dumped her in the alley behind my hotel, and far as I saw, it never even made the papers. I guess that was why I figured I could get away with killing Constance."

"Jesus." I just stared at him, trying to make this make sense. He didn't look any different; he didn't look like a monster. He was a smiling old man with thinning white hair and liver spots.

But he admitted killing almost a dozen women, just for fun.

"After all the fuss over Connie, though, I stuck to strangers from then on."

"Jesus," I said again.

"It was especially easy in the late '60s and early '70s, with all those hippies hitchhiking all over the place, but there were always hookers – as long as I never picked 'em up the same place more than twice, no one ever noticed. So I'd go to New York one time, and the next I'd drive out to Pittsburgh, or whatever."

"How many?"

He shrugged. "Don't know," he said. "I didn't count. Maybe three or four a year, most years; I slowed down in the 1980s, when my health started to go."

"That'd be more than a hundred!"

"Could be, yeah. Probably more than a hundred. Old Herman Mudgett killed maybe two hundred, they say."

I just stared at him for a moment, trying to absorb that.

He looked calmly back at me.

"So what are you going to do about it, now that you know?" he asked.

"I don't know," I said.

"If you turn me in, I'll be dead anyway before they finish all the appeals and crap, and you'll have to live the rest of your life with it."

"What, I should feel *guilty* for turning in a mass murderer?" I burst out. "I mean, you may be family, Grandpa, but my *God*...."

He held up a hand. "No, no, Jim boy, I don't mean that. Christ, give me a *little* credit!"

I subsided.

"I mean," he said, "you'll have to live with the notoriety of having me as your grandfather. Think Susie would like that? Think any woman would?"

I thought immediately that yeah, some women *would* like it – the sort of women who wrote to convicted killers in prison.

I didn't think I *wanted* those women interested in me.

He could see what I was thinking; he smiled.

"So it's off to the nursing home after all, then? Hey, you can send me off to jail any time, if you change your mind – have you looked at the rest of the stuff in that footlocker yet?"

"No."

"Souvenirs. All the books on serial killers tell you, we like to take souvenirs. Clippings, photos, locks of hair, all kinds of things."

"Like Constance Happerson's head."

"Yeah. I only did that once, though."

"*Why* did you do it?"

He shrugged. "Why does anyone keep souvenirs? To help me remember, of course – to remind me how good it felt." He blinked, then sighed. "I'd let too much slip away lately; I'd almost forgotten some of it. Haven't looked in that trunk in ages."

I sat there, not saying anything, again, just staring at him, with his bifocals and dentures and crooked nose, that familiar face I'd seen leaning over my crib when I was a baby, that face that had been there watching at my Little League games, that face that had been so proud when I graduated from college – that face that had been the last thing those women ever saw.

Finally he shifted in his seat and said, "Go ahead and ask; I know you want to."

I didn't pretend not to know what he meant. I asked.

"What *did* it feel like?"

And he told me. He told me details that would never be in any of the books; he told me about doing things I couldn't imagine thinking of doing. Cutting off Constance Happerson's head and keeping it in a jar was just the beginning; he'd done unspeakable things to women, alive, dead, or dying. He'd violated every opening, and then made his own and violated those. He'd used knives, saws, ropes, whips, needles, and his bare hands.

Some of the women had lived for days.

"Did you ever kill a man?" I asked.

He nodded. "A couple," he said, "as experiments, but that just wasn't as good."

That didn't stop him from describing the experiments, though.

He'd gone back to women, reminiscing happily about torture and mutilation, sounding more cheerful than he had in months, when we heard the car pull up. He stopped abruptly – he had been talking about skinning a hooker on a rooftop in Newark. We both turned and watched the door, waiting for Susie to walk back in.

I realized, when I shifted, that I had an erection.

I felt sick, that I could react like that.

Susie didn't notice, or at least didn't say anything.

We finished cleaning out the house, and got Grandpa safely installed at the nursing home; I took the trunk of souvenirs home and stashed it safely away, securely locked.

When we left Grandpa at the home he gave Susie a hug, then shook my hand.

And as he did, he gripped my hand with those bony fingers and winked at me, and said, "Bet she'd be a *lot* of fun."

I snatched my hand away; I wanted to punch the old man in the face for that, but I resisted.

No one would understand – not unless I told them the whole thing.

I wondered again whether maybe I *should* turn Grandpa in – but he was a dying old man, and I'd never escape the stigma. What good would it do now, so long after the fact? He didn't remember most of the names, if he'd ever known them; it wouldn't clear up any mysteries that still mattered.

Let it die with him, I thought.

But I knew it wouldn't, because I remembered every word he'd said, and I had the trunk of souvenirs. I knew that memory wasn't going away.

And that night, in bed with Susie, I couldn't help thinking what it would feel like if, while we were making love, I were to slip a knife under her ribs. I imagined the convulsive shock, the thrashing under me...

The next day, while Susie was out, I looked through the trunk. I found Grandpa's pictures, and his diary. I read it; I couldn't resist.

I've never been good at resisting temptation.

And every time since then, when I touch Susie, when I embrace her, I imagine her dying struggles, her gasping for air, her blood spilling out. I imagine her limp and lifeless on the bed.

And every time, I wonder all over again whether I should turn Grandpa in, quickly, before he dies – it'll only be days now.

And every time, the idea of a scandal seems better and better.

Because my life's ruined anyway, one way or another – the temptation, the curiosity, grows stronger all the time; at least, if I turn him in, I probably won't ever dare to act on those horrible imaginings he's left me. I'd be too obvious a suspect. If I turned him in, I wouldn't dare to give in.

At least...

Well, not with Susie.

end

~~~~~~

Jim Tuckerman's Angel

Jim Tuckerman wanted to see angels more than he wanted anything else on God's green earth.

He couldn't easily explain why. When his friends or family would ask him what was so goddamned special about angels, he got tongue-tied and awkward, but would eventually, with the proper coaxing, manage a few fragmentary sentences about how glorious God's own messengers must be, and how wonderful it was that God sent them among ordinary folks.

Whereupon Jim's mother would either sniff disdainfully or growl angrily, depending on her mood, and point out that the Good Book said that God had created *Man* in His own image, and while Man had fallen from his high estate back when Eve pussywhipped Adam into eating the wrong thing, it still seemed to her that angels that were created just as God's errand boys wouldn't be half so magnificent as a good-looking young man in tight jeans.

"Bunch of half-assed things, neither man nor woman," she said. "You want to see folks can't make up their mind whether they're pitching or catching, you just go on out to San Francisco and cruise the streets a bit, you'll see plenty. And I figure angels probably aren't much better. You'll notice God never wastes much time talking to *them* in the Bible; no, He knows that men are a hell of a lot more interesting, got more *to* 'em, than the bunch of dickless choirboys He's got fetchin' and carryin' for Him!"

"The Bible's for men and women, Ma," Jim said. "That's why it's about us and not the angels. They don't *need* an instruction book to know what God wants of them; they're God's will made manifest. That's why I want to see 'em, meet them and talk with them; they know God better than we do."

"Hmph."

Jim didn't try to convince his mother of anything; he knew her better than that. She'd settled her mind on its path a long time ago, probably when he was still in diapers, and he couldn't see her turning aside from it for anything short of the Second Coming – and at least she wasn't expecting that to happen next Tuesday, the way Aunt Aimee was.

But he wasn't letting her turn *him* aside, either. He looked around at the world God had created, the cast-aside world that God had left to Adam and Eve after they disappointed Him so much, and he saw the glory and wonder of it all, the magnificence of the vast blue sky and the bright green leaves, the smell of woodsmoke or wisteria or a pretty woman, the sound of the birds in the trees and the water in the creek, and it was all so beautiful he could scarcely stand it – and this was the *fallen* world, while the Lord's angels never fell. How much more beautiful would they be, then?

Jim knew that for a lot of folks, God and His angels were something you talked about on Sunday mornings that didn't have a thing to do with the everyday world. But Jim didn't see it that way. He knew other people didn't see any angels, but he didn't let that stop him. He was pretty sure, from what the other fellows said, that he saw things not everyone saw – that he saw *more* than most people. He hoped that meant that he might be able to see an angel where other men wouldn't, because he *needed* to see one.

Angels were the only glimpse of Heaven a man could hope for while he lived, and Jim wasn't anywhere near sure enough of himself to think he'd be seeing anything but flames once he died. He knew he was a shiftless fool, since everyone had told him as much every day of his life, and he didn't see as how there'd be room for such a one in God's Heaven. Oh, Jesus loved him, he knew that, had been told it since before he could talk, but Jim didn't figure that meant he wouldn't catch Hell for his sins when he died, any more than old Ticker hadn't caught Hell from Jim when he'd dig out under the fence to chase rabbits. Despite that Jim loved the old dog, he'd whacked Ticker across the nose and tied him up when he misbehaved and left him to whimper, and Jim wasn't expecting anything kinder from God when his time came. A man should know better than a dog how to behave.

With that in mind, Jim didn't think he'd be singing hymns in Heaven for eternity. He was pretty sure he was bound the other way. He accepted that, but before he went he wanted to get a look at what he'd be missing, and here on Earth that could only mean an angel.

He didn't explain this all to his friends, for fear they'd tell him what a fool he was. He'd been talked out of a good many things in his life, and usually he wished later that he hadn't been, and he wasn't going to let that happen with this. It was too important. It was so important, in fact, that he didn't intend to just quietly wait around home in hopes an angel would stop by Ballard, Kentucky on business. He intended to go out looking for one.

He didn't tell his friends *that*, either.

Angels went everywhere, of course, going about the Lord's business; everyone had a guardian angel watching over him. That was what Preacher Bill said, and Jim had never heard anyone question it. God's messengers had errands to attend to in every corner of the world.

Jim hadn't seen any of them, though, and he'd been looking. He wasn't sure whether they were invisible even to him, or moved so quick he never caught a glimpse of them, or watched from afar with telescopic vision like Superman in the comics, but he never saw them.

He wanted to see one. It wasn't enough to know they were there; he wanted to *see* one.

He'd tried praying for a glimpse, but as yet he hadn't got an answer, unless the answer was "no." God helps those who help themselves, though, so he wasn't going to just wait. He was going looking.

He'd thought it out. Angels were God's messengers, watching over people. Didn't it follow, then, that there'd be more angels, and more of a chance of seeing one, if he was somewhere with more *people* in it? Ballard, population 115, was not exactly bustling.

So one day in August he drove the old Dodge 150 out of the barn, called to his mother, "Goin' into town, Ma. Not sure when I'll be back," and headed up the highway past Winchester to the interstate. He had a few hundred dollars he'd saved up stuffed in his pants, and a bag of clothes and the like tossed in the back of the pick-up, and when he got to I-64 he headed east, because everyone knew it was more crowded back east on the coast than it was anywhere else.

It didn't *look* more crowded at first, there where I-64 headed up into the mountains and through the Daniel Boone National Forest, but he knew he'd get to the real east eventually, and come out in Washington or New York or someplace like that.

He drove up past Ashland and Huntington and on to the east, staying on I-64 clear across West Virginia and into Virginia, where I-81 came in from the south. He drove past mile upon mile of rich green country, tall straight trees and fine

210

green fields, all washed in God's golden sunlight, and he marveled at the beauty of it all. The world was lush and lovely, and he gloried in it as he drove.

When I-64 split off from I-81 again and turned toward Richmond he stayed on I-81, because the signs said that could get him to Washington DC, and he thought that if ever there was a place on God's Earth that needed angels, it must be Washington. Those senators and presidential staffers and all surely needed the Lord's guidance to keep God's country in its proper order, and wouldn't there be angels to bring that guidance to hand?

By then he'd driven the day through. The sky was dark now, and he was tired, and the right headlight on the Dodge didn't work the way it ought, so he followed the signs to a motel in New Market and got himself a room, and bought himself supper at the family diner across the road.

After he'd eaten he went back to the motel and sat in his room reading the Bible – the story of Lot, mostly. When he finished the chapter he said his prayers and went to bed.

In the morning he got up and got himself showered and dressed, and went out to the Dodge with his bag in one hand, but he didn't get behind the wheel right at the first, because there was a man on the ground between Jim's pick-up and the next car over, which was an old blue Chevy with taped-on plastic where the passenger side window should have been. The man had one hand under the Chevy, and his head pushed up to the underside of the Chevy.

He looked up at the sound of Jim's footsteps, and Jim recognized his face as one he'd seen at supper the night before. It was a handsome face, with a narrow jaw and deep-set eyes.

"Got some trouble there?" Jim asked.

"'Fraid I do," the man said. "The engine turns over fine, but there's no power to the wheels. I was thinkin' it might be a

211

busted driveshaft."

"More like to be the transmission gone bad," Jim said. "Not that that's so very much better."

"You're probably right about that," the man said. He glanced at the Dodge. "That your truck?"

"Yessir."

"And I'm blockin' you, aren't I? Sorry 'bout that." He rolled over and sat up. Then he looked up at Jim again from where he sat. "You wouldn't happen to be on your way to DC, would you?"

"I might be," Jim admitted. "Why?"

"I got no right to ask you this, and if it's any bother you just tell me no, but I sure could use a lift. I've got a job interview in Washington this afternoon, and there's no way *this* heap is gonna get me there." He slapped the Chevy. "Probably be a week's work to get her runnin' again, and that's assuming they can get the parts and they'll trust me to pay 'em, which frankly, *I* wouldn't. Hell, the repairs are probably gonna cost more than the damn thing's worth." He got to his feet, and said, "What do you say?"

Jim had to think about this a little. Ma had always told him he was too trusting of strangers, but giving a man a helping hand was the Christian thing to do, and it wasn't as if Jim had anything much this fellow was likely to be after stealing. The Dodge was in better shape than the Chevy, but not by much, and the stranger couldn't know about the cash in Jim's pants; if he was looking to rob someone, he wouldn't have picked Jim.

He wasn't any sort of pervert or anything, either, Jim was pretty sure. He didn't look a bit like Ma's descriptions; wasn't a touch of make-up on him, and his clothes were just good decent clothes, no leather or silk.

And it could be that the Lord had put this man in his path for a reason. After all, God knew what Jim was up to, and why wouldn't He want to give Jim a hand? Sure, Jim was hellbound, but that didn't mean God wouldn't cut him a break while Jim was still drawing breath. Jesus loved him, after all.

"I could do that," Jim said.

"Awright! *Thank* you, friend! I'll pay my share of the gas. Let me get my gear and turn in my key, and we can go soon as you're ready."

"All right. I'll be turning in my key, too." Jim had been thinking about maybe getting himself some breakfast, but now he thought he'd put that off a bit.

Jim tossed his bag in the back of the Dodge, then went back to check on his room and make sure he hadn't left anything; then he went to the office to drop off the key, and got there just as the other man stepped up to the counter.

A moment later the two of them walked out to the truck together. The rider tossed his big old backpack in the back, next to Jim's bag, then held out a hand and said, "My name's Nick Lichtman."

"Jim," Jim said, shaking the offered hand quick and firm.

Then the two headed for the two doors. Jim climbed behind the wheel, while Nick slid into the passenger seat. "It's real generous of you to give me a lift," Nick said. "I could really use this job."

"It's not so much," Jim said. "What line of work are you in?"

"Reclamation," Nick said. "Been working freelance these last few years, but I'm hoping to get a government job – I wouldn't mind having a pension and a health plan. What about you?"

"My folks have been farming for nigh onto a hundred years, out in Ballard, Kentucky," Jim said. "Corn and tobacco, mostly." He started the engine.

"A son of the soil, huh? Lot of hard work, farming."

"Can be," Jim acknowledged, as he shifted into reverse.

"So what takes you to the nation's capital?"

Jim concentrated on getting out of the parking space and didn't answer.

Nick seemed to take the hint, and shut up, at least for the moment. He let Jim get out of the parking lot and up the state road and onto the interstate in peace.

That seemed to be all the quiet he could stand, though. "Where you bound in DC?" he asked. "My interview's on 14th Street, right downtown."

"Don't rightly know," Jim said, concentrating on the traffic. He wasn't used to driving as fast as folks did on this side of the mountains.

"You're not after work, then? Nor visiting family?"

"Nope."

"Not much of a talker, are you?" he said.

Jim glanced at him. "Don't suppose I've much to say just now," he said. "I'm keeping my mind on the driving."

"In my experience, a man who don't talk's got something he wants to keep to himself, and he's afraid it'll slip out if he opens his mouth."

"Can't say as that's been *my* experience. Might be any number of reasons to keep a mouth shut." He glanced at the eighteen-wheeler in the rear view mirror; it was coming up fast behind them, and he wasn't sure whether he'd best get out of its way, or just let it pass.

"But when a man answers a civil question with a bunch of dodges, I think there's something he doesn't want to say. Why *are* you going to Washington?"

"Don't see as it's any of your business," Jim said.

"It's not, but you're doin' me a favor as it is, I know that, so I was thinkin' I might do you one in return. You said you didn't know just where you were going in Washington; if you tell me

214

what you're after, I might be able to help you out with that. I've been there before, know the city pretty well. I can tell you the best route to the White House, if that's what you want to see."

"It's not."

"But you're lookin' for *something*, aren't you?"

Jim sighed. "I am," he admitted.

"What is it?"

Jim remembered his earlier thought, that the Lord might have put this fellow Nick in his path for a reason. Besides, what was he going to do if he thought Jim was crazy? He was in Jim's truck, after all, and the .38 under the seat was on Jim's side.

"I'm looking for an angel," he said.

Nick considered that carefully for a moment before replying. He looked Jim over, then looked out the windshield at the highway for a bit, then looked at Jim again.

"There's them that if they said that, I'd think they meant someone with money to invest, but you don't strike me as that kind," Nick said. "There's them I'd think meant they were lookin' to get laid, but you don't seem one of those, either. I'm thinkin' you mean it just the way you said it – you want to see one of God's own angels, and not any sort of human being at all."

"That's right," Jim said, a trifle uneasy at how Nick was taking this.

"Not a dead friend or relative?"

Jim snorted. "Dead souls ain't angels," he said. "Anyone who thinks that ain't read the Good Book or paid attention in Bible school. The dead in Heaven are saints, not angels. Angels are God's messengers, made before Man."

Nick nodded and looked out at the road again. "I know that. Just makin' sure you did."

"'Course I do."

The eighteen-wheeler roared past them in the left lane, and Jim gripped the wheel to keep the Dodge straight on the highway.

A moment later Nick said, "How do you know *haven't* seen an angel?"

"What?"

"Well, they can look human if they want to, can't they? That's in the Bible, that some have entertained angels unawares. And the ones who visited Lot in Sodom, they were beautiful, but the Sodomites thought they were human."

Jim frowned, remembering what he'd read the night before. Nick was right, but still...

"Then I haven't seen an angel, have I? Just an angel's disguise."

"It's still an angel."

"It's not what I'm looking for."

"So you want to look on beauty bare, is that it?"

Jim glanced at him. "You could say that," he said.

"Are you sure? Remember that a lot of the angels in the Bible were terrible to look upon – half the time the first thing they say is 'Fear not.' You really want a look at something like that?"

"Yes, I truly do," Jim said, letting up on the gas so as not to gain on the eighteen-wheeler on the upgrade they'd just hit.

"Why?"

"Because I reckon it's the closest I'll ever get to looking on the face of God."

Nick didn't answer that right away, but just looked at Jim, his expression growing thoughtful.

"Not optimistic about your post-mortem prospects, I take it?"

Jim glanced at him. "What?"

"Not expecting anything good when you die?"

Jim looked back at the road before answering. This fellow was smart, maybe smarter than Jim entirely liked.

"No reason I should," he said.

Nick nodded. "Well, you'd know that better than I."

For a moment neither man spoke; then Nick asked, "Why Washington?"

"It's a big city. Lots for angels to do."

"You think more people means a better chance of findin' an angel? Seems to me that's huntin' a needle in a haystack."

"God's got a plan for us all," Jim said. "Seems to me He'd send His angels to keep an eye on that plan."

"God sees every sparrow's fall, though. He and His angels would be everywhere."

"Not that I've seen. People have guardian angels, though. I reckon if I get around enough people, I've got a better chance of spotting me an angel."

Nick considered that for a moment, then shook his head. "I don't think it works like that. I never heard of anyone seein' guardian angels in New York, 'less you mean those punks with the berets."

"I wouldn't know about that," Jim said. "But if I don't look in the cities, where *do* I look?"

"I don't know," Nick admitted. "I never heard of anyone went lookin' for angels and found 'em. I'm not sure you *can* see 'em." He grimaced. "Not what you wanted to hear, I suppose."

"Can't say that it is. But I see things other folks don't, sometimes, so I'm thinking I might see an angel if there's one to be seen."

"But you haven't seen one yet."

"Nope."

"So you don't know if you can?"

"Not for certain, but my heart says I can."

They drove on in silence for some time then, making the turn to the east onto I-66 through Front Royal. They'd gone another ten miles when Nick spoke.

"Seems to me," he said suddenly, "that you gotta look at this logically. You been thinkin' about guardian angels, but hardly anyone ever seen one of those, at least not and known it. But there's other angels."

"Don't know how to find them either, though," Jim said gloomily.

"But there's one angel that you know where he's gonna be, sooner or later. And it's one that doesn't bother with disguises."

Jim glanced at him. "There is?"

"The angel of death."

Jim didn't answer right away; he took his time to think about that.

Finally, though, he said, "No man knows the hour of his passing, so where do you reckon I'd find the Angel of Death?"

"A hospital," Nick said. "The terminal ward. Maybe the emergency room."

Jim considered that long and hard, and had to admit there was some promise to the idea.

"You don't hear much about people seein' the angel of death in the E.R.," Nick mused, "but then, they aren't lookin'."

"Might be there's a good reason for that."

"People don't much like to think about death, that's for sure."

That wasn't what Jim had meant, but he didn't say so.

They drove on in silence again for some time after that.

Finally, though, as they were cutting through Arlington and the Washington Monument was just visible ahead on the left, gleaming white in the sun, Jim said, "I don't suppose you'd know much about hospitals in Washington?"

"Not a lot," Nick admitted. "There's one at Georgetown University." He pointed past the monument.

Jim nodded. "Where'd you say your appointment is at?"

"Fourteenth Street, just across the bridge. Stay straight on this highway across the river – it changes number, but don't let that throw you, and as soon as you're across the river the highway curves to the right, but you bear left onto Independence Avenue and then turn left again onto 14th, and it's just a few blocks up."

A few minutes later they were indeed on Independence Avenue, and Jim saw a sign for 14th Street. They were driving through the largest city Jim had ever seen. "It looks like something off the television," he said.

"Well, yeah," Nick said. "Can you pull over up ahead there? I think that's the building." He pointed.

Jim managed to maneuver the Dodge over to the curb without causing a collision or encouraging much honking, and let Nick out. He fetched his pack from the back, then leaned back in and said, "Thanks for the ride. You serious about findin' a hospital?"

"Reckon I am."

"Well, if you go on up 14th across the Mall, then turn left on Pennsylvania Avenue up ahead, that'll take you into Georgetown, and maybe there'll be signs."

"I'll give it a try, then. Good luck." He waved, and pulled back into traffic.

When he looked back on it later, Jim was amazed he managed to get anywhere in that city without getting the pick-up's fenders more banged up than they already were. There were more cars in every block than in all of Ballard, more on every street than he'd seen in all his life, and about half of them were apparently being driven by crazies. Somehow, though, he got through it without hitting a thing.

219

He thought maybe his own personal guardian angel might have a thing or two to do with it, but he never did see any such being. If there was an angel at work, it was doing its best to stay out of sight. God's handiwork wasn't so obvious as that here. Man's creations were everywhere, but except for a few trees and the sky above, the hand of the Lord was less evident.

But God had created Man in His image, and that image was everywhere. The streets were crowded with more people than Jim had ever seen. It was greatly distracting, and it took him more than an hour to find his way from one blue H sign to the next and finally to a hospital.

He wasn't entirely sure whether this was the Georgetown University one that Nick had mentioned, or another, but it didn't much matter – it was a hospital. He found a place to park the Dodge and walked into the hospital lobby.

There he stopped to look around, wondering where he might best go to have a chance of seeing the Angel of Death. No man knows the hour of his passing, as he'd told Nick, but Jim was sure that in a big place like this, full of the sick and injured, someone must die pretty much every day, and it was just a matter of finding the right person and staying by him until the Angel came for him.

There was a directory on the wall near the elevators; Jim went to take a look. He thought the cancer ward might be a good place to start, but when he read the list he didn't see cancer; he saw any number of long names he didn't know, like endocrinology and oncology, and he guessed one of those must be a doctor's word for cancer, but he didn't know which.

But there was an emergency room, and that was probably as good a place as any to look.

He almost expected someone to stop him and ask what he was doing there, or demand to see a visitor's badge, or some such a thing, but no one did; he walked down the corridor and through the sliding glass door into the emergency room and looked around.

There were empty beds in darkened alcoves, and people in beds behind screens or curtains, and doctors and nurses dressed in white. It was quiet – not at all like the emergency rooms he had seen on TV, but of course those had been made-up stories about exciting times, not about ordinary days.

He stood for awhile, trying to decide what he should do. He felt a bit like a vulture, standing there hoping someone would die; it didn't seem right.

But then, maybe he might see another sort of angel here. Guardian angels must be busy in a place like this. He found a chair in an open area and sat for a time, taking it in, listening to the murmur of the nurses' voices, and the louder words of the doctors, and the tapping of fingers on keyboards, and looking around, trying to understand what he was seeing.

No one troubled him; they were all busy with their own concerns and none of his.

After a time – he wasn't sure how long, but it might've been an hour – he grew restless. He had been sitting there waiting for something to happen, and it wasn't any better than waiting back home in Ballard. He got back on his feet and began walking along, looking at each occupied bed, or at the screens and curtains, hoping for some sign of God's messengers.

As he did, a doctor hurried past, and then another, and he turned to see that they were gathering at the big glass door where a sign read AMBULANCE ENTRANCE – STAND CLEAR.

Then he heard a siren, and the roar of an engine, and the squeal of tires, as the door slid open, and a big boxy red ambulance was pulling up, the doctors hurrying out to meet it. Men in heavy coats swung open the rear doors and began hauling out stretchers. Jim stared, his heart in his throat, as three stretchers were unloaded, their wheels unfolded, and then they were rolling into the emergency room, and a nurse was suddenly at his elbow asking, "Can I help you find someone, sir?"

"No," Jim said, keeping his gaze fixed on the stretchers. "I was... I was on my way out and I saw..."

"Don't get in anyone's way," the nurse said. Then she was hurrying toward the stretchers herself.

Two of the stretchers had been rolled away already, but the third was still by the door, with people clustered around it and doctors bent over, and then it was there, above the stretcher. Jim saw it, and he knew instantly what he was seeing.

The Angel of Death.

It was a darkness and emptiness that filled the room without being in it at all. It had no shape but it had great black colorless wings and blind, all-seeing eyes. For an instant Jim saw it, saw the utter all-consuming nothingness of it, like an endless hole in the universe, there above the body.

And beyond it, *through* it, so briefly that Jim could not be sure he really saw anything at all, was something that might have been a light, or might have been nothing at all.

Then it was gone, and the doctors were stepping away from the body, and someone was swearing repetitiously, saying the same two words over and over, and Jim felt tears on his cheeks.

He stared at the place where the angel had been.

It had been so *quick*. He hadn't had anything like a good look at it.

He had seen an angel, right enough, but he hadn't seen *enough* of it. He wanted a good hard look at it.

The stretcher with the corpse on it was rolled away, out of his sight somewhere, and the doctors were gone with it, and Jim stood staring at the big glass door. It had closed again, and the big red ambulance had driven away, without sirens or lights.

He reached up and dabbed at his eyes, blinking away the tears.

"Did you see what you came for?" a voice asked, a familiar voice, and Jim turned to see Nick Lichtman standing there behind him.

"Reckon I did," Jim said. "What brings *you* here? Wa'n't you getting interviewed?"

"I got interviewed," Nick said. "They said to come back tomorrow, ten a.m., for a follow-up, which is promisin', but it left me a bit at loose ends for the rest of today, y'know? So I thought I'd come see if you found the place and got what you were after."

"I found it," Jim said.

"Did you see your angel?"

"I saw it."

Nick blinked. "Did you really?"

"I saw it," Jim repeated, remembering that vast dark emptiness, and the tantalizing hint of something more, something *beyond*.

Nick stared at him. "I will be damned," he said. "What did it look like?"

"Can't rightly say. Big. Dark. Empty."

"That doesn't sound real attractive."

Jim looked at Nick the way he'd look at a hound that wouldn't back down when called off. "I wouldn't think the Angel of *Death* ought to be real pretty," he said.

But even as he said it, he knew he was wrong. The angel had been beautiful in its utter desolation, in its purity and simplicity. There were no complications to it, no uncertainties – it was exactly and entirely what it was, no more and no less, without doubts or reservations. Jim remembered his mother talking about the glories of a man's body, and he supposed she had a point; certainly a *woman's* body was beautiful in its complexity and contradictions, the combinations of softness and strength, the smooth surfaces that were actually an intricate mass of fluids and follicles and a hundred other things.

The angel had had none of that, no flesh, no real shape, nothing but a single iteration of divine will, absolute and infinite, and it had been terrible and beautiful.

Jim ached to look on it again, to drink in the sight of that essence.

"I suppose not," Nick said. "Nothin' pretty about death. So you're satisfied? Ready to go back home to Kentucky?"

"No," Jim said slowly. "Can't say I am." He wanted to see it again. He wanted to see what lay beyond it, whether there was really anything there at all, or whether he had imagined that because his mind could not comprehend so total an emptiness.

"No?" Nick looked around the emergency room. "What are you thinkin'?"

"It was too quick," Jim said. "I didn't get a good look at it. And it was almost like I could see something *through* it." The words didn't convey his meaning well, but human speech couldn't.

Nick's expression turned suddenly solemn. "Through it?"

"Yup."

"You don't just mean the wall, do you?"

"No." Whatever he had or hadn't seen within and beyond the angel, it was nothing there in the emergency room.

"Was it... you know, the light? *The* light?"

"Might've been. Couldn't say for sure." Jim hadn't really thought about it in those terms. To reduce whatever he had glimpsed to human words like light, or Heaven, or Hell, or even the Face of God, seemed to diminish it somehow.

224

"You *saw* it?"

"Can't say for sure. Thought I might've."

"You mean it? You aren't pullin' my leg?"

"I'm not joking." Jim's expression left no room for doubt.

For a moment the two men stood silently thinking. Then Nick said, "There's some would say you must be nuts."

Jim smiled crookedly. "It's a sad world, my Ma says, where people don't know what they're seeing, and if seeing angels means I'm crazy, I'd say she was right – that's pretty sad. The Bible talks about people seeing angels, and people have seen 'em all along, now and again. I don't reckon one's got to be crazy."

"Most people don't see angels."

"Most people aren't looking."

"So you saw the Angel of Death, and you want another look at it?"

"That's about the way of it."

"What're you goin' to do about it?"

"Hadn't made up my mind as yet."

"Gonna wait around here until someone else dies?" Nick glanced around at the quiet room – there were voices from somewhere off to the left, where the doctors were working on the others who'd been brought in by that ambulance, but this area was deserted for the moment. "Could take awhile."

"It could," Jim agreed.

Nick looked around again, then leaned close and whispered, "O'course, you could hurry things up a little."

Jim blinked. "What?" Astonished, he looked at Nick's face.

"You could find some poor bastard who hasn't got very long, and help him along," Nick said quietly. "Maybe a pillow over the face. So you won't blink at the wrong time, or be in the john when it happens. Be a shame to sit with someone for days waiting for him to die, and then miss the show."

"You... you're saying I might kill someone?" The idea was horrible – but at the same time, the idea of seeing the Angel of Death again was horribly alluring.

It was a temptation, truly it was. Jim look at Nick.

"Someone who's dying anyway," Nick said. "You'd be putting him out of his misery, y'know? It'd be a kindness, really."

Jim looked into Nick's eyes – brown eyes, dark and deep-set. Jim looked into those eyes long and hard, and he saw what there was to see there, and he shivered.

He saw emptiness there, and darkness, and a deliberate hiding of any light that might lie beyond. There was a purity and simplicity to that darkness that was not quite like anything Jim had ever seen in a man's eyes before.

He remembered his mother saying that men were more interesting than angels, that there was more *to* them, and he knew she'd been right.

"It's not for us to play God," Jim said.

"What?" Nick said, backing off a little from Jim's gaze. "Okay, maybe that's not such a great idea, killing someone, but just waiting..."

"You can stop now," Jim said, interrupting him and looking away.

"What?"

"I know you. I've seen enough." Jim looked up at the ceiling, at the off-white acoustic tile.

"Jim, I'm just tryin' to be helpful..."

"You're tempting me, Nick, and I don't want that. I've seen enough. I'll be going home now." He started to turn away.

Nick caught his arm. "Home? But you wanted another look at the Angel of Death!"

"Reckon I've seen enough angels for now," Jim said. "More than my share, I'm thinking."

"One quick look at the Angel of Death?" Nick sounded almost angry. "That's enough for you? I thought you'd said you'd been waitin' all your life to see and angel, and you get half a glimpse, and you're ready to pack it up and go home?"

"I've had more than a glimpse," Jim said. "Seems to me I drove halfway across Virginia with an angel beside me."

Nick frowned. "Your guardian angel, you mean? You think you needed an angel to protect you from me, because I suggested you might want to end the sufferin' of some poor sick old man?"

Jim shook his head. "No, Nick," he said gently. "I *know* who you are. I'll be going now."

"You think so, do you?" Nick's voice was suddenly strong; he did not bother with further denials.

"I do, Nick. And I reckon I might have a better shot at Heaven than I thought, or you wouldn't have troubled yourself with me." He thrust out a hand to shake. "I thank you for that, Nick. A fallen angel is still an angel, and I reckon that one way or another every angel, fallen or not, is God's will made manifest."

Nick looked down at the hand, then back up at Jim's face.

And then he vanished, without taking Jim Tuckerman's hand, and he left nothing behind but the odor of brimstone.

end

~~~~~

Impostor Syndrome

Gordon knew Janice liked to paint; Cheryl had mentioned it at the party when she first introduced them.

"She paints?" Gordon had asked, while Janice was at the buffet stocking up on scallops in bacon.

"Mm-hm," Cheryl said, pulling a toothpick from the hors d'oeuvre she'd just put in her mouth.

"Is she any good?"

Cheryl had held up a hand until the hot little tidbit was out of her mouth, then said, "Don't know – I've never seen any of her work. She's shy about it."

Gordon had nodded and not thought any more about it at the time. Oh, he'd been interested – he was interested in everything about Janice just then, and besides, he'd majored in art history, and even if he'd wound up a broker instead of an artist or an art critic or a museum curator, he was still interested in art.

But it didn't seem especially important at the time.

They'd had dinner together two days later, and met for lunch the day after that, and one thing led to another, and six weeks after the party he had moved his belongings into the big old house on Thornton Street that her parents had left her.

She'd made it clear, though, that she didn't want him prying into the closed-off rooms on the second floor – not that there was anything terrible about them, but they were private, full of family relics.

And Gordon hadn't been pushy; he liked Janice very much indeed, liked her shy, crooked little smile and the way she seemed to always be looking sideways at him, liked her childlike, high-pitched laughter. She had a sly wit and a slender, sexy body, and their tastes in any number of things – movies and music and manners – were neatly aligned. He didn't want to antagonize her. If she wanted to keep a few rooms to herself, that was fine with him. He hadn't exactly told her the whole story of his own life, either. They had plenty of time to get to know each other better.

So he kept himself to the ground floor and the big master bedroom, and that was plenty of space, far more than he'd had in his old apartment.

Janice liked to paint, Cheryl had said, and it did occur to Gordon that he hadn't seen any sign of it, hadn't seen an easel anywhere, or any of her paintings on the walls anywhere, but maybe she'd lost interest, maybe she'd just taken a few classes and then given it up.

He didn't worry about it.

But then, about three months after they met, he came home one wintry evening and found the downstairs dark and empty, even though her car was in the driveway.

Puzzled, he turned on the hall light, then put down his briefcase and hung up his scarf and overcoat.

"Jan?" he called.

No answer.

He walked down the hall and stuck his head into the kitchen, and that was just as dark and deserted as the front of the house.

"Hello?" he called, in case she was in the pantry or down in the basement, but no one answered.

Taking a nap, perhaps?

He walked back to the front and up the big staircase, and turned to head for the master bedroom, then stopped.

The door of one of the other rooms was open, and light was pouring out into the unlit hallway.

Curious, he stepped over and looked in.

She was sitting there on a tall stool, working on a large painting, a painting done mostly in cream and shades of grey, a painting of a mother in late 19th-century dress stroking a young girl's hair.

"Wow," he said.

Janice started and dropped her brush. She turned and stared blankly at him for a moment.

"I'm sorry," he said, "the door was open, and I couldn't help..."

Before he could finish the sentence she bustled off the stool and slammed the door in his face.

He stood there, blinking, trying to decide what to do next, and absorbing what he had seen.

He'd heard that she liked to paint, of course; what he hadn't heard was that she was *good*.

He hadn't had a proper look at it, of course, but from the glimpse he had had, the painting was excellent – a bit sentimental and old-fashioned in its choice of subject, perhaps, but the composition was original and very, very good, the colors subtle and effective with the warm creamy hues of the woman's face and clothing in vivid contrast to the cool background.

Mere technical details such as light and shadow and perspective didn't even come into it, so far as he could tell – they were all perfect.

That was why he had said "Wow," instead of clearing his throat or otherwise politely making his presence known.

Smart and sweet and sexy – and *talented*, too. He'd really found himself a prize!

Then the door opened again, the light in the room went out, and he was still standing there stupidly as she pushed past him and closed the door behind her.

"Hi," he said.

She looked nervously up at him. "Hi," she said. "I'm sorry about the door..."

"Oh, it's okay – I'm sorry if I intruded."

"I shouldn't have left it open, but it gets chilly in there with it closed – the radiator doesn't work right."

"Maybe I could fix it."

"Maybe," she said, in a tone that clearly meant no.

"So, you paint?"

"Sort of," she said, looking down.

"What I saw looked really good."

She didn't answer, and in the dim light from downstairs he couldn't really see, but he thought she might actually be blushing.

"Come on downstairs," she said. "I'll make us some dinner."

She didn't want to talk about the painting; she made that obvious as she conveniently didn't hear his comments and questions over the bustle of cooking supper. He let it drop – for the moment.

He knew he should probably let it drop for good, but the image of that woman in the creamy Victorian dress haunted him – something about the expression on her face would not leave him alone. He would stop sometimes on his way along the upstairs hall and stare at the closed door.

He didn't try to open it, though. He wasn't going to sneak around. He valued her too much for that.

It was almost a week later that he brought the subject up again.

"So, did you ever take art classes?" he asked over dinner.

She nodded, not looking up from her plate. "Years of them," she said.

"I thought that painting you were doing was very good," he said. "From what I saw of it, anyway."

She shrugged. "It's nothing special," she said.

"Yes, it is," he told her. "Not everyone can paint like that. I'd like to see it again, sometime."

"Maybe sometime," she murmured.

"Are there others?"

She looked up, finally. "What do you mean?"

"I mean, do you have other paintings you've done?"

"Well, of course," she said. "You didn't think that was my first, did you? I thought you said you liked it."

"I *do* like it – I think it's wonderful!"

"Then it couldn't be my first, could it? Painting takes practice."

"No, but... oh, I don't know, I thought maybe you'd given the others away, or thrown them out, or something."

She shook her head and looked back at her plate; she fumbled with her fork.

"No," she said. "I still have them all. All the ones that I thought were any good, anyway; I burned the early junk."

"Could I see some of them?"

"No," she said – then softened it. "Maybe someday, when I know you better."

He nodded. "All right," he said. He knew not to push it any further, and changed the subject. "Say, did you see the news today?"

Gordon was patient. It was six months later, six months of carefully avoiding the subject and never looking in even when

232

she was painting with the door open, weeks after he'd asked her to marry him and she'd put off a decision, that she finally told him one Sunday afternoon, "I want to show you something."

He looked up from his magazine and asked, "What?"

He wasn't thinking about paintings; he'd been involved in an article on Vatican politics. He blinked at her, and realized she was nervous about something. He put the magazine down.

"A painting," she said.

His eyes widened, and he got up quickly. "Please," he said, "I'd love to see it."

She led him upstairs – and he noticed, as they climbed the steps, that she was breathing fast, and her hand on the banister was trembling.

She wasn't just nervous, he realized; she was *scared*.

Of what? Of his reaction to her painting?

That was silly; even if it was trash, didn't she trust him to be tactful?

She led the way into one of the rooms she ordinarily kept locked – a small bedroom at the back of the house, full of dusty sunlight and faded pastel furniture.

The painting was the brightest thing in the room; it stood propped up on the dresser. He stepped over to look at it.

She stepped out of his way, not saying a word.

It was an odd scene – a little girl in a pink party dress standing in a littered alleyway against a nighttime background of pawn shops and strip joints, handing a single red rose to a man in a black leather coat. The dress, the rose, the neon signs, the red bandana the man wore at his throat, all seemed to shimmer, patches of brilliant color against the washed-out, greyed and decayed background.

The faces looked oddly familiar, but Gordon couldn't place them; he supposed they were just models he'd seen in magazines, or something.

He stared at the painting, taking in every bit of it.

A pawn shop window held a display of watches, and he could read the time on each one; a barroom window reflected a bow in the little girl's hair, and also a woman in a tight black skirt who wasn't in the foreground.

Everything was perfectly realized, no detail missed. The neon lights colored the little girl's shiny black shoes and the man's leather coat; the man needed a shave. The rose was ever so slightly past its peak, the petals just beginning to droop.

"It's wonderful," Gordon said.

"You like it?" Janice said, smiling shyly.

"I *love* it. Did you... what did you use for models? All the little touches..."

"No models. I made it all up."

"That's amazing!" He turned and glanced at her – she was radiant, basking in his acceptance.

"I'll leave it here, then," she said, "and I won't lock the door."

"Could we put it out on display, somewhere?"

Her smile vanished. "Oh, no!" she said. "I couldn't let anyone else see it." She saw the disappointment on his face, and added, "Not yet."

"All right," he said. Then he went back to staring at the painting.

She didn't just have talent, he thought; she was a *genius*.

Why did she hide it so completely?

He looked at her with a whole new sense of wonder. Who *was* this woman he was living with? She obviously had depths he hadn't even imagined.

He turned back to the painting.

Why had she painted that particular scene?

Why was that the painting she had chosen to show him, rather than the one of the Victorian women?

It was a mystery.

When he looked again she was gone, slipped silently away.

He took to reading in that little back bedroom, where he could look up at the painting every so often.

It was a month later that the second painting appeared. He went into the room, book in hand, and stopped dead.

The two paintings were side by side on the dresser, the girl in the alley and the new one, of a plump man standing in a forest clearing, smiling beatifically, arms spread wide as he looked up at something that wasn't in the scene, bands of sunlight spilling down between the trees and streaking bright colors across the mysterious dark green forest gloom, the brightest light bleaching the man's face almost white.

Again, it was a stunning work. Gordon stared.

"Do you like it?" Janice asked at dinner that night.

Gordon didn't pretend not to understand.

"I love it," he said.

She beamed at him, and hummed to herself later, when she cleared away the dishes.

Two more paintings appeared a fortnight later – a woman in a white gown trimmed with red, blue, and gold, standing in a ruined church; and a man reading a newspaper on an otherwise-empty subway platform as an express ran by. The newspaper headline was SUBWAY KILLER STRIKES AGAIN, and it was only after he read that that Gordon noticed the bloodstain on the concrete by the man's foot.

Why had Janice painted such a thing? Why had she chosen that as one of the handful he was allowed to see?

And why didn't she let him see the others? Why didn't she let anyone *else* see any? Her younger brother had visited, and had been forbidden entrance to any of the locked rooms, including the back one that had become Gordon's private gallery.

Didn't she know how good they were?

He asked her that flat out at dinner.

"Do you know how good your paintings are?"

She blushed. "No, they aren't," she said. "They're just... just playing around."

"They're *art*," he said. "First-rate art. They should be hanging in galleries and museums!"

"Oh, Gordie, it's sweet of you to say that, but I could never let them be displayed anywhere."

"Why *not*? They're nothing to be embarrassed about – they're fine, fine work!"

"No, they aren't, Gordie. And speaking of work, did you know they promoted that obnoxious Karen Baker?"

Having thus changed the subject, she steadfastly ignored any attempt to change it back, babbling on about her office.

At first, Gordon thought she was just trying to distract him, but then he began to listen to what she was saying.

"You should have had that promotion, shouldn't you?" he asked.

"Oh, no, I wouldn't want it – all that responsibility!"

He let it drop – but the next morning he stayed home from work, and around mid-morning he phoned Cheryl, who was a manager in the same office as Janice, and after some chit-chat asked, "Isn't Jan about due for promotion?"

"Janice? She didn't tell you?" Cheryl asked, startled.

"Tell me what?"

"We *offered* her a promotion – twice, in fact. She turned it down."

He pressed her for more details. By the time he hung up he was seriously dismayed, and thinking back over other incidents that had taken place during his relationship with Janice.

There were little things, like thrown-away lottery tickets, and bigger ones, like the secret paintings and the refused promotions, and even the postponed marriage decision.

Janice, he realized, was systematically avoiding success.

A promotion was obviously a success, and she surely must realize how good her art was, so keeping it secret was a way of avoiding success. And marrying him – well, he couldn't help thinking of that as a form of success, too.

He'd heard of this sort of thing – sometimes it was called "impostor syndrome," the belief that one didn't deserve success, that any success would lead to disaster because it was undeserved, that sooner or later everyone would realize that one was undeserving, an impostor, and the success would be snatched away, to be replaced with disgrace.

He was angry with himself for not having realized months ago that Janice had it.

He'd read about it. Sufferers would sabotage their own lives, doing it to themselves before anyone else could do it to them, so that their imposture wouldn't be discovered.

He remembered how she had been frightened when she showed him the first painting. She must have been afraid he'd tell her she couldn't paint, he realized – that he'd expose her as an impostor.

He stood in the hall, one hand still on the telephone receiver, thinking it all through.

He had respected Janice's wishes about the paintings, and the marriage, and everything else, up until now; he'd assumed she had sound reasons for her actions. Maybe not logical reasons, but reasons.

But if it was this phobia that was responsible, that was different. She shouldn't let it run her life.

He glanced up the stairs, and let go of the phone. Then he changed his mind and picked up the receiver again while he pawed through the phone book.

One of his old college classmates, a fellow art major, owned a gallery now.

Gordon handled the four paintings with the utmost care as he loaded them in his car and drove them to the gallery for Ian to inspect.

He brought them through the back door, one by one, and leaned them up on a framing table.

Ian, at first casual, grew more respectful when he got a look at the first canvas.

"You know the artist?" he asked, looking sideways at Gordon.

"I'm living with her," Gordon explained.

Ian whistled a note through his teeth. "Must be interesting," he said, looking back at the painting of the girl in the alley.

He inspected the four paintings carefully.

"Do they have titles?" he asked.

Gordon admitted, with some embarrassment, "I don't know; I never asked."

"We'd need to frame them before we could hang them."

"You'd be willing to display them?"

Ian glanced at him, startled. "Are you nuts? Of course we'll hang them! The only question is whether I have the nerve to ask what they ought to be worth."

Gordon blinked.

"They're not for sale," he said.

Ian sighed. "Then what the hell are you doing here? We're not a museum, Gordie; we're a business."

"I was thinking you... you know, as a favor, for publicity, I thought you might display a couple, just to see what sort of reaction you get."

Ian stared at him.

"Why?" he asked.

"Well, see, I want to convince Janice how good they are. She's... well, she doesn't believe she's talented."

Ian looked back at the paintings.

"She's talented, all right. She's fucking brilliant." He considered, then said, "Look, Gordie, I'd like to help – but I'd also like a chance to sell these. You think there's *any* chance this Janice might be willing to sell something? Maybe not these particular pieces, but you say she's got others?"

"I think so," Gordon said. "These are the only ones I've seen, but I'm pretty sure she has others put away."

"Think she might want to sell any?"

Gordon hesitated.

"I don't know," he said at last.

"Well, find out," Ian said.

"I can't. Look, Ian, suppose I were to loan you more than a dozen paintings, enough for a one-woman show, and I promised you'd be the exclusive agent if she ever *does* agree to sell any? Would you do it?"

"Do what? A show?" Ian considered that. "Yeah," he said slowly. "It'd be good publicity, showing these – get people into the gallery. One day only, on a Saturday. I'd need at least... let's see, three on that wall... at least twenty paintings, to do it right, but I could maybe get by with one room. A dozen would be the absolute minimum, and they'd all have to be good-sized. How many will she loan me?"

"I don't know," Gordon said. "I'll find out and get back to you."

That night at dinner Gordon sat across the table from Janice, watching her closely, trying to gauge her mood, how she would react to the suggestion of a gallery show.

She was being unusually quiet, though, and his attempts to guide conversation to the subject of her painting – or for that matter, her fear of success – were unsuccessful. She would only speak of trivia.

Finally, he asked straight out, "Jan, are you afraid people would make fun of your paintings?"

She looked up, shocked, from her pecan pie dessert.

"They wouldn't, you know," he said quickly. "The paintings are really *good*."

"That's not it," she said.

"Then are you afraid they'd *praise* them? And that you don't deserve it?"

"No," she said, looking down at her pie. "That's not it, either."

"Then why won't you let anyone else see them?"

She looked up, looked him right in the eye. "You don't know?" she asked.

"No, I don't. I can guess, maybe, but I wish you'd tell me."

"If you don't *know*, Gordon... no, I'm not going to tell you."

She pushed away and left the table, left her pie unfinished.

He watched her go, and debated going after her.

She was lying, he was sure. She was afraid people would laugh at her work – or that they wouldn't, that they'd tell her it was wonderful, and she'd never be able to live up to it.

But she wouldn't admit it.

He got up and followed her, and found her standing at the foot of the stairs, looking up into the darkness. He came up behind her and put his arms around her.

"I'm sorry," he said. "I'd never do anything to hurt you, Janice – I just want everyone to see how wonderful you are!"

"I'm not wonderful," she said. She pulled away.

He had to show her, he thought. She *was* wonderful, and he had to convince her of it. She had no self-confidence, that was the problem; she didn't think, "Nothing ventured, nothing gained," she thought, "Nothing ventured, little lost."

But *he* believed in "Nothing ventured, nothing gained"!

And two weeks later, opportunity fell into his lap.

"I need to go up to Chicago," Janice told him. "My uncle Eugene's moving, giving up his house and taking an apartment, and he's asked me to come help him sort through stuff, see if there's anything I want."

"Oh?" Gordon asked.

"Yeah, he's got a lot of the old family stuff. My cousin Charlotte will be there, and maybe Aunt Grace, if her health holds." She hesitated. "Would you like to come?"

"When would this be?" he asked.

"I'd be leaving Thursday, coming back Tuesday. I've got vacation days I can use."

He looked at her, then said, "*I* don't; I'm afraid I'll have to pass."

"Oh, I thought you did," she said.

"Nope."

He was lying; he did have leave time available.

But this was his chance to put on that show at Ian's gallery.

She seemed disappointed, but he thought about how her face would light up when she saw the reviews, when she heard people raving about her work.

"You go ahead and have a good time," he said.

"All right," she said, a bit coolly.

A few minutes later he excused himself and called Ian.

Ian complained about the short notice, but agreed. Gordon provided him with Polaroids of the four he'd already seen, so that he could advertise the show.

And Thursday, as soon as Janice was gone, Gordon took the keys from her dresser jewelbox and unlocked all the upstairs rooms, his hands trembling with anticipation.

How many paintings would there be? Would there be enough good ones?

Then the door of the first room, the room where he had seen her working on her painting, swung open.

There was the easel, and the stool, and the lamp – and behind the door a stack of canvases.

A *large* stack of canvases – sixteen in all.

The Victorian woman and child were there; so was a stunning self-portrait that showed Janice's face subtly distorted, her teeth almost fangs, her expression predatory. There was a painting of a steam train, one of a pair of horses, one of a man chopping vegetables as a little girl watched...

"Jackpot," Gordon whispered to himself.

He was wrong, though; the jackpot was in the next room, where the canvases were stacked on all sides – portraits, landscapes, still life, even abstracts.

Altogether, there were over a hundred and twenty paintings.

Some of them were obviously early work; some were so bizarre Gordon didn't know what to make of them. Even so, when he arrived at Ian's gallery Friday morning, he had sixty-six canvases packed into his car.

That was all he could fit and still have room to drive.

Ian, after a few moments of shock when he saw the number, and several moments of awe and delight when he looked through the available material, weeded them down further, and in the end, forty-three were hung.

The show was a wild success.

And Tuesday, when Janice came home, clippings of the rave reviews were set out on the living room coffee table, waiting for her.

The reviews were all just from the local papers, there hadn't been time to get any serious attention, but it was a start. He couldn't wait for her to read them.

He met her at the door, kissed her, and took her bags.

"There's a lot more stuff in the car," she said.

"I'll help you with it," he answered. "Let me drop these in the bedroom."

As he hauled the luggage up the stairs he glanced back and saw her drifting into the living room, looking at the clippings, and he smiled nervously.

She might be angry at first, he'd taken a really great liberty, but when she saw what everyone *said* about her work...

He dropped the suitcases by the bed and hurried back down.

She was sitting on the couch, holding one of the clippings, staring at it, stunned.

"I'm sorry," he said, "I know you were afraid that people wouldn't like your paintings, but I *knew* they were good, so good I had to share them – and see? Everyone loves them!"

She finished reading the review, then turned and stared up at him.

"You really don't understand, do you, Gordon?"

"Sure I do, Jan," he said, but she was already on her feet, pushing her way past him.

He turned and followed her out to her car – as she had said, it was full of boxes and bundles. She circled around to the driver's side and opened the door.

"What should I get first?" he asked, reaching for the passenger door.

"Lost," she said, as she tapped the power lock switch. Then she climbed into the car, slammed the door, and started the engine.

He stood and watched helplessly as she pulled away.

She was angry. He should have known. But she'd have to come back sooner or later, and maybe he could make her see that he hadn't done any harm, he'd been saving her from her own fears.

He turned and went back into the house.

She'd be back. And she'd see that he'd done her a favor.

She'd be back.

But she wasn't back when the phone rang about eight, and he snatched it up ready to apologize, ready to beg, but the voice on the other end was Ian's.

"Does she want to sell any?" the art dealer asked. "I think I could get ten thousand for that big one of the old woman and the cobwebs right now."

"I don't think so, Ian," Gordon said. "I'll talk to you later." He hung up.

Janice hadn't come home by midnight, and Gordon finally gave up and went to bed.

He was awakened by the phone; he snatched it up.

"Hello?" he said. "Janice?"

"No," said a man's voice, "this is Lieutenant Arneson, with the police."

"Police?" He blinked and sat up.

"Is this Gordon Webber?"

Nightmare scenarios ran through his mind – Janice in a car wreck, Janice mugged, Janice raped.

"Yes," he said, "I'm Gordon Webber."

"If you could come to the Holiday Inn on Route 35, we'd like to talk to you."

"Is this about Janice?"

"Yes, sir, it's about Ms. Fletcher."

"Is she okay?"

"No, sir, I'm afraid she isn't. If you could come to the hotel, please?"

"I'll be right there."

He hung up the phone, and quickly got dressed. Fifteen minutes later he hurried into the hotel lobby.

There were three cops standing by the entrance to a first-floor corridor; he approached them and shakily said, "I'm Gordon Webber – I think Lieutenant Anderson wanted to see me? About Janice Fletcher?"

"Lieutenant Arneson," one of them corrected him. "Room 122; he's waiting for you." He pointed down the corridor.

At the door of the room he was ushered inside, and met by a man in plainclothes who introduced himself as Arneson.

Janice wasn't there; Gordon had half-expected to see her lying dead on the floor.

The bed was unmade, he noticed.

"Where's Jan?" he asked.

"The hospital," Arneson said.

"Then why am I *here*?" Gordon demanded, starting to turn.

"The hospital *morgue*," Arneson told him.

Gordon stopped, and sagged.

"I thought it would be easier here," Arneson said. "We'll be going over there later, so you can confirm our identification of the deceased, but I thought we should have a little talk here, first."

"How'd it happen?" Gordon asked, not looking at anyone or anything in particular.

"Pills," Arneson said. "Sleeping pills. Lots of 'em."

Gordon blinked.

"She left this," Arneson said, holding out an envelope.

Gordon looked at it, and saw his name and their shared phone number written on it. He took it and pulled out the sheet of paper inside.

"That her handwriting?" Arneson asked.

"Yes," Gordon said, starting to read.

"Gordon," it began, and at the omission of the customary "Dear" his eyes began to tear. "I know you don't understand what you've done to me. You thought I was afraid I'd be laughed at, afraid of failure, but that was never it. You thought I was afraid to marry you for the same reasons – but that wasn't it. I couldn't marry you because you didn't understand. You didn't see what my paintings were about. I didn't show my paintings because they were *private*, Gordon – they were my innermost soul put down on canvas. I was never good with words, so I used my pictures. I never cared one way or another about money or success, I had enough of both and didn't need any more, but I cared about my privacy – and you put my soul on display, you invited the public to trample through my most secret feelings, feelings you never understood. In a way, you raped me, Gordon – a psychic gang-bang. I can't live with that. So I've left you these two notes, and I'm saying goodbye. I hope you'll understand at least *one* of them."

It was signed "Janice," and underneath was a P.S.: "Not Jan, you son of a bitch."

Gordon swallowed hard, then looked up from the note to Arneson's hostile face.

"It says *two* notes," Gordon managed to say.

Arneson nodded, and gestured to one of the other cops.

The man picked up a piece of board, about two feet square, that had been leaning against the wall. He handed it to Arneson, who held it up and displayed it to Gordon.

Gordon looked at it, at Janice's final painting, done in cheap hobby-shop pigments on masonite, and finally understood.

It wasn't anywhere near as finished as any of her others, parts of it were little more than hasty sketches, but it was still a fine work of art in its way.

The painting showed a magician and his assistant, standing on a stage before a crowd of reporters. The magician was a man in top hat and cape – and Gordon recognized his own face.

And seeing it there, he also realized that he was the man in the leather coat in the first painting she had shown him, and that Janice had been the little girl.

The assistant was Janice, as well – Janice standing stark naked, teeth clenched as she fought against pain; the magician had sliced open her belly and pulled out a double handful of her intestines, and was displaying them to the applauding crowd with flamboyant gestures.

Blood dripped through the magician's fingers, but he smiled proudly, oblivious to the blood and the woman's agony as he performed for the crowd.

And Gordon knew that that smile, and the entire painting, would haunt him for the rest of his life.

end

HAZMAT

~~~~

Stab

You still remember it, don't you?

You remember the feel of the knife going in.

You remember the pressure on your forearm as you pulled him to you. You remember the smell of his breath, and of his sweat, and the feel of the rough cloth of his shirt. You remember the sound of his breathing as he struggled. You remember the firm, hard grip of the knife in your hand, your brother's fancy military knife that you borrowed without asking, and how it pulled the skin tight across the insides of your knuckles as you shoved it up through the shirt, under the ribs, into the flesh. You remember the resistance, how you had to push harder than you expected.

You did, though, you pushed hard, as hard as you could, and the blade went in, and his breath suddenly all came out in a gasp, and his face came forward, smacked against your shoulder, his cheek brushing yours, and you felt his body tense, and then relax. You smelled urine, and when you felt the moisture you realized you had your leg between his, pressed into his crotch. You heard his own knife fall.

You remember the fear, the shame, the confusion, and the rush of adrenaline you felt. You remember the weird relief, relief you didn't understand.

Then you let go of him, and stepped away, and pulled the knife out. He fell, a dead weight, and his arms and legs flopped against you and almost knocked you over, and you stepped back.

He fell to the ground and didn't move, and you turned and ran, your shoes slapping the pavement. You were overwhelmed by terror, by the enormity of what you had done, the knowledge that you had taken a human life, the certainty that you would be caught and punished.

But you weren't, were you?

You never were. You were just a scared kid in a gang fight, and they never caught you, never knew who did it.

And that fall you went back to school. The next June you graduated, with a scholarship nobody expected you to get, and you went off to college, and you did fine there, got your engineering degree. You were quiet, never bothered anyone, never went back to the old gang – you remembered it all, but you didn't want to think about it.

So you didn't think about it.

You thought about stresses and linkages and tensile strengths, and about the people around you who had never fought in the streets, the girls who were more impressed with your GPA than your scars.

You thought about the future, now that you knew you'd have one.

You went for your MBA and you got it, and you got a job, and a promotion, and you took women to bed and finally married one.

And you never mentioned the gang fight and the knife going in and the other boy falling to the ground in his own blood. You never thought about it.

But you always remembered it.

And your wife had a baby, and you argued, and she left, taking the mewling little brat with her, and you turned your energy into the company.

You fought. You schemed. You did everything you could to bring in money, to make the company a success, to let everyone know you were bringing in money. You had power.

And before all that long, you had the company.

CEO, they call you. Sir, they say when they speak to you. You have women – not cheap floozies, not confused college girls, not your wife fighting you for control, but sleek young women who want to be close to power and wealth. Men respect you, fear you. You eat well, eat anything you want at the best restaurants. You drink fine brandy. You sleep on the finest linens, cool and smooth. Anything you want, you can buy.

But you still remember it.

And now you do think about it. You have time now. You look back and remember, and sometimes you lie awake sweating as you recall it all.

You killed a boy.

You committed a murder, and got away with it. No one could ever suspect you now.

And if they did suspect, what could they do?

You got away with murder.

You lie there, remembering the feel of the knife going in, and you smile.

You know that you have something the men around you, the men you compete with, don't have. You have that knowledge in you, that calm certainty that you have the ruthlessness you need to destroy your enemies. You've killed. You could do it again.

It gives you the edge, doesn't it?

You remember the feel of the knife going in.

And you know that you will never again experience anything that powerful again.

You know that that murder, at the age of seventeen, was the high point of your life.

You know that everything since has been basking in the afterglow.

And you lie there on your fine smooth sheets, the woman beside you stroking your cheek, and you remember the feel of the knife going in.

end

~~~~~

Slash

He reached down and stroked her cheek gently.

She sighed softly in her sleep, and he smiled. Still smiling, he took the straight razor and ran it caressingly down that same cheek, along the same path he had just stroked, pressing down gently.

It left a clean red line, but then the line broadened, and the blood began to run down across her cheek, down to her mouth and nose, and she blinked and woke up, startled.

He dropped the razor to the floor, out of her sight.

"Hey, you're bleeding!" he said.

"What?" She sat up and groped for the drawer of her bedside table.

"Let me get a towel," he said. He ran to the bathroom and pulled one of the little white guest towels from the bar, and glanced back to see her staring into her hand mirror, astonished, her eyes widening, her lips pulling apart. Her free hand flew to her face, smacked wetly into the blood, and he was there beside her again, with the towel.

She put it delicately to the wound, and a small wordless noise leapt from her lips, a tiny sound of pain and terror, like something a kitten might make.

"What happened?" he asked, as he helped her dab at the slash with the towel.

The cloth was mostly red already.

"I don't know," she said, staring at the mirror. "I don't know!"

"Was there a piece of glass in the bed or something?"

"I don't know," she said again, baffled. "I didn't feel anything."

"How bad is it? Do you think we need to see a doctor?"

Gingerly, she prodded her cheek, wincing slightly as her fingers made contact. He watched the fingertips press, saw the indentations they made, saw fresh blood spill out, red and new – it was only when he saw the new bleeding that he could tell that the blood on the towel had already started to dry, had already discolored.

His fingers pressed his own cheek in sympathy; he felt the hardness of bone, the soft hollow below, and from the corner of his eye he could see his knuckles as a pinkish blur.

"Maybe I'd better drive you to the emergency room," he said.

She took her hand away and looked at her fingertips, at the vivid redness. "Yes," she said unsteadily, "I think that might be a good idea."

#

The cut was clean and not deep, and the doctor didn't bother stitching it up beyond a few butterfly sutures. "Head wounds always bleed like crazy," he said, as he applied the bandages. "Nothing to worry about."

"Thank you," she said, in a tenuous whisper.

"How'd it happen?"

"We don't know," the husband said. "We were hoping maybe you could tell us."

"Me?" The doctor glanced up at the husband, threw him a grin. "Well, I don't know – how can you not know what happened? It's fresh, not more than, oh, two hours old, at the outside – very clean, so it was something sharp, a good knife or a straight razor, maybe."

"It happened in bed," the husband said.

The doctor looked up at him questioningly.

"I just woke up this morning, and there it was," she said. "We thought... we thought maybe something was in the bed."

The doctor eyed the bandage critically. "Can't imagine what," he said. "Broken bedsprings I've seen; never saw one could do a slash like that, though. Maybe mirror glass, if it broke right, but I didn't see any bits of glass, and there usually are some."

He considered, and said, "Beats me."

#

As they waited at the light he turned and looked at her, at the long white bandage that covered her cheek, and he wondered why he had done it.

He didn't hate her.

He wasn't completely sure whether he loved her or not, he hadn't been sure for years, but he knew he didn't hate her.

Slashing someone with a razor, though – wasn't that hateful? Wasn't that a horrible, vicious, depraved thing to do?

He didn't feel vicious or depraved. He didn't feel any hate, or any of the bitter satisfaction he had felt on those occasions when he had taken a successful revenge on someone he hated.

Instead he felt a sort of calm pride, and a certain excitement, a feeling of power. He had done it, and he had gotten away with it, and she was still there, his handiwork just beneath that bandage, carved into the living flesh of her face. She hadn't fled; the possibility that he had been responsible for the wound never seemed to have occurred to her.

But then, why should it? Why would he have even contemplated such a thing?

He didn't know the answer to that himself. In fact, he had hardly contemplated it at all; he had simply done it, on a whim, on a sudden impulse. He had held the razor, and he had seen her face, and he had drawn that red line, with no more thought than a child might give to trying out a bit of chalk.

How was it possible that he could do that?

The light turned green, and he transferred his foot from the brake to the accelerator.

He wondered whether the cut would leave a scar, and if so, what it would look like. Surely, a cut like that would scar! He tried to imagine her with a scar down her cheek, and could not quite picture it.

Well, he would see it soon enough. He found himself looking forward to it.

For an instant, revulsion set in. He might have just permanently disfigured his wife, a woman who had done him no real harm, who claimed to love him and might well mean it. She gave him affection, she cared for him, she helped him in a thousand little ways, and he had repaid her with a slash down the side of her face. What was *wrong* with him? Had he gone mad? Had he become some sort of monster? Was he a sociopath who had just been fooling himself all these years, pretending to care about other people?

Then the revulsion passed. He turned into their street and guided the car toward their driveway.

#

He hurried to the bedroom while she was in the kitchen, dropping her purse on the breakfast table. He had to find the razor, clean it, and put it away. He couldn't let her see it, or she might realize what had happened.

He couldn't allow her to know he had done it deliberately. She would want to know why, and he couldn't tell her – after all, he didn't know himself. She would be astonished, and hurt.

She would be frightened of him. She would want him to see a psychiatrist. She might even leave him. He didn't want that. He wanted her to stay, to go on as before. If she realized what he had done, she could not possibly fail to respond somehow.

She wouldn't go to the police, though. He knew her well enough to be sure of that.

He looked down at the razor in his hand, at the faint red smear on the blade, and wondered whether he really *did* know her that well. He thought he did, but then, he had just discovered he didn't even know himself. He had never thought he was the someone who could slash a woman's face with a straight razor for no reason at all.

He turned and headed for the bathroom. He needed to clean the razor and put it away. He needed to clean it very thoroughly, very carefully. He wanted it sharp and clean, no nicks, no possibility of infection.

After all, though he didn't know why, he knew that sooner or later he was going to use it on her again.

end

About the Author:

Lawrence Watt-Evans has been a full-time writer for more than thirty years, with more than forty novels and well over a hundred short stories to his credit. He served two terms as president of the Horror Writers' Association, and won the Silver Hammer award for service to HWA. His story "Why I Left Harry's All-Night Hamburgers" won the 1988 Hugo for short story, as well as the Asimov's Readers Award. He lives in Takoma Park, Maryland, with his wife and a second-hand cat.

His website is at www.watt-evans.com.

www.ingramcontent.com/pod-product-compliance
Lightning Source LLC
Chambersburg PA
CBHW070905180626
46817CB00003B/928